Praise from Readers

"I don't usually go for romance novels, however, this author has the captivating ability to pull you in and submerse you into Mina's world, I found myself lost in this book for hours, a real page-turner!!!"

—Jasmine

"It was a pleasant read and certainly delivered on the romance and k-pop world as promised. I really got into the whole K-entertainment world drama very fast and enjoyed it!"

—Erni

"I felt like I was reading from a more established author than a first timer, this book made me smile from page to page and I found myself becoming lost in their story of strength and growth."

—Riggs

"The author's writing is beautifully detailed, but without the unnecessary filler that comes with similar writing styles. It's perfectly balanced."

—Aria

"This book is a relatable narrative for any K-pop fangirl, descriptive enough to make your heart swoon, and exciting enough to make you turn every page till the last; The Strings Between Love and Race will make you relive the fantasy of Mina's life at Underground Entertainment."

—Jennifer

THE STRINGS BETWEEN LOVE & RACE

Fatima Alabi

Global Book Publishing

The Strings Between Love & Race
Fatima Alabi

ISBN: 978-1-956193-89-3
Book Design & Publishing done by:
Global Book Publishing
www.globalbookpublishing.com

To Mum,
Adijat Idowu
whose dream,
was seeing my dreams come true,
Rest in Paradise, my Angel.

Trigger Warning

"There are a few scenes of physical altercations and an off-page recollection of an almost traumatic event that triggers PTSD which might be triggering for sensitive readers, please note we take mental health issues seriously and don't wish to cause anyone distress."

Prologue

"Joon, where are you off to so late?" Mum asks.

"Just going out for a ride to get some air," I say, with my bike in hand, shutting the door behind me and head for the lift pressing the call button.

I ride around for a while ending up in London Bridge. Getting off, I lock my bike by a nearby pole and begin strolling but come to a halt when I spot her standing by the bridge, looking up at the stars making heart race.

Once again, fate has led us to each other. She is probably feeling conflicted, stuck and frustrated, unable to decide which way to go. Torn between choosing herself or sacrificing her happiness once again for the sake of others. Being the creature of habit that she is, I am certain of the choice she will make, and my heart aches at the thought.

Although we've been here before, it never gets easier, but I hope that a day will come when she eventually follows her heart. Until she's brave enough to take that step, I am willing to wait as long as it takes because I know Mina is worth every second. Even in her silence, I can always tell what lies deep in her heart.

I sigh, knowing I would have to watch her from a distance for a while, but I know our hearts will lead us back to each other just like today.

My eyes widen as she clenches the star pendant necklace yanking it off her neck, swinging it in the air but halts midway, sobbing. I sigh, walking in closer, clutching her hand, lowering it. She gasps, and her eyes widen as they meet mine. I exhale, finding that look in her eyes ever so present, exposing her involuntarily.

Chapter One

"Mina? Mina? Has anyone seen the Maid of Honour?" Sheila, the wedding planner, calls out. She must have noticed my absence.

I'm cooped up in the bathroom, reading breaking news on N.O. The past decade has transformed them, they're now older, and hotter. But four years ago, my beloved bias, Kim Dong-min, forcibly departed amidst scandals, shattering fans' hearts, including mine. Yet, his loyal fandom's outcry granted him a solo chance at redemption, a flicker of hope to reclaim the public's faith.

He was replaced by Liam Choi, a charismatic soloist, who embodied South Korea's allure. Natives and foreigners are stunned by his good looks, which earned him the nickname "Man-Jjit-Nam," meaning a man who seems like a character from a comic book or animation because of his perfectly aligned facial features. He's also referred to as "Um-Chin-Ah," meaning a person who has it all.

Liam is great at sports, was always the topper in his classes and speaks English fluently. His arrival transformed N.O., catapulting them to global stardom. His mesmerising deep voice bewitches hearts but is said to have a cold demeanour.

Though unhappy with the change, as the president of the UK fan club, I choose to stay unbiased. The fan club group chat has been buzzing all morning. I click on the link being passed around. It's an article about Liam Choi making his drama debut.

Headline: Fans will get a glimpse of Liam Choi's tender side in a romantic drama with Go Ae-ra, singer and actress.

Rachel's presence under the spotlight feels unfamiliar. After leaving the UK a few years ago, Rachel debuted with the name Go Ae-ra through her father's company, Underground Entertainment, which is also the same company N.O. is signed to. I have been keeping track of her career; she's the only link I have left to find Joon and Ji-won. I grip hold of my phone as a jolt curses through my body.

Shoes appear in front of the bathroom stall, followed by a sharp knock on the door.

"Miss Mina, I know you're in there; hurry up and come out. We are all waiting for you."

I check the time and gasp, leaping up from the toilet seat hurriedly before opening the door. Sheila glares at me through her sharp-edged glasses, with a clipboard in hand; her fitted black pencil skirt and blazer, along with a white blouse, gives her the look of a teacher scolding her student as her eyes shoot lasers.

"I'm ready," I mutter, grinning but her gaze remains stern.

She pulls me by the arm all the way to the bridal room. I halt and gasp as I glance at the bride. She's wearing an ivory sweetheart neckline mermaid dress with a six-foot-long train, with her hair in a braided updo. Her flawless natural makeup look brings out the beauty in her chestnut brown skin, and my eyes get teary as I watch my beautiful sister in all her glory.

I pinch myself, remembering that being this close to her ten years ago seemed impossible. Although our journey was strewn with challenges, every single thorn I encountered along the way was worth it.

"Oh, my goodness Dina, you are the most beautiful bride I have ever seen," I murmur, embracing her.

"Ladies, ladies, remember we need to fight back the tears. We can't have your makeup ruined," Sheila nags, tapping her clipboard, and Dina and I giggle.

She orders the makeup artist to touch up Dina's makeup, and I go over to the mirror to fix mine; my hair is slicked back in a ponytail; although it took two broken combs to tame down my afro, my gold Maid of Honour silk cow neck gown wraps around my body like a glove, and I am still getting used to having a figure and wearing clothes that embrace my curves.

Luckily, the brow gel has my bushy eyebrows tamed, and I glare back at my chestnut-brown eyes. Seeing my face with no glasses is still strange since I switched to wearing contact lenses last year. I grab my light pink lip gloss and reapply it to revive the shine on my lips and add some highlighter on my cheekbones, magnifying my golden-brown skin and smiling back at my reflection, a new daily practice of mine. However, it's a habit I have yet to master internally; the old me would shiver. Back then my reflection felt like a curse, one I've convinced myself has been broken.

"Ladies, it's time," Sheila says, bringing me back to the present.

We make our way to the wedding hall, hand in hand, grinning from ear to ear, surrounded by exquisite art from around the world. The five-star hotel looks every bit like royalty. I smirk recalling Dina's husband-to-be, insisting the wedding be held at the most luxurious hotel in London, accepting nothing less than perfect for Dina; I smile, reassured she will be cherished by him.

"Are you all packed up?" Dina asks.

I sigh, lowering my head, remembering I will be leaving soon.

"Yes," I respond.

We get in front of the wedding hall, and she turns to face me, reaching for my hands.

"Mina," she calls.

I look up to meet her gaze.

"Don't worry so much, of course. Mum and I will miss you like crazy, but we'll be okay; it's time that you finally choose yourself," she says.

"This will be the beginning of great things for us both as we embark on a new journey separately. I love you so much; never forget that," she adds, making me choke up.

"I love you too," I say.

She uses her handkerchief to wipe off my tears, and I collect it reciprocating.

"Ladies, not again," Sheila scolds and we chuckle.

Sheila orders the doors to the wedding hall to be open over her walkie-talkie. Linking hands, we make our way to the groom who watches welling up. I gasp mesmerised by the fairy-tale decor. White roses with green leaves droop down from the high ceiling like a waterfall, the floor is completely covered in white rose petals, the scent of freshly bloomed roses fills the room, and white chairs with matching tables each has big floral centrepieces on them, the guests all dressed in white get on their feet.

It looks just as Dina envisioned, and I must admit, Sheila has an exceptional eye for detail. As we reach the end of the aisle, the groom's radiant smile shines through tear-filled eyes, and his gaze locks onto his bride. I gently place her hands into his with a firm stare. It's still surreal to see him with a full-grown beard and bulging muscles that strain against his ivory tuxedo. I choke up reflecting upon the journey that shaped him from a boy into the remarkable man he has become.

"Yo, best make sure you look after my sister."

I warn, and he smirks, taking her hands.

"Aye Mina, come on man, you know man's got her for life. Thank you for entrusting your sister with me," he says and Dina blushes.

I grin, walking over to fix Dina's dress train, carefully spreading them out.

"Thanks for having her back," he says giving me a fist bump, and I walk to the sitting area, taking my place next to the other bridesmaids dressed in white.

With no dry eyes in the hall, they exchange their vows along with their rings and share their first kiss and the whole room cheers. They stroll together as Mr and Mrs. They visit each table and greet their guest as food is served.

The menu is a perfect blend of both their heritage. I opt for a mixture, choosing a side of Nigerian and Ghanaian jollof rice, along with waakye, taliyah, gari foto, salad and plantain, but I don't stop there. I also request a portion of ayamase and ofada rice with boiled egg and assorted meat. Everyone else at the table gawks at me, but I ignore their puzzled glances.

I eat as much as I can manage, aware I wouldn't find these food options when I leave. Time flies by as I stuff my face and then the MC announces it's time for the first dance. The groom heads over to our table, asking Mum for her hand.

Mum is wearing a traditional Yoruba Iro and Buba in white with a gold gele to match. I grin recalling Mum and Dina arguing about the colour she chose being too plain as Mum initially wanted to include a bright coloured Ankara which is the usual African fabric traditionally used at a Yoruba wedding, but Dina insisted on having everyone wear white with the only exception for gold being her shoes, my dress, Mum's gele, and the grooms bow tie. Eventually, Mum caved in to keep Dina happy, however the Grooms parents were the exception to her rule, with his mum wearing a two piece Kente corset kaba top with a mermaid slit skirt, while his dad is wearing his Kente in a traditional toga style along with oheneba slippers. Dina and I tear up as we watch. I choke up wishing Dad could have been here with us. Mum looks so youthful, grinning as they dance to some old-school fuji music by Mum's favourite artist Wasiu Ayinde.

After the song ends, he returns with Mum to our table. She joins Aunt Amira, who wipes her tears. The groom approaches, asking for my hand. I hesitate, fearing a mishap. Dina insists, urging me on. I eventually yield, taking his hand as the DJ changes the song to "Best Friend" by 50 Cent featuring Olivia, and we both chuckle.

"Excited for your new journey?" he asks.

I nod, giving him a bittersweet smile.

I grin as we pull out of our embrace as the song ends.

"I hope you find him along the way, but… I am a bit worried he might not recognise you, seeing as you no longer look like a teenage boy," he whispers, and I raise my hands to hit him then instantly recall everyone in the room is watching us.

"You better behave yourself or else I'll give you a beat down in front of all these people," I murmur, and he smirks sticking his tongue out.

I exhale reminding myself he's no longer just my annoying best friend, but now my brother-in-law, then I turn walking off.

"Yo M, can you please help me bring my wife to the dance floor?" he asks.

Pointing at Dina, who is smiling from ear to ear, I nod, grinning, and grab her hand.

"Your husband is asking for you, Mrs," I say.

I lead her to him, embracing them both, tears flowing like a grieving child, and then Dina gazes wide-eyed pointing to the wall clock.

"Oh no, Mina, the time; you need to hurry before you miss your flight," she says.

Through teary eyes, I glance at the clock, motionless. How can I depart the wedding early? Dina grasps my hand, shaking her head with a faint smile.

"Mina, it's okay, really, go find your smile again," she says, and I exhale.

"Hurry, go go."

After a final hug from the couple and Mum, I quickly change into leggings and a hoodie. With my suitcase and backpack in hand, I wait outside the hotel for a cab. Suddenly, Emily's red Audi pulls up.

"Need a ride?" she asks, grinning.

She steps out, adjusting her white mini dress and flaunting her fresh bleach blonde pixie cut. We lift my suitcase into the car's boot. I grab the newspaper from her dashboard, stashing it in my bag as we get in. With Emily's fearless driving, we navigate through red lights, dodging traffic, and we arrive at the airport just in time.

We embrace, saying our goodbyes and I hesitantly release her and head through check-in, tearing up as I reflect on our decade-long friendship. As the plane prepares for take-off, glancing out the window, I bid farewell to my home and the people I love as I embark on a new journey. As the plane ascends, tears stream down my cheeks.

Transfixed by the captivating night view of London, I etch its illuminating beauty deep within my heart, a treasured image to reminisce upon on the days when I yearn for home.

I grab the newspaper I took from Emily's car and flip through it to the daily horoscope page. A wide smile spreads across my face as I am instantly transported a decade into the past, back to the day that altered the course of Joon's and my life forever.

Chapter Two

Looking back, everything changed after that horoscope reading ten years ago. Ji-won pulled me to sit on a wooden school bench with that day's newspaper in hand. I didn't believe in horoscopes, but Ji-won insisted we needed a sign to stay optimistic about getting tickets for the N.O. concert. They were coming to the UK for the first time, and we were desperate to attend by securing tickets before they sold out.

Ji-won, an avid follower of daily horoscopes, was obsessed with signs and omens. Yet, despite her fervent belief, their predictions for me had always proven inaccurate.

Well, except for that day's warning of a dark cloud hovering, which I ignored and almost received a bird's unwelcome gift in my hair. But I indulged her because it seemed important to her. How could I refuse those irresistible puppy-dog eyes, accentuated by her cute, fringed bob. But beyond that, Ji-won was worth the effort and more.

She stayed by my side, non-judgemental and didn't pry me with questions about why I lived like a ghost or asked why I was nothing like my sister, Dina, the epitome of charm and grace.

Dina was like freshly bloomed roses in every sense, capturing people's hearts instantly.

Then there was me; I was like a parched rose left out for far too long, all weltered and dry, but that was intentional. Being ignored by others gave me a surge of pride and satisfaction. Being invincible was how I atoned for my past mistakes, but Ji-won saw past it all.

When we first moved into the neighbourhood, Ji-won ran up to Dina and me, saying we were beautiful, fascinated by our identical appearance, and asked if we could be friends. I loved her pink dress and her puffy hair bow. Ji-won reached out her hands, and I raised mine to take them.

But Dina pulled my hand away walking off. The next time we saw her, she came running again smiling and asked if we could play together, but I felt Dina's glare, so I walked away. When we finally started school, she begged our form tutor to let us sit together, and we've been best friends ever since. Though opposites in many ways, we had a few things in common.

Both our families migrated to the UK when we were young, mine from Nigeria, and Ji-won's from South Korea. We both had bad grades, but most importantly, we both loved N.O. Ji-won introduced me to K-pop when I visited her house for the first time; it was love at first listen. I didn't understand most of the lyrics, but felt a deep connection to the music; it made me feel understood.

We would listen to K-pop while singing along and dancing in her room. I felt free, light as a feather; my guilt and burden evaporated. But when the music stopped, it all came rushing back. Music became my drug of escape, my ecstasy.

The first time N.O., short for "Neighbourhood Oppa's," debuted, Ji-won, and I watched the live broadcast of their debut song "Wounded Soldier." That was when I learnt the word "Oppa," meaning older brother, or male friend. N.O.'s songs made me feel liberated, and the lyrics took the words I couldn't utter right out of my heart.

My favourite lyric from their debut song written by Kim Dong-min, the group's leader, was "I am a wounded soul with invisible scars." Those words resonated, assuring me I wasn't alone, and I became a hardcore fan instantly.

People think fangirls are teenagers chasing after aesthetically pleasing boys or men, but it's much more than that; we defy stereotypes; diverse in age, nationality, and gender, and we unite in our shared belief in idols' message expressed through music and their authentic presence on and off stage. Hence, we demonstrate unwavering loyalty as devoted fans.

Ji-won was interested in learning about African culture. So, I introduced her to Afro beats, which she loved, but could never get the dance moves right. The sight of her rhythmless feet trying to do the legwork or azonto was unbearable to watch.

I shook off the thought, crossing my fingers in hopes that my horoscope would be positive. Then, inhaled turning towards Ji-won as she read mine. She cleared her throat, and I adjusted my brown-framed glasses as I listened.

"Gemini, as the sun rises in your sign, embrace change and newfound faith. A lucky charm will fall into your arms, sparking a transformative union. Healing and self-discovery lie ahead, guided by a compass to an extraordinary destination."

Ji-won's hands sunk along with my heart; we locked eyes, and I sighed.

"Why can't they ever be direct? What do they mean by compass?" I groaned deeply.

I glanced at Ji-won who tossed the paper aside and firmly grasped my shoulders.

"Mimi, don't worry. Mine is good, so we still have a chance," she said, with a confident grin. I nodded.

As the school bell rang, we walked along the brick pathway to class. Our school buildings were divided into blocks, each with a vibrant colour: Block A in sky blue, Block B in lime green, Block C in red, Block D in purple, and Block E in orange. Probably to inspire a bright future, but I remained unconvinced. Certain, my fate held only darkness.

Someone wrapped their arms around Ji-won and me.

"Yo, what's good, ladies?"

Ji-won and I looked at each other and smirked, pulling his arm off, and carried on walking.

"Hey, where is the love man?" he mumbled.

Terry was like gum on your shoe. He used to be in Dina's classes but was moved to mine due to poor grades. But he always appeared whenever I needed him, like when a bird nearly pooped in my hair, he stepped in taking the hit. Even in P.E., he always shielded me during dodgeball.

I felt reassured whenever he was around, although I never said it aloud. He did a good enough job complimenting himself, but I knew his intentions were rooted in humour.

"Hey, T," Bianca Johnson from science called, giving him a flirtatious smile.

Subjectively speaking, Terry ticked many boxes: from a wealthy family, charismatic, charming, tall, dark, and handsome.

His Ghanaian heritage and upbringing played a significant role in his mannerisms. He regarded females respectfully, often getting him in trouble. They mistook his etiquette as flirtation.

Bianca seemed to be Terry's latest victim, half Italian, half Jamaican, with long brown curly hair and an hourglass figure matching her pretty face. Boys at school swarmed her, desperate to date her. But she only had eyes for Terry, which landed him in a few rows.

"Hey, B, you good, yeah," Terry responded, and she nodded with a grin and headed off with her friends.

A few guys passing by gave Terry a grim stare-down, but he pretended not to notice. Ji-won and I exhaled and carried on walking.

"Guys, wait up," Terry yelled, running to catch up to us.

A few girls from our year group walked by, flaunting their bodies.

"Mimi, when do you think we will finally hit puberty?" Ji-won asked, and we giggled.

But I was glad we hadn't started puberty yet, as it would invite unwanted attention. Which was why on my fifteenth birthday, I wished my body would remain unchanged.

We followed the pathway to Block B for our first lesson, covered in dried yellow, orange, red, purple, and brown fallen leaves. I hugged my jacket tightly, bracing against the strengthening wind. Turning the corner, I spotted Dina with her friends.

I crouched to tie my undone shoelaces for cover, but Terry reappeared beating me to it. Glancing back up, I exhaled as Dina walked towards Block A. Facing disapproving glares, I gently removed Terry's hands.

"It's fine, I'll do it," I muttered.

"Hold up, almost done," he insisted.

"Are you guys shooting a movie?" Ji-won blurted, chuckling.

"All done," Terry said.

Grinning, then tilted his head to the side, his smile suddenly faded, and his eyes widened.

"I'll catch you lot later yeah. Gotta run," he said, taking off.

"Stop right there, Terry Jones."

From his Congolese accent, it must be Mr Dean, Terry's basketball coach, taking off his face cap, exposing his bald head. He chased him likely for skipping practice again. Ji-won, and I chuckled, heading inside Block B, walking up the lime-green hallway to the first floor.

We walked into the room buzzed with conversations. Everything in our classroom was white, including the board, tables, and chairs, except for educational posters on the walls. Perhaps to minimise distractions, possibly the reason why our school uniform was navy blue and white, the diagonal gold stripes on our navy-blue ties were the only pop of colour.

We headed for our spot at the back next to the window. Though I was blind as a bat, I preferred it there to avoid unwanted attention. Fortunately, my glasses were powerful enough to see the board from there, although I didn't pay it any attention.

Our English teacher, Miss Andrews entered wearing her customary two-inch heels, an oversized black skirt, and a white blouse. However, her self-proclaimed uniform didn't complement her brunette mushroom bowl haircut. She asked for silence, instructing us to open our textbooks to page ten. Her disappointed gaze caught mine, but I looked away.

I was a constant disappointment to her. In our last assessment, she said, “Mina, I think you deliberately under-perform to avoid attention, not because you lack ability, but because you’re afraid to stand out.” She saw through my facade; she didn’t fall for my act like the other teachers. While they gave up on me, she didn’t. Deep down, I was glad someone heard my silent plea for help. I averted my gaze, opening my notebook to doodle.

With ten minutes left until class ended, my eyes were glued to the door, tapping my legs mimicking the ticking clock, waiting for the bell to ring. The tickets for the concert were about to go on sale, and the school’s internet connection was terrible. Luckily, two years prior, I discovered a spot with the best connection, so I was responsible for booking the tickets. We had saved every penny we could for six months, scraping together just enough for standing tickets. As the bell rang, I quickly rose from my seat.

“Good luck!” Ji-won called out. I nodded and headed for the door.

“Mina Adebayo,” Miss Andrews called, making me halt.

“What does she want now,” I mumbled, exhaling before turning to meet her gaze.

“Yes, Miss.”

“Where is your homework from yesterday?”

I sighed as my head sank.

“I don’t have it, Miss.”

“Detention after school.”

I rose my head grinning.

"Okay, Miss, I'll be there."

I sprinted towards the door before she could respond. Detentions were nothing but sort of a routine for me. It offered a brief respite before returning to my personal hell called "home."

I hurried through the crowded hallway, dashing down the stairs, taking a shortcut to my hideout in Block E. Suddenly, I paused, noticing a group of girls congregating outside, shrieking with excitement. I followed the noise to find out what the fuss was all about, peeping from a corner to catch a glimpse; they surrounded a male senior whose face I couldn't see.

I tilted my head, racking my brain to recall where I had seen his yellow and blue baseball jacket, and then it hit me, Joon Oppa. I recalled seeing Ji-won's brother wearing the same jacket a few days ago; they must have been drooling over his new haircut.

I caught a glimpse of it when I took the trash out yesterday. Joon Choi was like a boy cut out of a magazine; having girls chasing after him was the price he paid for looking like that. Joon's reality was my absolute nightmare. Having people chase, follow, or even look at me was what I dreaded most.

That was why I avoided being in the same space with him, although he didn't appear to like the attention either. That we had in common. He had an icy cold demeanour, which I thought would chase the girls away, but it gave the opposite effect. Fuelling his "bad-boy" demeanour, making them swoon. I rolled my eyes and snuck off, heading for the orange-painted hallway leading to the storeroom.

"Yo, Mina," I heard Terry's voice from behind.

"Is Mr Dean still there?" he asked, ducking behind the stairwell.

I peeked out, surveying the hallway. Mr Dean's booming voice echoed from the other side as he conversed with Miss Nafiseh, the head of the science who towered over Mr Dean. I turned to Terry and nodded, and he sighed, then my phone buzzed with an alert, indicating that the tickets were now available for purchase.

"Gotta go," I said, running off.

"Mina!"

Ignoring Terry, I headed for the storeroom and waited for the connection to get stronger. The scent of bleach and disinfectant filled my nostrils and I grinned, recalling my first time here. I frightened the cleaning lady when she walked in to find me huddled in the corner with the lights off.

Startled, she fell to the ground, screaming, causing her frizzy red wig to fly off. Though she was initially spooked, she eventually grew accustomed to it, even leaving me treats occasionally. Her pitiful stare remained constant, stating, "You must not have any friends."

But I didn't mind; isolating myself was intentional. After the connection got stronger, I selected standing tickets and went to the payment tab. Startled, I looked up and gasped as the door swung open, causing me to lose grip of my phone, which fell to the floor.

Someone barged in, shoving me against the wall, a tall figure looming over me. Was it Terry? The partially opened door allowed a sliver of light inside. But the build didn't match Terry's or the cleaning lady's. I raised my head to get a better look as the light outside reflected off his baseball jacket.

Joon!

Chapter Three

My eyes grew grim, meeting his gaze. Why was he here? He stared at me sternly, and my brows furrowed. I moved to speak, but he placed his hands over my lips.

"Joon, Joon."

We turned towards the door, hearing female voices outside calling him.

I'm sure he came this way."

They must be the girls from earlier, but why did he choose to hide here, of all places? My palms began to sweat, and my heart rate spiked. The light from my phone caught my eye, and I gasped remembering the tickets. I attempted to crouch down and retrieve my phone, but Joon held me firmly in place.

"The tickets," I mumbled.

Pointing at my phone, but he didn't flinch. A shadow approached and the voices outside grew nearer. I gasped as Joon spun me around, pushing his back to the wall, and pulling me in by my waist. I stood frozen, lost in his gaze, as we exchanged breaths.

It'd been a while since I'd been in such proximity to Joon, I knew I should've run for the hills, but instead, I found myself immobilised, frozen in time, breathing him in, digesting every little detail.

Coconut scent lingered in the air, probably from his shampoo. His classic fade haircut enhanced his already captivating face, marrying his meticulously groomed bushy eyebrows, long lashes that complemented his caramel brown eyes, and flawlessly smooth skin with no blemish in sight. His lips had a slight cherry hue, adding to his allure.

I swallowed as his gaze grew intense. I felt exposed, like he could see through me, unveiling my mask. Blinking rapidly, my breath hitched, and my eyes welled up.

"Breathe, Mina," he whispered.

The light from my phone flickered, snapping me back to reality. I wriggled out of his hold but lost my balance and fell backwards. He tried to catch me, but his grip slipped, and in my effort to regain stability, I unintentionally pulled him down. We tumbled out of the storeroom and crashed onto the hallway floor.

"Ahhh," I yelled out as I hit the ground with his weight on top of me.

I blinked, confused by his stillness. Looking to the side, I noticed a crowd surrounding us, their gazes demanding explanations. Joon sighed, unhappy about being caught. They began taking pictures of us, and I placed my hands over my face for cover.

"Omg, what were they doing in there?" one girl asked.

Uncovering my face, I noticed a pair of familiar black shoes approaching. I peered through my fingers and gasped at the sight of Dina with Terry beside her, shooting me a piercing glare; pushing Joon aside, I snatched my phone and manoeuvred through the crowd of students.

"M," Terry called, but I don't stop.

I entered the girls' bathroom, for refuge. Got into the last stall, lowered the toilet seat, and sank onto it. Curling up, I embraced my legs tightly as tears streamed down my face. All my efforts to remain invisible were shattered in an instant. Dina wouldn't let me hear the last of this. I had unintentionally hurt her yet again. I froze as I heard a few girls enter the bathroom.

"Omg, who was that girl with Joon?" a high-pitched voice muttered.

"No clue, she must be a nobody. I don't think I've seen her around before," another added.

"We need to find out who she is. How dare she get mixed up with Joon?" the first girl said, and I felt a pit in my stomach.

They left, and I exhaled. My phone buzzed. Thankfully, it was Ji-won.

"Mimi, got the tickets?"

I gasped recalling the tickets and checked the website, but they were all sold out, and my tears overflowed. My year-long wish was dashed because of Joon Choi. Why did I have to get mixed up with him, of all people? I had also become a target of those girls.

The bell rang, ending break time, but I remained frozen. How do I tell Ji-won? What if I bumped into Dina? Shaking my head, I buried my face between my knees. All cried out, and I exited the stall.

I cautiously stepped out ensuring no one was nearby and walked to the sink. Adjusting my glasses, I stared back at my reflection; my golden-brown skin looked haggard, like a fallen autumn leaf. I glared at my face, resentful of every detail, from my coiled black afro tamed in a bun, my bushy arched eyebrows, and chestnut brown eyes.

I was reminded of the weight my face carried, especially with an identical copy in the world. My actions would either bring its copy peace or tragedy, but I only seemed to give Dina the latter. Switching on the tap, I splashed water on my reflection, exited the bathroom, raced down the hall to my class, and tried sneaking into my seat quietly.

"Mina," Mr Johnson's deep husky voice made me halt.

He was our maths teacher, who was always impeccably dressed in his neatly styled wavy hair and had a deep and distinctive voice that made the female students swoon. Having recently moved to the UK from South Africa, his strong accent added to his allure. I faced him with my head sank.

"Why are you late?" he asked.

My hands trembled as the class stared in suspense.

"Sorry, I'm late, sir," I muttered.

Thankfully, he let me off with a stern look, nudging me to head for my seat; as I approached the table, Ji-won's eyes danced with excitement.

"Did you get the tickets?"

My face fell even lower as I shook my head.

"I'll explain later," I muttered, and her smile dissolved into despair.

She didn't pry me any further, knowing I wanted to go just as bad. I laid my head on my elbow, fighting back my tears. After class, I filled Ji-won in on what occurred earlier, and she quietly listened. Afterwards, she parted my shoulder with a faint smile.

"Don't worry, I'll think of something," she muttered and I exhaled.

"Oppa and his fangirls, wait until I get my hands on them," she said, making a fist and I chuckled, then she gasped.

"Mimi, hurry, you'll be late for detention."

We grabbed our bags and headed out, watching for Dina, who was thankfully nowhere in sight. I was still not ready to face her outburst. As we reached our destination, I waved Ji-won goodbye.

Heading for my spot at the back, laying my head down, I played back today's events. I rolled my eyes as I recalled my horoscope prediction about luck falling on me. But all that fell on me was Joon and a lot of complications. I sighed deeply. My phone buzzed; it was a text from Terry.

"Yo M, sorry I couldn't come to you; got caught by Mr Dean, so I'm stuck in practice until late. Let's link up and I'll walk you home." I hit reply.

"Okay, cool."

I hit send, and laid back down, drifting off.

I woke up and the room was empty, left behind by everyone yet again. Checking the time my eyes widened. It was already five o'clock. I grabbed my backpack and left in haste.

Walking through the empty halls when dark out always sent chills down my spine. I quickened my pace towards the sports hall but halted when I heard voices downstairs.

"You must think you're special because you have junior girls chasing after you?" a deep male voice said.

“Get out of my way,” another boy responded, but his voice sounded familiar.

I got closer but could only see shadows. The clock had gone backwards, making it dark out early.

“Where do you think you are going? I’m not done talking to you,” a high-pitched male voice muttered.

“If I ever see you with Leighann again, it’ll be the end of you,” the high-pitched male voice added.

Then he grabbed the boy in the middle by the collar, pushing him against the wall.

“They are only using you to live out their fantasies. So, don’t get cocky,” he continued.

“Get off me,” the boy with the familiar voice muttered.

“Well, I’ll move if you agree to leave this school or, better yet, this country.”

They all laughed. I turned on my heels, heading back upstairs. I couldn’t afford to get caught up in any more drama. Then I halted as they got louder.

“You dare push me? You’re dead now!”

The boy with the high-pitched voice said then I heard scuffling.

My hand started trembling. I bit my bottom lip, thinking of a way to help. What if they seriously hurt him? I paced back and forth, then it hit me. I turned on my flashlight and faced it towards the stairwell.

“Hey, stop whatever you’re doing over there. I have called the police, and they’re already on the way,” I muttered in a deep voice.

They scattered in haste, leaving the wounded boy behind. I descend a few steps to assess his condition. He was crouched in the corner.

"Hey, are you okay?"

He winced, but he didn't respond attempting to get up but fell back down.

"Hold on. I'll get help."

I turned to leave, then felt pulling on my ankle.

"Mina," he called out.

I gasped as my heart raced. How did he know my name?

"Don't call anyone," he said, releasing my ankle.

Slowly turning, I shone my flashlight on his face; he squinted at its brightness.

"Oppa? Joon Oppa?" my jaw dropped.

"Oh my gosh, you're bleeding."

I reached out to assess his face, but he shoved me off.

I sighed watching him struggle. Still cold-tempered even in this situation.

He attempted hauling himself up again, using the wall for support and finally managed to rise back up, wincing continuously.

"Are you sure I don't need to call someone?"

"No!"

Lifting my hands in surrender, I turned to walk off; getting involved with him would only lead to trouble.

He yelped again, making me halt; I turned to find him gripping the stairwell. I sighed, reaching for his arm to support him, but he resisted.

"Stop being stubborn and let me help you!"

I grabbed his arm again, and he pulled it off. I squeezed my eyes shut and reopened them.

"Fine! If you don't let me help, I'll call for help instead. You choose!" I said, folding my arms.

Exhaling with a frown, he complied. I grabbed his arm and we hobbled over to the nearest classroom. I walked him over to a table to sit.

"Why won't you let me call for help?" I muttered, with my lips pressed into a hard line and he gaped at me.

"It's no big deal; stop fussing," I pressed on his ribs, and he cried out.

"Really? Are you sure about that?" I said, and his expression softened.

"Fine, if you want to help, go to my locker and bring my spare clothes; can't leave looking like this," he said, pointing to his dirty shirt.

His attempt at sarcasm felt out of place. I reluctantly agreed. He shared his locker combination, and I made my way. It was typical of Joon to have a backup plan for every situation or perhaps that wasn't the first time.

I got to his locker, and it looked exactly as you'd expect; it was clean and well-organised, and his spare clothes were well-ironed and neatly folded. I grabbed them quickly and stopped by my locker for supplies.

Being clumsy, I kept a first aid kit in my locker. I retrieved it and returned to Joon, knocking before entering. His glare fixated on the box in my hand.

"How'd you get into the nurse's office?"

I scowled at him.

"I didn't; this is mine."

"Why do you need a first aid kit?"

"Because I'm always getting injured," he chuckled.

"You are very clumsy," he smirked.

Ignoring him, I opened the kit, grabbing disinfectant wipes to clean the blood on his lips. He stops my hand mid-way, snatching the wipe.

"I'll do it," he insisted, dabbing at his lip.

"You missed a bit."

He moved his hands to another corner.

"Not there, just beneath your chin."

"Here?" I shook my head and sighed.

"Pass it."

Grabbing the wipe from him, I held his chin in place, gently wiping and he winced, making me smirk.

"Cry, baby," I murmured.

In silence, he stared at me as though for the first time. The room was dimly lit by my flashlight. I paused, wishing I could read his thoughts. Then a flashback of us in the storeroom replayed in my mind and I swallowed blinking rapidly as the silence intensified.

"Finished?" he asked, making me jump.

I grabbed ointment using a cotton bud to apply it.

"All done," I said.

"How did you know it was me back there?" he brows frowned.

"Who wouldn't recognise your annoying voice?" my jaw dropped.

Then he got up unbuttoning his shirt, and I swallowed turning around instantly, but caught a glimpse of his muscular chest.

"What are you doing?" I asked, catching my breath.

"Why were you looking?" he smirked, and I rolled my eyes.

"You could have warned me," I said, walking towards the door.

"I'll wait outside."

"Suit yourself."

I got to the halls, fanning myself. Moments later Joon stepped out limping towards the stairs.

"Hey, wait up," I said.

But he didn't respond. I rushed back into the room, grabbed my stuff, and ran to catch up with him.

"Why did you leave me behind?"

"Caught up, didn't you?"

I clenched my jaw, stopping to catch my breath. "Let's stay calm, Mina," I repeated. We got to the bike shed, and my eyes widened. They must have gotten to his bike cutting off the chains. Joon sighed, clenching his fists then exhaled grabbing it and pushing it down the hill. I jogged on to catch up with him.

"Who were those guys?" I asked, but he said nothing.

"Has this happened before?" he still didn't respond.

"Shouldn't you report them?" I added; he halted and dropped his bike walking towards me.

I backed up slowly, gulping until my back hit the wall. He placed his arms on either side of my head caging me in, glaring at me panting. I gasped trembling as I saw the veins on his neck bulge.

"You better not say a word of this to anyone, especially not to Ji-won, do you understand?" he yelled.

My heart rate spiked, and I clenched my fists; I attempted to speak, but he picked up his bike and walked off; I gasped, clenching my teeth. How could Joon treat me this way? After everything he put me through today, instead of thanking me, he was making threats and demands; I ran up to him, grabbed his bike and made him halt.

"Do you know what you've put me through today?"

"Because of that storeroom incident, rumours are spreading about me in school. Also, I helped you earlier with those boys and your wounds!"

I squeezed my eyes shut as my words failed me.

"But instead of thanking me, you're making threats and demands?"

I walked in closer, raising my head to meet his gaze.

"Don't worry about me saying anything to anyone because getting involved with you is my literal nightmare," his eyes faded.

I turned on my heels and walked off without looking back.

I held back my tears, refusing to let them escape. Joon wasn't worth it.

Chapter Four

Getting to our building, I halted exhaling as I glared at the old brown chipping brick walls of our estate, covered with graffiti, the scent of fish and chips oozing from the nearby takeaway making my belly rumble, but I ignored it.

I exhaled knowing the overwhelming events I had been through that day were nowhere near the flames of hell I was heading towards. Slowly pacing up the stairs, I finally arrived in front of hell's gate, hesitant to go inside. My phone buzzed, making my heart jump. It was a text from Terry.

"Yo M, why didn't you wait for me? Hope you got back okay," I clicked reply.

"Yes, I did. Sorry, something came up," I hit send.

I swallowed and turned in my keys, saying a silent prayer before pulling the door handle, but it was unexpectedly quiet inside. I took my shoes off and placed them on the shoe rack by the passageway, then spotted Dina's shoes already in place, making my heart rate spike.

Although our living room was always gloomy with the charcoal curtains drawn, it looked grimmer. I peeked in, checking for Mum at her usual spot on the black sofa, but she wasn't there. Then the lights abruptly switched on.

"Why are you back so late?" Mum asked.

Readjusting her Ankara wrapper tied around her waist over a black t-shirt. I gasped, taken aback by her sudden appearance; she was sitting in the dining area.

"I slept off at detention," I said, looking down at my fingers.

The door to Dina's room suddenly slammed open, and she came charging at me; I stepped back instinctively, but I could not get away fast enough. She slapped me, making my glasses fly off. My eyes widened as I stared back at her, holding my cheeks tingled with sparks.

"Dina!" Mum called out, running towards us.

She ignored Mum, grabbing onto my shirt.

"Haven't I warned you to lay low and remain invincible?" Dina said, with her eyes burning with rage.

"Dina, ḱi lọ́ dé?" Mum asked what's going on in Yoruba.

She tried to pull Dina away, but Dina didn't let go.

"Why were you with him in the storeroom? Do you realise how much danger you've put me in? What if people mistake me for you again!"

Her eyes darkened, making me tremble.

"Do you want to see me go crazy?"

She shook me continuously, before finally shoving me to the ground. I hit my head against the wall. Mum rushed over to help.

"Are you okay?" she asked.

But I remained speechless, glaring at the floor, panting heavily.

"Stay hidden and invisible, Mina," she breathlessly warned.

"If you feel any remorse for what you did, you will do as I've said."

She stormed off, slamming the door. I remained stagnant, trembling.

"What did you do to your sister this time?"

"Haven't I warned you not to make her angry?"

Mum then rushed towards Dina's room and tears cascaded down my tingling cheeks. Time stood still as I sat, fixated on the shadowy wall of our living room. My eyes were swollen, my heart heavy, and my legs had turned to jelly.

Mum returned, picked up my glasses, and guided me to my room. She turned on the light, illuminating my N.O. posters, and laid me on my N.O. printed bedding.

"Get some sleep; we will talk about this later," she said.

I placed my glasses on the bedside table and sighed, observing my aged Mum. Despite being in her early forties, she appeared much older. Her once black afro was now grey, her eyes tired and wrinkled, and her complexion dry and worn. The stress of dealing with Dina and me and the responsibilities of being a widowed single parent had taken its toll.

"I'm sorry, Mum," I murmured, and she sighed.

"Get some sleep," she said, closing the door.

Ignoring my growling stomach, I dismissed any desire to eat. Dina's piercing stare consumed my mind. I squeezed my eyes shut clutching my shirt. It was in those moments I yearned for my dad's presence.

I grabbed his wedding photo from my bedside table clutching onto it, gazing at it through my teary eyes. Dad's radiant smile on that joyous day, dressed in a burgundy and gold Yoruba agbada with a matching Fila, grinning through his moustache. I held it close, sobbing continuously.

My heart ached, reminded I was also to blame for his absence; I hit my chest repeatedly, weeping silently. After a while I plugged in my headphones, playing "Not Alone" by N.O. The part of the song I related to the most was the bridge, "I will give all I have for just a second longer with you." I shut my eyes, letting their soothing voices send me into a slumber.

My alarm beeped jolting me awake. I groaned at the bright light streaming through the windows, feeling my body ache. I sat up, put on my glasses, and admired my N.O. plastered walls. Their smiling faces energised me, helping me forget yesterday's events.

On my centrepiece poster, Kim Dong-min stood at the far right. The tall and muscly leader with beautiful brown eyes. Next was Lee Min-woo, the lead dancer, known for his bright and fun personality, earning him the nickname "Rainbow" due to his colourful hairstyles and fashion sense. Park Sung-mo, the lead singer, was nicknamed "Flower Boy" for his stunning looks and visible abs. Jin Tae-hee, the cheeky maknae, was playful and competitive. As I admired them, their impact faded catching the reflection of my swollen cheeks in the mirror.

I pondered how to distinguish myself from Dina running my hands through my unruly afro, an idea struck me. I recalled Mum still had Dad's old clippers. I retrieved them from storage and locked myself in the bathroom.

Plugging the clippers, I shaved my hair as low as possible. After cleaning the floor, I took a shower and quickly got dressed.

Quietly, putting on my shoes and left for school, avoiding Mum and Dina like I usually did in the mornings.

Though we lived together, we rarely interacted. I usually ate alone to avoid arguments with Dina to avoid upsetting Mum. But yesterday felt different. Dina spoke to me more than she had in years, which was oddly comforting. Others often admired our twin bond, assuming we were close.

I'd smile and nod to preserve their fantasy and avoid confronting my reality, but we weren't always like that. Once, those fantasies were our reality; Mum, Dad, Dina, and I lived happily, surrounded by joy and laughter. Thoughts of the past flooded my mind: Dad grilling in the backyard of our old house, Mum relaxing in the hammock reading a book, and Dina and I chasing each other with water guns.

The lingering fragrance of Mum's roses remained etched in my memory. Dina and I watered them daily. Back then, we shared everything, our room, bed, clothes, secrets, and endless laughter. We were inseparable. Well until I ruined everything.

I got on the lift, and it stopped on Ji-won's floor. I looked up hoping Ji-won was finally up early for school. The doors sprung open, and I swallowed as my hope faded. Joon stared at me wide-eyed, wearing his signature baseball jacket with white t-shirt and grey trousers. I looked away, avoiding his gaze.

"Aren't you getting on?" I asked as he stood wide-eyed gawking at me.

I caressed my cropped hair biting my bottom lip. He got in, and we descended in silence. I glanced at his lip, which had gotten less swollen. Exiting the building, he followed behind as we headed up the hill to school. The wind whipped around wildly, sending chills down my scalp, realising I had chosen the wrong season to cut my hair, but on the plus side I was glad knowing I no longer had to spend time taming my afro before school.

I thrust my feet through the dry, crackling leaves. Watching Junior students giggle, making angel wings on a pile of leaves. The air was filled with the aroma of pumpkin spice and cinnamon latte from the local café, where seniors posed with their coffee cups for pictures.

Reaching the school gates, Joon strode ahead, and I rolled my eyes, brushing aside thoughts of him. Hoping my new hair would stop people from recalling I was the girl mixed up with him.

I exhaled heading straight for the girl's bathroom in Block A. Entering a stall, I sat on the covered toilet seat and plugged in my headphones. Playing, "Good Time" by N.O. An upbeat song from their first album. Folding my legs into an embrace, listening until it was time for my first lesson.

Walking down the halls, I felt glares and whispers. Didn't I trim my haircut well? Then I gasped as the thought crossed my mind. Could they have figured out that I was the girl with Joon yesterday? I quickened my pace until I got to class. Ji-won stared, doing a double take as I pulled out my chair to sit.

"Mi-mi-Mimi, is that you?" she muttered, blinking.

I glared at her puzzled.

"Does it look bad?"

Then she leaned in closer making me gasp.

"Oh my gosh, I can't believe you cut your hair!"

"Does it look weird?"

"Amazing, you look amazing!" she gushed.

"Mimi, were you always this beautiful?" she muttered, and I turned tomato red.

"Beautiful?" I mumbled in disbelief.

My aim was to blend in, but I might have failed again, creating the opposite effect as the whole class stared at me.

"Who's the new girl?"

Ginger-haired Jacob asked, and then the second bell rang. I exhaled as Mr Peter, our social studies teacher, entered, telling everyone to sit. He recently began power walking to class to lose weight. Ji-won continued gawking at me making me squirm.

"Ah, that reminds me, I might have found a way to get us tickets," Ji-won muttered, and I gasped.

"How?" I asked as my eyes widened.

"Who's talking?" Mr Peter asked.

Pulling up his ill-fitted trousers. Then paused, staring at me as though for the first time.

"Are you new?" he asked.

"It's Mina, sir," Ji-won said.

"Who? Detention, Mina," he said, and everyone chuckled.

"Be quiet," he yelled.

He glared at me in disbelief.

"Mina, have you done your homework?" he asked.

I looked down at my fingers.

"No, sir."

"I guess the new hair doesn't come with a new brain," he said, and everyone chuckled.

"Detention for you, Mina," he said, banging his table with a ruler.

"That's enough now. Quiet down, everyone, and open your textbook to page six."

I sunk my head onto the table.

Ji-won sighed, tapping my back and I forced a smile.

After the lesson, I turned to Ji-won.

"So, tell me, how can we get tickets?"

"Rachel, a family friend of ours, is the daughter of the C.E.O for underground entertainment," Ji-won said, and my jaw dropped.

"You mean the same record company N.O. is signed to?" she nodded.

"Ji, why have you never mentioned this?"

"Well, I was hoping I wouldn't have to ask. I'm sure she has a lot of people bothering her for favours," I nodded in agreement.

"That's true, so what's the plan?" I asked.

"Well, she's a student here."

"Wait, what, she is?" my jaw dropped.

"Yes, she is in most classes with Joon Oppa," I sighed at the sound of his name.

"I'll meet her after school and ask," I squeezed her hands, grinning.

"Okay, let's give it one more shot," I muttered, but her brows furrowed suddenly, and her smile faded.

"Wait Mina, what happened to your cheek? You have a scar on the side," she said, reaching out her hands.

I turned away from her, placing mine over it.

"It's nothing," I said, grabbing my bag.

"It's time for our next lesson. See you at lunch," I said.

Heading for the door, she hurriedly followed me out of the class.

"What happened, Mina? Tell me," she insisted.

"Hey, you're Ji-won, right?"

We both turned, and I gasped.

It was a junior who constantly chased Joon around the school. She also witnessed the storeroom incident; she tucked her long blonde hair behind her ears, exposing her trail of piercings. Thick winged liner and a skull necklace. Her skirt rolled up with her shirt unbuttoned at the top, exposing her chest. I turned my gaze away, keeping my head down.

"I am, and you are?" Ji-won asked.

"Someone interested in your brother," she smirked.

"Does he have a girlfriend?" Ji-won chuckled.

"I don't think I need to disclose my brother's personal life to you," she said, and the junior smirked.

"Well, from your reaction, it doesn't seem like he does," she said.

"Well, if that's all, I'll be on my way," Ji-won said.

Turning to leave, the junior grabbed her arm, stopping her.

"One last thing; I'm sure you've heard about what happened yesterday. Who was the girl that fell out of the storeroom with him?" she asked.

My heart tightened and my hands began to tremble. Ji-won jolted her arm free of her grip.

"I don't know whom you're talking about, but whomever it is probably moved schools already to get away from crazies like you looking for her," Ji-won said.

The girl's jaw dropped. Ji-won turned to me, grabbed my hand, and pulled me away.

We got to the end of the hallway, turning the corner, and I crouched, panting.

"Mimi, you, okay?" Ji-won asked. I nodded panting.

"Sure?"

I exhaled, getting back on my feet.

"I'm fine, Ji. You go ahead. I'll see you later," I said.

Giving Ji-won a reassuring smile, she nodded and headed to her next class, and I headed to mine at Block E with my heart still pounding.

Ascending the stairs, I spotted Joon coming down. I gasped and turned towards the opposite direction and accidentally collided with someone in the hallway. Rubbing my head, I looked up and saw a group of sixth-formers.

Unfortunately, I bumped into their leader, a tall, slim mixed-race boy with grey eyes. Accompanied by his minions clad in black tracksuits and red bandanas, the emblem of their gang. They had a reputation for skipping classes and chasing girls. He grinned exposing his unkept gold teeth.

Chapter Five

"Sorry," I muttered.

"It's cool, babes. You good, though?"

My brows rose, and I stepped back; his high-pitched voice sounded familiar, sending chills down my spine.

"I'm good, thank you, and sorry again."

I moved to the side, but he stepped in front of me.

"Yo babes, chill; what's the hurry?" he said and I scrolled.

"I don't want to be late for class," I said.

Taking another step and he blocked my way again.

"It'll only be a sec b," he said, and I sighed meeting his gaze.

"Are you new here? Coz there's no way I wouldn't have noticed a pretty thing like you. That low cut looks good on you."

I rolled my eyes at his corny pickup line. Then he lifted his hands to touch my hair, and I ducked out of his reach.

"I think you know better than to touch a black girl's hair," I said, stepping back.

"What's the big deal? I was admiring it; why you acting up?"

He reached for my hair again, but this time, someone grabbed his hands midway from behind.

From his expensive watch and name-brand shoes, I exhaled.

“Bro, she said don’t touch her hair, so allow it.”

As always, Terry showed up right when I needed him. Stepping in front of me to face the boy directly.

“Who the hell are you, and why are you getting involved? Are you her man or what?” the senior asked.

His minions gathered around, surrounding us.

“She’s my bredrin. She told you to stop, so let her go,” Terry said.

As they argued, I slowly backed away, and then I felt a pull on my arm from behind, whisking me away.

It happened so fast that I almost lost my footing, and my glasses fell halfway down my face. I readjusted them to see who it was, and my heart leapt spotting his yellow baseball jacket. I tried pulling my hands out of his hold, but his grip got tighter.

“What are you doing? Let go.”

But he didn’t respond; although I only saw his back, I could tell from his heavy breathing, he was furious.

“Let go,” I repeated.

Pulling, however, my strength was no match for his; luckily, most students were already in class. Hence, no one noticed us.

We finally got to the third floor, and he halted abruptly; releasing my hand, I turned, and we were at my next lesson; my brows frowned, wondering how he knew I had that class. He then began walking off.

“Joon Oppa!”

He turned panting with his brows frowned, and hands formed into a fist, charging towards me.

I swallowed, stepping back, gripping the edge of my navy-blue skirt. He attempted to speak, but his mouth settled into a grim line as he exhaled. What was he so mad about? I thought to myself; my school tie suddenly felt too tight, making it hard to breathe. He ran his hands through his hair, breathing heavily.

"Didn't I warn you not to say anything to anyone about yesterday?" he said, and my brows frowned.

"I didn't say anything to anyone," I muttered.

"Then why were you speaking to those boys? What makes you so fearless, Mina? What if they had hurt…" he paused.

Squeezing his eyes shut, as his words failed him, I glared at him, puzzled.

"What does that have to do with them?"

His eyes widened and his brows frowned.

"Joon."

A female voice from behind called; we turned to find a gorgeous senior. She was tall and slim, with long silky black hair, wearing all-white skinny jeans and a wool jumper. Her makeup looked seamless, as though a professional makeup artist did it; she looked like a runway model. I gawked at her as my mouth went dry.

"Aren't you coming to class? You're going to be late," she said.

Then reached into her white Chanel purse, took out two banana milk and offered one to Joon; it looked just like the ones I saw in Korean dramas, the same kind Ji-won offered me whenever I visited her house. She must be South Korean too, and then her eyes fell on me. I spun around instantly, and Joon leaned in.

"Don't make me repeat myself, Mina. Keep your mouth shut."

I met his gaze, and he wore the same tortured look he had yesterday, making my heart clench, but I ignored it, upholding my disdained expression.

He sighed joining the senior; I watched as they walked into their classroom two doors down from mine; the senior halted looking back at me, glaring; I lowered my gaze and entered my class.

Luckily our teacher hadn't arrived yet. I sat replaying my encounter with Joon; *why was he worried I was speaking to those boys*? Then I gasp recalling yesterday's incident. That's why that senior's voice sounded familiar. I bit my finger and tap my feet repeatedly. *But why isn't Joon reporting them? What if they hurt him again or worse*? I thought. Judging by how he questioned me, he seemed on edge.

"Oh, that was close. Thank God Mr Harris isn't here yet," Terry muttered breathlessly, sliding into the chair beside me.

My eyes widened.

"Are you okay? Are you hurt?"

He raised his brows, blinking rapidly, and cleared his throat.

"If you cared so much about my well-being, why did you run off?"

I looked down at my fingers.

"I'm sorry, they didn't hurt you, did they?" I muttered.

"Hey, come on now. It's me you're talking about here," he smirked.

"Don't worry; I went easy on them," he added, making me chuckle.

Then my smile faded, recalling I left him alone.

"It's cool. I'll let you off this time, well, because I like your new haircut," he said, gawking at me.

I gently patted my hair, squirming in my chair.

"It looks weird, doesn't it?" I muttered.

He didn't respond, but I felt his eyes on me, so I turned to meet his gaze.

"What's with the look?"

"You're right; it is weird," he said, and I gasped.

"You've become prettier," he added, and I looked down at my fingers.

"I guess now I have to make sure I go to the gym more regularly, so I can fight off all your new admirers," he added, flexing his muscles, making me chuckle.

"What admirers?" I murmured.

"Like those boys from earlier; there will be a lot more, mark my words," he said. I shook my head, shrugging off his comment.

"Quiet down, everyone."

"Our history teacher, Mr Harris, or as most students liked to call him behind his back," Mr Hairy said.

"Sorry, I'm late. I had issues with the printer again," he continued.

Scratching his overgrown grey and unkept beard with a pen cover.

Terry leaned in close, nudging me.

"Yo M, who was the guy that pulled you away?" he asked.

Resting his chin on his palm, intensely waiting for my response.

"Isn't he the same guy from yesterday?"

I hoped Terry would have forgotten about yesterday's incident or at least pretended to; I cleared my throat.

"Who?" I asked.

He raised his brows, and I bit my bottom lip, realising I couldn't play coy.

"You mean the guy from earlier?" I stuttered.

"Obviously, who is he?"

"Ji-won's, brother," I muttered, and he leaned back with his arms crossed, then forward again.

"Hmm, I see," he mumbled.

"But what were you guys doing in the storeroom yesterday? And why did he grab you earlier? He seemed angry."

"Oh, that, he was trying to get me away from those boys, just like you were. Besides, Joon always looks angry."

"Quiet over there!" Mr Harris yelled.

"Terry, enough with the twenty-one questions. I don't want to get in trouble."

"Fine, but this conversation isn't over," he whispered.

"At lunchtime, I attempted dodging Terry, but he cornered me, insisting I join him for lunch. I declined to walk off, but he blocked my path, until I gave in as always, on our way, we bumped into Dina outside," she gasped glaring at me.

"Yourrrrrr, your hair."

Terry's brows frowned.

"D, are you just seeing it for the first time? Don't you guys live together?"

"Oo of course, I've seen it already, just still surprised she cut it," she muttered, clearing her throat.

"Well, we are going for lunch together. Want to join?" Terry asked.

"Sure, but I need to speak with Mina. It'll just be a minute," she said.

Wearing a forced smile, she pulled me to the side.

"What the hell are you up to this time, Mina? Cutting your hair to seek attention?" she asked, panting.

"You've forgotten my warning already? First, it was that boy, Joon, or whatever his name is, and now Terry?" she added, panting.

"Dina, it's not what you think. I was only trying to," she lifted her hands cutting me off.

"Save it. I'm not interested in any of your excuses or lies. Stay away from them both understood?"

Putting on her fake smile, she pulled me back to Terry.

"Oh no, T. It looks like it'll just be us having lunch. Mina isn't feeling well; she's going to the nurse's office," Dina said.

"Mina, what's wrong? Are you okay?" he asked.

Terry reached out to check my temperature, and Dina stopped him midway.

"She'll be fine. I offered to go with her, but she insists on going alone. She doesn't want us to miss lunch because of her. How considerate," she smirked, pulling Terry away.

"But…" Terry muttered.

"Don't worry; she'll be okay. Feel better, Mina, and text me later, okay?" Dina said cutting him off.

I forced a smile, as they walked off, and she gave me a smug glare. I headed to my usual spot in the girl's bathroom, plugged in my headphones, and played N.O. to transport me, eating my leftover shortbread for lunch. My attempt to protect Dina had failed once again. I sighed, fighting back my tears, but they came sprawling down my cheeks.

After school, I headed to my usual extracurricular activity. On my way I spotted Ji-won, and Emily waiting at the end of the hall waving and I rushed over to join them.

Emily had her food diary in hand, doing thigh exercises while chewing on a nutritional bar. She had gone from size sixteen to size eight, battling body dysmorphia. Constantly monitoring her diet and exercising, she even dyed her hair blonde to create the illusion of a smaller face.

Ji-won and I reassured her she was beautiful, regardless of her weight, but to no avail. I linked arms with them, and we walked towards Block A.

"Ji-won."

A familiar voice called out, we all turned, and it was the senior I saw with Joon earlier.

"Rachel unnie," Ji-won called, grinning.

"Mimi, remember the family friend I told you about?" she said.

"You mean the one that could get us tickets?" I asked and she nodded.

"I'll be right back," she said, running over to meet her.

I silently prayed as she approached her. Rachel looked at me, then smiled and nodded at Ji-won, who screamed hugging Rachel tightly, before giving me a thumbs up. I felt a surge of sparks, knowing I would finally see the boys who gave my life a new meaning. Waving Rachel goodbye, Ji-won re-joined us.

"Oh my gosh, Mimi, she's getting us V.I.P tickets and backstage passes too," Ji-won said.

My knees grew weak hearing those words. We screamed, linking hands, and jumping around in circles.

"All that's left now is getting our parent's permission," Ji-won said.

My face sank as the image of Mum saying no popped into my head.

"What's wrong?" Ji-won asked.

I shook my head.

"Nothing," I said, putting on a forced smile.

"Let's start with your Mum," I suggested, and she nodded.

"Okay, then let's meet at my house tonight," she muttered.

Emily rolled her eyes at us as she had no interest in K-pop. I waved them goodbye racing to detention, getting in just in time. I sank into my seat as the joy I felt earlier faded, knowing Mum wouldn't let me go. Arriving home, Mum and Dina were engrossed in their favourite reality show, "Love in the Jungle," wearing matching pink pyjamas. After greeting Mum, I headed for my room.

"Stop right there, Mina," Mum said.

"Why did you cut your hair?" she muttered.

Turning off the TV as she walked up to me.

"What is going on with you lately?"

From the smirk on Dina's face, she must have told Mum.

"Isn't it obvious she did it for attention," Dina said, I glared at her, clenching my teeth. Mum sighed.

"That's enough, Dina. I don't want a repeat of yesterday," Mum said.

Pulling me in to check my haircut, and sighed then asked me to change and grab the dinner she left for me in the kitchen. After changing, I grabbed the food and retreated to my room avoiding Dina.

Mum rarely showed concern for me, always prioritising Dina. She felt guilty for what happened to Dina and blamed herself, which led to me being overlooked. It took shaving my hair off to finally capture her attention, and it was oddly comforting.

After finishing dinner, pounded yam and ogbono soup, I received a text from Ji-won inviting me over. I exhaled, grabbed a random textbook from my bag, and made my way back to the living room.

"Mum, I need to go to Ji-won's house to return her textbook; she needs it for her homework," I swallowed, and Dina smirked.

"Since when did you and that dummy start caring about homework?"

"That's enough, Dina. You can go, Mina, but hurry back."

I pressed my lips together racing out. I got to Ji-won's pressing the doorbell; our building was just like every other red-bricked estate in London, making it nothing to brag about. It had no outstanding features or unique selling point, but it had grown on me.

"Umma, I'll get it," I heard Ji-won, saying from inside.

She opened the door, wearing pink leggings and a dolphin-print top. Hand in hand, we headed to the bustling kitchen where her mum and grandmother were preparing dinner. Her mum wore a beige apron over a yellow midi skater dress, while her grandmother donned colourful floral print trousers and a pink blouse. The enticing aroma was of bibimbap.

"Annyeong-haseyo," I said.

I said my greetings with a bow, the way Ji-won taught me to show respect to an elder in South Korean culture which is somewhat different to mine, in Yoruba culture we kneel to show respect to our elders and the lower you go the more respectful its deemed.

"Hello, Mina; wow, I love your haircut. It suits you," Ji-won's Mum muttered, and her grandma nodded in agreement.

"Thank you."

Ji-won's house was a vibrant haven, adorned with warm colours and filled with laughter. It felt like stepping into a different world. Her youthful mum, always impeccably styled, radiated brightness, unlike mine. She wore colourful attire and maintained her silky brown hair. Her spring-like smile and sparkling eyes enlivened every conversation.

Ji-won's grandma treated me like family, sharing her delicious homemade Korean meals and warm hugs. Her impeccable fashion made her stand out among the grandmas in the neighbourhood. She always praised me for enjoying her spicy tteokbokki.

Clearing her throat Ji-won nudged closer.

"Umma," she called out.

"Yes?" she responded, but Ji-won began to tremble.

"Erm," she mumbled.

Biting down her bottom lip, fiddled with her fingers, her Mum sighed as Ji-won hesitated.

"Ji-won; what is it?" she asked.

Despite Ji-won's mum's generally sweet nature, she disapproved of our fangirling activities, and Ji-won remained frozen, unable to speak.

"Mina, you tell me, what is going on?"

As I prepared to speak, Joon emerged from his room. He walked past towering over me, and the warmth I felt earlier turned cold. Despite his loving upbringing, Joon was nothing like his family.

He sighed and slid into a dining chair, arms crossed; perhaps suspicious I might mention yesterday's incident, I rolled my eyes at the thought.

"Well, would one of you speak!" Ji-won's Mum muttered folding her arms.

Ji-won nudged me, and I pushed back, raising my brows, and her Mum sighed.

"Either one of you speaks, or you can both forget it."

"Mum, can we please attend the upcoming N.O. concert?" Ji-won blurted out.

"No," she said instantly.

"You should both be focusing on your upcoming mock exams instead of thinking about going to a concert!"

"But Aunty, we can do both," I insisted, sounding as desperate as I felt.

"How is that Mina?" she asked, folding her arms.

"At the moment, you and Ji-won have one of the worst grades in your year group," she added.

Ji-won and I looked at each other, lowering our heads, and her Mum sighed.

"All right, girls, how about we strike a deal? You can go if you both get a C grade in your upcoming mock exam."

Our jaws dropped, and Joon chuckled.

"Joon," she called out; he turned to meet her gaze.

"Can you tutor them for an hour every day after school and on the weekends?" she said.

His laughter faded as he leapt up, wide-eyed. Then she turned to me.

"Mina, I'll call your Mum and tell her about the lessons," she added.

My face sank; how had I become intertwined with Joon again? I wobbled as my knees grew weak, Joon's face turned red, and his jaw clenched.

"But why do I have to tutor them? I have a lot of studying to do," he muttered.

"Joon, it'll only be for an hour," she replied.

He sighed looking away. Ji-won pulled my arm, leading me to her room.

"Should we just do it?"

"Are you having a laugh, Ji? For our last mock exam, I got an E, and you, my darling, got an F our next mock exam is in a month. Do you really think we can both get a C in such a short amount of time?" I said, folding my arms.

"Mimi, didn't we promise to go to the concert together? If we're true N.O. fans, shouldn't we do our best to make sure we get to see them live?" she asked.

Wrapping her arms into mine, displaying those puppy doll eyes.

"It's an hour after school, huh? Say yes, Mina?" she insisted, wiggling me and I sighed.

"Give me a second to think," I muttered.

Chapter Six

Biting my fingers, I pondered. What if Joon noticed my intentional underperformance? But without his tutoring, sudden improvement would raise questions. However, being intertwined with him was equally dangerous. I sighed.

I glanced back, Ji-won's hands folded in a plea. Perhaps tutoring with Joon was my escape. He could vouch for my change in grades. Convincing Mum to keep it from Dina was crucial. I exhaled meeting Ji-won's gaze.

"Fine, let's do it," I blurted out, and she jumped for joy.

On our way back to the living room, I halted.

"What's wrong?" she asked.

"What about Joon? He seemed to be against it," I muttered, and she smirked.

"Don't worry, Mum will handle him, let's go."

"Mum, we're in," Ji-won muttered.

"I'm not," Joon said, leaving, and his Mum grinned.

"Well, if you help, I'll get you that new bike. What do you say?" she proposed.

He pivoted and exhaled.

"Fine, but only until exams start," he said, with a stern glare.

"Both of you, come with me."

Suppressing our grins, we trailed behind him. Entering his room for the first time. A world globe poster and certificates for attendance, top grades, and volunteer recognition adorned the wall above his desk.

His walls, painted sky blue, showcased a black bookshelf lined with neatly arranged educational books. The double bed, adorned with grey and white bedding, exuded tidiness. The spotless room stood in stark contrast to mine. Above the bed, a wooden acoustic guitar adorned the wall.

My eyes widened, glancing at him and then back at the guitar.

"Joon Oppa, is that really yours?"

He scrolled at me but didn't comment.

"He plays really well. Dad taught him. You should hear him sing too; he's good," Ji-won exclaimed.

I stared in disbelief, and he gazed intensely at Ji-won, who covered her mouth. My attention shifted to a family photo on his white study desk. As I reached out to grab it, he swiftly snatched it away, holding it high above his head, making me stumble, crashing into his arms. We tumbled backwards, landing on the chair beside his desk, and my forehead collided with his nose.

"Ouch," I cried out.

Rubbing my forehead to ease the pain, I lifted my head, and our eyes locked. I swallowed, captivated by his gaze—a mix of wonder, safety, and fear. But above all, I felt exposed; could he see right through me?

"Get off," he said.

Ji-won's laughter snapped me out of my daze. I wiggled my way out and back on my feet.

"Oh my gosh, Oppa, you're bleeding!" she exclaimed, pointing at the blood trickling down his nose, as her laughter faded.

"I'll get tissue," Ji-won said running out.

I stretched out my jumper sleeves, pressing them against his nose, and pushed his head back.

"I'm so sorry," I said.

"What are you doing?" he asked, escaping my reach.

"Keep your head back and hold still," I muttered.

Pushing his head down again, he tried pulling me away, but I resisted, and his hands landed on my chest. My eyes widened, and he gasped, immediately taking his hands off.

"That wasn't intentional," he said, clearing his throat.

"Besides, why were you pushing my head back? It's a common misconception about nosebleeds," he scolded.

Stunned, I stayed motionless, trying to comprehend the situation. Ji-won brought tissues and handed them to him.

"Does it hurt?" I asked.

He blanked me, holding the tissue to his nose, then got up placing the picture above his shelf. I swallowed, heading for the door.

"Where are you going?" Joon asked.

"Sit," he muttered.

Pointing at his bed.

He then pulled out his desk chair sitting to face us.

"I hope you will both take this seriously."

"We will, Oppa!" Ji-won said.

Then he glared at me.

"We will," I muttered.

"Good. Lessons start at 6 pm sharp, after school for an hour. No phones or chatting," he cautioned, his gaze firm.

"Note the subjects you struggle with for review tomorrow," he said, jotting in his navy-blue planner.

"On weekends, we'll have one-on-one sessions."

"Mina, you're up this weekend," he said, and I nodded in agreement.

"That's it for today."

I leapt up, leaving, and Ji-won followed behind.

"Everything will go well, right?" I asked.

She grinned, placing her hands on my shoulders.

"Of course, it will," she said, and we headed to the living room.

"Mina, I've informed your Mum about the lessons," Ji-won's Mum said.

My eyes widened, and my knees grew weak.

"I should get back home now. See you tomorrow."

I rushed out the door, screaming inwardly. I hoped to tell Mum myself. I ran my hand through my hair, biting my fingers. Rolling up my sleeves to hide the bloodstain, I exhaled and headed upstairs. Getting in, Dina and Mum were nowhere in sight. Trembling, I headed for my room. Hearing the running shower, I exhaled realising Dina hadn't overheard Mum's phone call. Opening the door to my room, I froze. Mum was sitting on my bed with her arms folded.

"Ẃa jòkó," she said in Yoruba, instructing me to sit.

Pointing at the bean bag chair opposite the bed, I sat down, folding my trembling hands.

"What's this I hear about you getting tutored by Ji-won's brother? Wasn't he the reason for your argument with Dina? What if she finds out?"

Fuelled by my longing to see the boys, I exhaled deeply, raising my eyes to meet hers.

"She won't, Mum, unless you tell her. The lessons will be at Ji-won's house, not at school, so it won't affect Dina."

"Do you even have tickets?"

"Yes, we do! Please, Mum, I never ask for anything, but just this once, can't I have this?" I mumbled, tears welling up.

"What happened that day wasn't within my control. But I've lived like a sinner for years, never complaining, even when you constantly favour Dina over me. In Year Seven, when we started ballet, Dina didn't want us seen together, so you asked me to drop out, and I did without hesitation. In Year Eight, I was chosen as the lead in the school play, but Dina went on a hunger strike in protest for me to give it up. And when you asked me to quit again, I did so without complaint. Then, in Year Nine..." Mum interrupted, raising her hands.

"—Ó ti t'o, that's enough," she said in Yoruba, choked up.

"Mum, am I, not your daughter, too?" I choked up.

Struggling to utter the words, tears streamed down our cheeks.

"I won't ask for anything else, Mum, so please, don't ask me to give up on this," I pleaded.

We both sobbed and finally, she exhaled, nodding, and I gasped.

"Just ensure your sister doesn't get hurt."

"I will."

"Thank you, Mum, thank you," I whispered.

Mum got up, opened the door, and gasped, colliding with Dina in the hallway.

"What's wrong? Why are you so startled?" Dina asked, frowning.

"Nothing, I was telling Mina off for cutting her hair; let's all go to bed," she said.

Closing my bedroom door, I leapt off the bean bag chair, silently cheering. Approaching the largest N.O. poster on my wall and kissed it. The next morning, Ji-won was waiting by the lift. I shared the news of Mum letting me get tutored and we both cheered.

Getting to school, we said our goodbyes and headed to our first classes. I arrived and Terry waved at me to sit beside him. Recalling Dina's warning, I walked past him sitting at an empty desk, and his face fell. Then Bianca rushed over sitting beside him.

"Hey T, is this seat taken?" she asked.

"Nope, you can have them both," Terry muttered.

He walked over and sat beside me, my lips pressed together, getting up to move, but our science teacher, Mr Idris walked in. Asking us to sit, placed his dreads in a hair tie and swapped his loafers for palm slippers.

"Mina, are you avoiding me?" he asked and I sighed.

"Did I do something wrong?" he continued; I forced a smile.

"I moved because I find it difficult to see the board from there," I muttered, and he tilted his head.

"Hmmm, but you always sat there with no trouble seeing the board."

"I guess my eyes have worsened from straining them," I replied.

"No talking," Mr Idris snapped.

Terry halted his barrage of questions, and I focused on the lesson taking notes diligently. Terry watched intensely and then leaned in.

"Mina, I don't think I've seen you so focused before," he said.

"It's time for a quiz," Mr Idris announced.

After the test papers were distributed, we got started. I tended to accidentally approach the correct answers but intentionally selected the wrong ones. Ji-won usually didn't notice as she was unsure about the correct answers, but Terry observed me closely, scrutinising my choices like a hawk.

To be safe, I used my elbow to create a divide between us. This time, I made sure to answer a few questions correctly, so my grades wouldn't be flagged later for overnight improvement. Soon after, our time was up, and we handed in our papers.

"Mina," Terry called.

"Do you purposely…"

Then he stopped mid-sentence.

"Hmmm?" I asked.

But he glared at me in silence.

"What is it?" I pressed him.

"Nothing, never mind," he said.

I grabbed my bag and waved him goodbye. After school, Ji-won, Emily, and I headed home. At the school gate, we saw Joon, Rachel, and another student I often saw with Joon Oppa. I think his name was Chris, a tall, slim boy with an Afro comb hanging out of his hair.

"Oh Ji, can't lie, your brother's buff."

Emily gushed, and Ji-won and I scrolled at her.

"Buff? More like annoying," I muttered.

"Girl with a face like that, he can annoy me all day long," she gushed.

Ji-won and I busted out laughing.

"Is that girl his girlfriend?" Emily asked, nudging at Rachel, who looked in our direction.

"Ji-won," Rachel called.

Ji-won jogged over to them, while Emily and I caught up slowly from behind.

"So, how did it go last night? Did your Mum give you permission?" Rachel asked.

"Well, sort of; we can only go if we get a C in the upcoming exam," she muttered.

Lowering her gaze, Rachel placed her hand on Ji-won's shoulders.

"Ji-won, you can do it, don't worry I'll help you," she said, and Ji-won smiled brightly.

"Thanks for the offer Unnie; however, Mum asked Oppa to tutor us," she said, and Rachel grinned.

"Really? Joon, can I join you guys? I want to help," Joon turned with a stern expression.

"I think it's best that I teach them alone; it would be less distracting."

"I disagree; we can split them between us. That way, they get more one-on-one time," she suggested.

"Oppa, Unnie is right. I think it might be too much for you to teach us both," Ji-won added, and Joon sighed.

"Don't you have the chemistry project to work on?" Joon asked and Rachel grinned.

"It's fine. I can still help while working on it. Besides, it's more productive to have study partners, don't you think?" she muttered.

Joon nodded walking off, seemingly defeated, and then Rachel turned to face me.

"It's Mina, right?" I nodded.

"Is it okay that I join you guys?" she asked with a faint smile.

I swallowed, stunned by her question, I nodded, and she gave me a crooked smile. Finally, we got to the end of the hill.

"I'll head home first to change and then come over to yours," Rachel said.

Joon nodded slightly, we waved her goodbye along with Emily, and we headed home too.

I got home spotting a black Swade loafer on the shoe rack; it belonged to Dina's private tutor Mr David a middle-age divorcee I once heard Mum mention. They were sitting by the dining area for their lesson.

Mum was sitting on the couch, doing needlework, with her hair freshly braided wearing her traditional Ankara dress. She was always overdressed whenever Mr David was around. I greeted them heading to my room to change.

I tucked my books into my clothes and walked past the sitting room, nudging at Mum signalling that I was heading out. Dina was completely immersed in her lesson, paying no attention to us. When I arrived at Ji-won's house, ringing the bell, Ji-won's Mum opened the door, wearing lilac yoga pants with a matching top, holding a laundry basket. I greeted her and headed for Joon's room.

The door was opened, but he was nowhere in sight, his study desk had been moved to the middle of the room to fit more chairs. I scanned through his bookshelf, picking a textbook about anatomy, and sat backwards on his bed flipping through it. I leapt up after realising I was sitting on a pile of clothes that fell off, so I bent to pick it up.

I gasped, throwing it in the air, and squeezed my eyes shut; it was a pair of Joon Oppa's pink boxers. It had landed on Joon's head as he walked in; he sighed, scowling at me, and cleared his throat as he pulled it off, and I smirked, holding back my giggle.

"Mum must be putting away laundry," he muttered.

He shoved them into his drawers, and I busted out laughing as I recalled Ji-won said she attempted to do laundry and ended up turning everything pink. But her Mum refused to throw them out, then the doorbell rang.

"I'll get it."

Ji-won yelled out from the corridor, Joon and I walked into the hallway.

Rachel entered, running straight to Ji-won's Mum and grandma, and embraced them. She seemed like a part of the family. I made my way back to Joon's room, with him following closely behind.

Soon after, Ji-won and Rachel joined us. Rachel looked around Joon's room, seemingly taking in the details as if seeing them for the first time.

"Oh, Joon, nice taste," she gushed.

Then walked over to the guitar, running her hands through the strings.

"I can't believe you still have this," Rachel exclaimed. "It's such a shame you stopped singing. My dad still talks about his wish to sign you to his label."

My jaw dropped. I had no idea Joon had any interest in music, wondering why he stopped; she turned, spotting his disdained expression, and she raised her hands in defeat.

"Okay, okay, I'll drop it," she muttered.

Chuckling, then her eyes fell on me.

"Hey, Mina," she said.

I nodded, twiddling my fingers; she looked dressed for a photoshoot wearing a fitted white crop top and white ripped slim-fitting jeans, and a rose-pink denim jacket. I looked down at my black jeans and khaki checked shirt, feeling underdressed. I guess it explained why Ji-won was wearing her favourite pink skater dress.

"Shall we begin?" Joon said.

We all took a seat. Joon and I sat opposite each other, and Ji-won sat at the end of the table facing Rachel. Then Joon and I reached for a pen.

“Ah.”

We both yelped getting a static shock, our eyes met, and I swallowed.

Ji-won giggled, bringing me out of my daze.

“Was that a static shock?” she muttered.

And continued laughing, while Rachel rolled her eyes.

“Joon, how about I help Mina instead,” Rachel suggested.

“Mina, swap seats with Ji-won,” she said.

I obliged, and we began; she gave me a few math problems to solve, and Joon did the same for Ji-won. Going through the questions, my hands subconsciously moved to the correct answers, but I moved them immediately. I answered four correctly getting the others wrong. I caught a few glances from Joon, as he watched my hands intensely.

About twenty minutes later, we gave them our books to review, and their faces fell at first glance. Joon sighed but walked Ji-won through the correct answers. However, Rachel glared at me with a stern expression.

“This is awful, Mina. How can you be so clueless for someone in Year Ten?” she muttered.

Chapter Seven

Folding her arms while furrowing her brows, my body tensed up.

"You need to take your studies more seriously instead of wasting time obsessing over K-pop."

I clenched my teeth, exhaling.

"Rachel, calm down. It's only their first lesson," Joon said.

My eyes widened, meeting his gaze, his lips formed a hard line, and Ji-won's gaze fell. Although Rachel's outburst reassured me that she had not caught on to my act, I wondered why she was being so intense. Then her face suddenly softened.

"Oh, was that too harsh? Joon, I was only trying to give her some critical criticism."

She said clearing her throat, and turned to me.

"Mina, I'm sorry if I hurt your feelings," she muttered.

"I'll help Mina instead, swap places," Joon said.

Ji-won's eyes widened, as she moved hesitantly, and the smile on Rachel's face dissolved.

Joon was patient, breaking down his explanation. After giving us homework, his timer went off, ending our study session. Grabbing my textbooks, my notepad fell out; I gasped, clenching my teeth.

It was what I used to secretly test myself correctly on an advanced level, I leaned down to grab it, but Joon got to it first, flipping through, I snatched it instantly. He glared at me, puzzled. I hid the book and my trembling hands behind my back.

"Oh, what's this doing here," I muttered, and Joon's brows furrowed.

"It's Dina's; she must have mixed it up with mine," I mumbled.

"Mina isn't that—"

"Oh, look at the time. I need to get going. Don't want to be late for dinner," I said.

I cut him off and grabbed my bag.

"I should get going, too," Rachel said.

We headed for the living room to say our goodbyes.

"Joon, walk Rachel to the bus stop; it's dark out now," Ji-won's Mum said, Rachel smiled brightly and Joon nodded.

We made our way out and onto the hallway, and Joon called the lift.

"See you tomorrow," I said, heading upstairs.

"Not getting the lift?" Joon asked.

I turned around, shaking my head.

"I want to stretch my legs a bit after sitting for so long. Besides, it's only two floors up, and you guys are going down."

Joon sighed, and Rachel pulled his arm, urging him to get on as the doors sprang open.

"Bye, Mina," Rachel muttered, grinning.

The doors shut and I sunk onto the stairs crouching down; that was a close call. I hoped Joon believed that it was Dina's notebook and not mine. I sighed, leaning my head against the stair rail, and shut my eyes for a moment.

"Mina, Mina."

My name echoed repeatedly and then I felt a tap on my shoulder.

"Mina, wake up."

I slowly opened my eyes, but my vision was blurry. I touched my face in search of my glasses.

"You reckless girl! How could you sleep out here? What if something happened to you?" Joon scolded.

I rubbed my eyes, then carried on searching for my glasses.

"Are you listening?" Joon yelled.

"Oppa, do you see my glasses?" I asked, ignoring his outburst.

"Is that important right now?" he snapped.

"Well, I can't see anything," I said.

Joon pulled my arm as I searched the lower staircase, causing me to stumble and fall into his embrace. The sound of his rapidly beating heart filled my ears, and then he pulled me off suddenly, clearing his throat, and I exhaled, regaining my balance, and continued searching, but bumped my head on the stair railing, and yelped. Joon grabbed my arm again.

"I thought you were only clueless when it came to your studies, but you are just as clueless about everything else," he muttered.

My lips pressed into a hard line, and my hands clenched into a fist. I stood up straight, pulling my hands off his grip.

"What's it to you? Why do you care if I get hurt or not," I said as my brows furrowed.

"Did you stop to think how much it would hurt the people who care about you if something bad happened to you?"

"People that care about me," I muttered under my breath and chuckled.

"Why does it matter to you? It's not like you're one of those people, so how about you stay out of my business," I said.

But he didn't respond, and my vision was too blurry to read his expression.

"Besides, what about you? Do you ever think about how those who care about you would feel if you got badly hurt? Don't you think it's reckless not to report those boys? Try taking your own advice," I muttered.

But he stayed silent. I rolled my eyes and used the stair railing as a guide, making my way up, and gave up on finding my glasses.

"Mina," Joon called out.

Sounding defeated. I halted, tilting my head to the side.

"Check your pocket," he said.

Then I heard keys muffling and a door slam. I reached my hands into my pocket and pulled out my glasses. I wore them and looked back to find him gone. I sighed, biting my bottom lip.

"Was I too harsh?" I mumbled to myself.

Then I shook off the thought; he had it coming; all I did was give him a taste of his own medicine. I got back home, and Dina and Mum were having dinner.

"Sorry I'm late," I muttered.

Dina rolled her eyes, but I ignored her. I told Mum I wasn't hungry and went straight to my room. I changed into my N.O. pyjamas and plugged in my headphones, playing N.O. "All Night Long." My favourite lyrics in that song were the chorus that went, "I just want to be here with you all night long." The upbeat tempo was uplifting.

Then I rolled my eyes recalling my argument with Joon, but at least one good thing came of it; Joon was still clueless about me failing intentionally, and he called me the clueless one. I smirked shutting my eyes for the night.

My phone buzzed waking me up before my alarm; it was a text from Ji-won.

"Hey Mimi, I completely forgot about my dentist appointment this morning. I'll see you at lunchtime. P.s., it's raining, so don't forget to take an umbrella xxx," I hit reply.

"Thanks for the heads up, Ji; see you at lunch ;)."

I got ready for school and grabbed my umbrella, quietly shut the door, and headed out; it was raining cats and dogs; I opened my umbrella, grinning from ear to ear, listening to its soothing sound. Dad used to say as a baby, I always fell asleep quickly whenever it rained.

Getting to the traffic lights, across the street was an elderly lady who was without an umbrella; her pinned-up grey curls had unravelled, and her bright pink suit was drenched. No one offered to share their umbrella, so when the green man flashed, I crossed, running to her.

"Excuse me," I said.

"Here you go," I muttered.

Handing her my umbrella, and her jaw dropped as she stared at me wide-eyed.

“What about you dear?” she asked, returning it. I placed it back in her hands.

“Please take it, I insist. My school is just up the hill,” I said.

Then ran off with my hands over my head before she could object any further, but the rain suddenly stopped, and a yellow umbrella appeared over my head. I turned and blinked rapidly, convinced I was hallucinating. I cleared my misty glasses, gazing up again, and it was really him, wearing a grey hoodie and blue jeans. I glared wide-eyed, taken aback by his unexpected gesture.

“I see you are still as clueless as ever, Mina, looking out for everyone but yourself,” he said.

I rolled my eyes, erasing my thoughts from earlier, then quickened my pace; he jogged ahead, catching up with me, placing the umbrella over my head again. I halted, turning to him.

“Why are you…”

He suddenly looked to the left, and his eyes widened, and I stopped mid-sentence, checking to see what caught his attention. Then he suddenly spun me around, wrapping his arms around my shoulders, and pulling me into an embrace. Then I heard a big splash of water and a car speeding past. His whole body fidgeted in response to the cold water drenching him. Luckily, only a few drops landed on my feet, and he slowly pulled me upright and out of his embrace.

“Are you okay? You didn’t get wet?” he asked.

Turning me full circle, checking for wet spots, and my eyes narrowed, I gazed at him, lost for words. What had gotten into him suddenly, and why was my heart racing?

“Mina?” he called. I blinked rapidly, taking a deep breath.

"You must've been startled, sorry," he muttered. I stared down at his wet clothes.

"Oppa, you're all soaked," I muttered.

Biting my bottom lip, lost for what to do.

"It's fine. Remember, I always have spare clothes in my locker?" he smirked.

My mouth went dry as I swallowed. It had been a long time since I saw him smile. I tilted my head, examining his unbecoming facial expression, then my brows frowned, suddenly feeling on edge, then I took a step back; what exactly was he playing at? I wondered, feeling the wall I'd built between us slowly crumbling. He stepped forward, keeping the umbrella above my head.

"Stay close, you'll get wet," he muttered.

I turned on my heel walking ahead of him. I looked around to check if anyone took notice of us. Luckily, they were all too busy avoiding the rain.

We walked up in silence, avoiding each other's gaze. He cleared his throat.

"About yesterday," he muttered, looking ahead.

"It seems like your sister can solve a lot of difficult math problems. Why haven't you asked her for help?" he asked.

I halted as my hands began to tremble.

"Oh, she does offer to help, but I am just too clueless to understand," I muttered.

"Although we are identical, intelligence wasn't passed down to me," I mumbled.

We got to the school gate, and he turned to me.

"It seems you both have identical handwriting, too," he murmured.

I gasped as my eyes widened.

"Oppa, I've got to run. I have somewhere to go before class. Thanks for the umbrella," I muttered.

Placing my hands over my head, ran into block A, and headed for the bathroom to dry myself; wondering why Joon was acting out of character. The bell went off and I was off to my first lesson. Walking down the hall, I saw Rachel approaching looking glamorous, wearing a lilac blazer dress with matching fishnet tights. I spun around.

"Hey, Mina," she called. I gasped, squeezing my eyes shut.

I turned back around with a forced smile.

"Hi, Rachel," I responded.

"Can we talk," she said, walking closer.

"I'm so sorry for coming on so strong yesterday. I was only trying to help," she muttered.

I fidgeted, flustered by her apology.

"It's fine; there's no need for an apology. Besides, everything you said was true. I'll try my best to do better going forward."

"I'm so relieved to hear you say that," she exhaled.

"Well then, I'll see you this evening," she said.

We went our separate ways. I arrived at history, and Terry pulled out a chair for me. I sighed, sitting next to him, knowing he would follow me if I moved.

"Hey," I said.

"Yo, you good?" he muttered and I nodded.

Mr Harris walked in, and I got my books ready for the lesson. I was focused on the board, taking notes diligently, and then Terry began writing a note in my book with a pencil.

"Why are you concentrating so hard lately? No doodling today?" he wrote, and I sighed.

I Rubbed it off and continued with the lesson. The bell went off. I checked to see our next lesson, then gasped.

"What's wrong?" he asked. I placed my head on the desk and sighed.

"Oh, don't tell me you forgot your P.E kit again?" he said, and I nodded.

He pulled me up, shaking his head, and we made our way to the sports hall. Terry had his elbow on my shoulders as an armrest as usual, so I dropped my shoulders, making his arm fall off, but he placed it back on again. We approached the end of the hallway, then I heard Joon's voice from the corner, and halted.

"Rachel, it's best you don't come to the study group anymore. I will teach the girls myself," Joon said.

Terry turned to me, and his brows furrowed.

"What's wrong? Why did you stop?" he asked.

I placed my finger on his lips.

"Shhhhhh," I murmured and carry-on listening.

"Why? Is it because of what I said to Mina? I already apologised to her this morning," she said, and Joon sighed.

Terry glared as he heard my name, and walked over to see who it was. I tried pulling his arm, but he wiggled me off and walked to the corner to peek, and his brows furrowed when he saw Joon.

"It's that guy again," he muttered bitterly.

"I think it will be best if you don't come to avoid any issues. Let's go. We will be late for class," Joon said.

Turning in our direction, I spun around, going the opposite way, but Terry pulled my blazer.

"Where do you think you're going, Mina? Class is this way," he said.

He grabbed my hand and led me straight through their path, as we walked past, I caught a glimpse of Joon's stern gaze. He was already wearing a change of clothes, black trousers, a blue button-up shirt, and a white shirt underneath. He lowered his gaze, staring down at my hands in Terry's grip, and his frown deepened.

I tried to pull my hands out of Terry's hold, but his grip got tighter; he pulled me walking past Joon and Rachel. I tilted my head back, and Joon was still glaring intensely, and Rachel stared back at Joon as bitterness crept into her face.

"Terry, you can let go now," I murmured, but he shook his head.

"We will be late. We need to hurry," he said.

After P.E. Ji-won was waiting outside the hall.

"Mimi," she called, smiling.

"Hi Ji, I can't go home with you today. I have detention," I muttered, and she pouted.

"Again, why?" she asked as her brows furrowed.

"Let me guess, forgot your P.E. kit, didn't you?" she said, shaking her head.

"When will that memory of yours improve?" she nagged.

"Anyways, I'll see you at our study session," she said.

I gasped, placing my hands over her mouth.

"Not so loud," I murmured, and then I felt an arm on my shoulder.

"Study session? What study session?" Terry asked.

I squeezed my eyes shut shrugging his arm off.

"See you later," Ji-won muttered.

Running off. I sighed, making my way into the detention room. Terry followed me in.

"Tell me, what study session was Ji-won talking about?" Terry asked.

"You don't need to know. Wait, why are you following me in here?" I asked, turning to face him.

"I have detention too. Remember I didn't have my P.E. kit either?" he smirked.

I rolled my eyes, knowing he lied just to get out of P.E.

"Mr Dean won't let you off easy for missing practice again," I muttered.

I placed my bag on the table, taking out my books to do the homework Joon Oppa gave us. Terry glared at me as his brows furrowed.

"Mina, you do homework now, too?" he gasped.

Placing a hand over my forehead.

"Are you feeling, okay? Do you have a temperature?"

I pulled his hands off, turning back to continue with my work.

"You know they say when a person changes suddenly, they're about to die," he muttered.

I sighed, shaking my head.

"Earlier, It seemed like they were talking about something to do with you. Did something happen?"

"It's no big deal," I muttered.

"You seem to get irritated whenever I bring him up."

"Because you keep asking unnecessary questions," I said.

"My bad, I didn't realise I was asking too much," he said.

Raising his hands in surrender. I sighed.

After completing the assignment, I laid my head down for a nap.

"Mina, wake up," Terry shook me.

"Huh," I mumbled, opening my eyes slowly.

"Times up. Let's go," he said.

I nodded, grabbing my bag, as we walked down the hill, I plugged in my headphones to avoid Terry's questioning.

I got home, and Mum was almost done preparing dinner, and from the lovely aroma, it must be egusi soup and pounded yam. My belly rumbled, as I said my greetings.

"Detention again," she sighed, and I lowered my head.

"Go change and join us at the table," she said.

After changing, I joined them and we ate in silence. I rushed my food and waited for my window of escape; Dina went to shower, allowing me to leave unnoticed.

I arrived at Ji-won's house, and the image of Joon's smirk this morning popped into my head; he seemed like a different person. Ji-won's grandma opened the door bringing me back to the present. I said my greetings and headed for Joon's room, and knocked.

Chapter Eight

"Come in," he said.

They had already started, so I joined them opening my textbook. I glanced at the empty seat, recalling Joon's conversation with Rachel. Then Joon suddenly reached out his hands to me, and I stared back, puzzled.

"Homework," he muttered.

I sighed, handing it to him. Looking through my answers, his brows furrowed. I only answered six out of twelve correctly.

"It's better than yesterday, but you still have a long way to go," he scolded.

We began and Joon taught us English literature. We delved into Shakespeare's "Macbeth," we completed exercises and received homework for the next day.

"I've got to go," Ji-won muttered.

Rushing to the bathroom. I got up, putting my books away.

"Thanks again for this morning, and sorry about your clothes," I muttered.

"It's fine," he responded.

"By the way, who was that guy?" he asked.

"What guy?"

"Are there so many you can't keep count?" he muttered.

I gasped as my eyes widened.

"The guy that had his arm around you," he said with a cold gaze.

I exhaled as the blood drained from my face.

"Terry is a friend. Why do you ask?"

"A friend?" he smirked.

"Do you let all your male friends put their arms on your shoulder like that?"

My lips pressed into a hard line, and my eyes narrowed as I glared at him.

"Mina, got all your stuff?" Ji-won asked, reappearing.

"Yes, let's go," I muttered, scrolling at him.

After saying my goodbyes, I left shutting the door behind me. I sighed as my palms formed into a fist, recalling Joon's comment.

What was he trying to imply? Shaking my head, I slammed the lift call button. I got back to my room and logged onto the N.O. fan chartroom to check on my fan sisters. Ever since I became a part of "Neighbours," the chosen fan name for all N.O.'s fans, it connected me with friends from all over the world.

We shared a unique bond; they scolded me for my recent inconsistency, which I explained was due to upcoming exams. Everyone buzzed with excitement about the boys' London concert, and some were even flying in to attend.

At 9 pm, I switched off the computer and got a start on the homework Joon Oppa gave us. After finishing, I got into bed, placed my glasses on the bedside table and snuggled my N.O. pillow as I drifted off.

I woke up to a note from Mum on the fridge; she and Dina were out shopping for groceries, so I could go for my one-on-one Saturday lesson unnoticed. After breakfast, I prepared my books but suddenly felt an intense cramp and gasped.

"Oh, no," I muttered.

I dashed into the bathroom to check if my suspicions were correct. I sighed, squeezing my eyes shut. Just as I thought my monthly visitor had arrived, I cleaned myself up, put on a pad, and returned to my room, pacing back and forth.

"Should I just cancel?" I murmured.

Then I recalled Joon saying if we missed even one lesson, it was game over; I bit my finger, pacing. I had only started getting periods two years prior, but still couldn't get used to the severe pain and purging. I checked the time and exhaled, grabbed my bag, and headed out.

My cramps were still mild, and I hoped they'd stay that way. I knocked, and Joon opened it. He was dressed in plain blue shirt and grey trousers, but with his build and face, everything he wore looked stylishly exaggerated.

"Coming?" he asked.

"Erm yeah, hi," I muttered.

Coming out of my daze, he nodded and walked off. I clenched my teeth, then rolled my eyes and walked in. Heading to his room, the house was quieter than usual. Joon walked over to sit at his usual spot, and I headed to mine, sitting beside him.

"Where's everyone?" I asked.

"Shopping," he muttered.

I swallowed, fidgeting in my seat. He glared at me, hitting his ruler on the table.

"Focus," he scolded.

I placed my hands on my chest, glaring back at him as I steadied my breathing.

"Homework?" he asked.

"Yes, here."

Handing it over to him, I swallowed as he went through it.

"You seem to be improving faster than I expected," he said.

Meeting my gaze, I looked down at my fingers, squeezing them together. Had he noticed something? Have I been caught?

"Let's go through the ones you got wrong," he said.

I exhaled, as he changed the subject, as we went through it, I struggled to concentrate as my cramps intensified and nausea set in. I clenched my thighs under the table, gritting my teeth. A few drops of tears landed on my book, and Joon glared up at me wide-eyed.

"Are you crying?" he asked.

And I wiped them off immediately.

"No, it's nothing."

"Are you sure?"

His voice was filled with panic. I was unresponsive, as an intense cramp hit, grabbing onto the table, squeezing my eyes shut and panting. Joon leapt up, placing his hands on my shoulders.

"Mina, talk to me; what's wrong? You don't look okay?" he muttered.

I suddenly felt nauseous, pushing my chair. I raced to the bathroom, heading for the toilet bowl, vomiting intensely while sweating profusely.

Knock knock!

"Are you okay? I'm coming in," Joon said.

Bursting in, he crouched beside me, patting my back. I threw up uncontrollably, only stopping to catch my breath occasionally.

"Hold on, I'll grab my phone and call for help," he said.

Summoning my last ounce of strength, I grasped his hand.

"Don't go, Oppa," I murmured breathlessly; he leaned down.

"You don't look okay. You've been throwing up non-stop."

I wiped my mouth with the back of my hands.

"Don't worry. It'll pass soon."

"Mina, you look like you are about to pass out. Shouldn't I call for help at least?"

"Oppa, you can't call 999 for period cramps."

Chuckling, but my laughter halted feeling the urge to vomit again, I released his hand, turning towards the toilet bowl, throwing up again.

After emptying the contents of my stomach, Joon brought me a glass of water. I rinsed my mouth and took a sip. I remained immobilised, completely drained of energy with my gaze fixed on the powder blue walls.

"Can you stand?" Joon asked.

I slowly shook my head. Then he leaned in, lifting me gently and carrying me to Ji-won's room. Too weak to protest, I wrapped my arms around his neck and rested my head on his chest. He laid me on the bed and covered me with a blanket. I gasped as he placed his hands over my head.

"You're burning up," he said.

He dashed out reappearing with a bowl of water and a towel. I met his fallen gaze, as he removed my glasses, and placed them by the bedside table, and winced as the wet cold towel landed on my forehead. I clenched my teeth as another cramp hit.

"Do you have painkillers I can take?" I murmured.

"What was that?" he asked.

Leaning in closer, my heart rate spiked. I swallowed, exhaling.

"Pain killer," I repeated.

He leaned back, shaking his head.

"Later. After you've eaten. You shouldn't take it on an empty stomach," Joon said.

Then suddenly, he lifted his hands to my head, caressing it.

"Get some sleep; I'll be right here," he muttered.

I slowly drifted off.

Under the beaming sunlight, Joon, Ji-won, and I were in our primary school playground at break time. Ji-won and I sat on the swings; her lengthy hair swished in the air, covering her face every time she went higher, while my afro bounced up and down when I did, taking in the view as I got to the top. I could see the blue merry-go-round, the yellow seesaw, and the green monkey bar, but the orange swings were my favourite. Joon Oppa stood behind us, pushing. We giggled, urging he pushed harder.

A few other girls asked if Joon could also push them, but he refused, focusing only on us.

"Oppa, push harder," I demanded.

He complied, but I lost grip of the strings and fell onto the grass, grazing my knees.

Joon and Ji-won rushed over to help me up.

"Mina, you are bleeding," Ji-won gasped.

Joon's face sunk, glaring wide-eyed through his overgrown mushroom haircut; I began sobbing, as the pain in my knee intensified.

"Get on my back, Mina," Joon said, crouching down.

I leaned in, wrapping my arms around his neck, and he clutched onto my legs, got back up and started running.

"Oppa, wait up," Ji-won said, following on.

He rushed through the green and white hallway adorned with hand-painted artwork. We arrived at the nurse's office. Joon gently laid me down on the blue cartoon bedding. The yellow walls displayed health-related posters and a human body chart. The nurse hurried to my bedside, adjusting her pink-framed glasses. Tears flowed as she examined my bleeding knee.

"Mina, it's okay. I'm so sorry. It's all my fault," Joon said.

He gently patted my head while holding my hand, as Ji-won clutched my other hand, tears streaming down her face. Nurse Jane Martin, trying to calm us down with no success, ran her hands through her unruly ginger curls, sighing. She then fetched a first aid kit, placing it on the nearby table and selecting the needed tools to tend to my injury.

"It's Mina, right?" she asked.

I nodded, panting breathlessly, and she smiled warmly.

"Mina, I need you to be a brave girl, okay? I'll clean your wound now, but it might sting a little," she said.

I swallowed, shutting my eyes, squeezing Ji-won and Joon's hands tightly; she began, and the pain began declining soon after.

"All done, Mina," the nurse muttered.

I slowly lifted my eyelids, looking down at my knees. She covered it up with a yellow cartoon bandage.

"Feeling better?" Joon asked, and I nodded, wiping my tears.

"It doesn't hurt anymore?" Ji-won asked.

As another tear escaped her eyes, I shook my head, and she exhaled.

"Sorry, Mina, I shouldn't have pushed so hard," Joon murmured.

Lowering his head and releasing my hands, I tightened my grip on his hold, glaring at his blood-stained white shirt and grey trouser and sighed.

"Oppa, it wasn't your fault; I kept asking you to push harder; besides, it doesn't hurt that much anymore," I said, smiling.

He met my gaze with a softened expression.

"Here, this is for being so brave," the nurse said.

Handing us lollipops, Ji-won wiped her cheeks, grinning, taking a cherry-flavoured one; I picked strawberry milk, and so did Joon. My eyes widened as he handed it to me, and I pushed his hands away, shaking my head.

"It's yours, Oppa; you have it," I said.

He shook his head, and my brows etched into a frown.

"No, Mina, have mine too; I did nothing to deserve this; you're the brave one, so take it," he said.

Placing it in my hands, Ji-won paused with her lollipop halfway into her mouth. She sighed, lowering her hands as her excitement waned.

"Here, Mina, have mine too," she said, handing hers to me.

"No, Ji, you have it. If I have all three, I will get a bellyache," I said.

Her grim expression turned into a grin.

"Ah, you're right, that won't be good," she mumbled.

Placing it in her mouth. I grinned, peering at the lollipop Joon gave me.

My eyes sprung open, waking from my brief slumber. I looked up at the pink curtains, recalling I was in Ji-won's bedroom. My cramps had subsided, and I turned to the side, gasping. Joon was lying next to me, still holding the wet towel, peacefully dozing.

I reached for my glasses to get a clearer view. Slowly, I turned my body towards him, studying his face intently. Despite my attempts to push thoughts of Joon away, I couldn't deny he still had an effect on me. I had forgotten how close we once were.

Back then, Joon was kind and caring, but he suddenly changed. Although I wanted distance between us at the time, he was the one who drew the line between us.

His hair swept over, covering his face, I smiled, stretching out my hands, gently tucking away the stray hairs behind his ear, brushing my fingers across his eyebrows, down to the bridge of his nose, inching closer to his lips.

"Feeling better?" he asked.

My heart jumped, and I gasped, quickly retracting my hands, and placing them on my chest to steady my breathing. He sat up, and I turned to face the wall. Then he placed his hands on my forehead, making my heart spike, but I remained still. He placed his other hand on his forehead, measured my temperature, and exhaled.

"Your temperature is back to normal," he said.

Smiling warmly, I didn't respond, squeezing hold of the bedding; he finally removed his hands, and I exhaled.

"Hungry?"

"No."

But my belly rumbled, betraying me; I chewed on my bottom lip, squeezing my tummy to quiet it down, but it only got louder. Joon smirked standing up.

"I'll get you some soup," he said, and I leapt up, shaking my head.

"No, Oppa, it's fine; I'll go home and eat," I insisted.

Unable to fathom the thought of eating in front of him. It would undoubtedly lead to indigestion.

"It won't take too long," he said.

I got off the bed and, on my feet.

"No need; I'll head home now," I said.

Heading towards the door, he grabbed my hands, leading me to the kitchen; I felt an electric wave coursing through my body, glaring down at our linked hands as he pulled me along, we got into the dining area, and he let go of my hands.

"Sit," he commanded.

He heated the pot on the stove, while I sat at the glass table, watching him move around the open kitchen. The curtains allowed sunlight to fill the room, illuminating the eggshell walls and nourishing the plants by the window. He retrieved a white bowl from the wooden cabinet.

He placed the bowl on the marble countertop and put on safety gloves to open the pot. The tantalising aroma of the soup filled the room, making my mouth water. After a few minutes, he filled a bowl with the soup and brought it over to me with a glass of water.

"Here, it's bean sprout soup," he said.

I met his gaze and choked up, taken back by his sudden kind gestures.

"What's with the look? Do you need me to feed you, too?" he said.

Giving me a grim smile, I shook my head profusely, taking a sip of the soup; he walked over and sat on the chair opposite me, lurking at me intensely, making it hard for me to swallow. I exhaled, rushing the spoon into my mouth.

"Ahhh," I yelped. Dropping the spoon and Joon smirked, shaking his head.

"Clumsy," he muttered.

Stretching his hands out, his thumb brushing past my lips, wiping the spilt soup, I squirmed, feeling a surge of sensations throughout my body. He licked his finger, leaving me speechless. Then he stood up, grabbing a towel to wipe the table. I watched him intensely, in case he made another unexpected move; I exhaled as he headed back to his seat.

"Make sure it cools down first," he scolded.

I could not respond with my eyes fixed on his lips; I swallowed, shook my head, and picked up my spoon again, but this time blowing the soup first; he watched me diligently, as I took each sip, reminding me of the time we were inseparable. After I was done eating, I got up to put my bowl away, but he grabbed it before I could.

"I'll do it," he said.

Chapter Nine

After washing the bowl, he retrieved ibuprofen from the cabinet and approached me.

"Here, you can take some now," he said.

Handing me two tablets, and I swallowed them with the remaining water. As I finished, he reached for the empty glass, but I pulled it away.

"No, Oppa, let me; it's the least I could do," I said, and he shook his head.

"It's fine. I'll do it. You should go get some rest," he said.

I looked down at my fingers, recalling the trouble I'd put him through, but I did as he said and got up but halted in the hallway.

"Oppa, shouldn't I at least clean the bathroom before I go," I muttered, and he hissed.

"Don't worry. I'll take care of everything here," he said.

He spun me towards the door and opened it giving me a faint smile.

I stepped out, exhaling as he closed it behind me. Returning home, I searched for my pink memory box under the bed, blowing off the dust and opening it. Inside were my first baby tooth, family pictures, a diary, and the lollipop Joon gave me. Grinning.

I flipped through old family photos. A picture of my parents holding hands brought a smile to my face, while a photo of Dina and me wearing matching dresses filled me with bittersweet nostalgia. When I reached the last page, I broke down.

Tears fell on the picture of a younger Joon, Ji-won, and me, with our arms linked. I choked up, feeling the distance that had grown between us. I yearned for those carefree days, Dad's presence, and Joon's joyful gaze. Light reflected on the mirror on my diary, I picked it up, staring back at my reflection.

Feeling disconnected from the girl who wrote those diary entries. Dad gave us this mirrored diary to reflect on our growth, but after that incident, looking at it only evoked hatred and despair. I flipped through the pages, stopping at my last entry titled "The End of Mina," remembering my dark mental space.

"Dear diary, I think I'm cursed. I must have done something awful in my past life, and as punishment, I was given a duplicated face in other to pay for my sins in this lifetime."

I choked up reading my own words. The next few lines had dried up tears with runny ink, but I could still make out the words.

"I've put her in danger again, but this time, because of the company I keep," I paused.

Transported to that incident years back, when Dina and I were in Year Four and Joon in Year Six. I took in a deep breath and continued.

"I saw a few girls shoving Dina to the ground at school today, warning she'd stay away from Joon. She crouched in the corner, unable to move having a panic attack. I ran to her, shielding her from them. Their eyes widened when they saw me, realising they had the wrong twin, and they ran off. I asked if she was okay, but she pushed me off."

"This is all your fault," she yelled.

"Haven't you caused me enough trauma already? Sharing this face with you has been my worst nightmare. I wish you'd just disappear, Mina, I hate you!" she screamed.

Pushing me away and running off in tears. That was the second time she had ever said those words to me.

"I HATE YOU!"

My hands trembled, recalling the power those words carried. I flipped through, skipping to the last page, reading the final paragraph.

"At that moment, I knew it was time to give up my last string of joy, one I wanted to hold onto desperately, Joon," I sighed and continued.

"It was the only way I could protect Dina, but I'm not brave enough to see it through. It would be easier if he wasn't so kind and caring and made life worth living, then I could let go with no regrets, but I have no choice. Mina must die for Dina to live, but I can only do so by cutting Joon off."

As I reminisced about that day, a heaviness settled in my stomach. I recalled running away whenever I saw Joon, ignoring him when he'd call out my name, but not respond. He left letters in my locker, asking what he did wrong, apologising for whatever it was. Each word was like thorns puncturing my heart.

Then, unexpectedly, he stopped approaching me, growing distant and cold. Finally taken the hint of my avoidance. Though it was what I wished for, witnessing his abrupt change was still unbearable. I heard the door open, quickly closed my diary, and stowed everything away under my bed. Removing my glasses, I covered myself with my blanket and drifted into a tearful slumber.

Buzz buzz. I searched around for my phone with my eyes still shut. I picked it up without checking who called.

"Hello."

"Mimi, sleeping?"

"Hmmm."

"Just calling to check on you. Oppa said you were really ill yesterday," I rubbed my eyes and sat up.

"Yeah, but I'm feeling better now."

"She's feeling better," she muttered.

"Who's next to you?"

"Oh, it's Oppa. He wanted to know how you were feeling."

My eyes widened.

"Oh, tell him I said thanks again for yesterday."

"Oppa, she said thanks for yesterday."

"Will you be able to come to school tomorrow?"

"Yes, I should be."

"Oh good, see you tomorrow."

"See ya," I responded and hung up.

Stretching my arms, I yawned, put my glasses on, and checked the time. It was 5:46 pm on Sunday. I had been in and out of naps since I got home yesterday, only leaving my room for a bathroom break or food.

Knock knock!

"Come in."

"How are you feeling? What would you like for dinner?" Mum asked.

"Can I have goat meat pepper soup?" I requested.

"Okay, but take it easy on the painkillers, I know you're hurting, but taking too much is not good," she warned, and I nodded.

After dinner, I struggled to fall asleep recalling yesterday's event. How do I face Joon tomorrow? I pulled my cover over my head silently screaming. Then I recalled him wiping the spilt soup off my lips. I swallowed, shaking off the thought and suddenly overheated, so I played my N.O. mix and drifted off.

The sky was unusually clear as Ji-won and I walked our way up the hills.

"Counting down the days until the concert, I get butterflies just thinking about it. Even Monday is exciting to me now," Ji-won gushed, grinning.

I smiled in response, but everything seemed to be going too well, which kept me on guard.

"What's wrong? Are you still in pain?" Ji-won asked.

Bringing me out of my train of thought, I shook my head, and her brows furrowed.

"Then what's the matter? You seem down."

I gave her a reassuring smile.

"It's nothing. I am just a bit worried something might go wrong," I muttered.

Then she suddenly stepped in front of me, making me halt, and placed her hands on my shoulders meeting my gaze.

"Mimi, I know you better than anyone else, and I'm certain that when you set your mind to something, you always succeed."

I smiled as my buried hope rose from the graves of despair.

"So, believe in yourself because I believe in you."

Stepping aside, she linked her arms with mine, grinning.

"N.O., here we come!" she yelled.

We ran up the hill, giggling, and then parted ways for our first lessons. As I walked to my science lesson, I turned a corner and froze. Joon leaned against the wall near my classroom, as though he was in a commercial shoot, wearing his baseball jacket in a white top, and black jeans. I tried to retreat, but he spotted me and approached. I bit my lip, stepping back.

I quickly scanned the hallway and exhaled as it was empty. I stepped back as he approached. Biting my finger, trying to figure out why he came. Back against a corner, he lifted his hands, and I shut my eyes, and my hands began trembling. Then, his hands touched my forehead, and I opened my eyes slowly.

He then placed his other hand on his own and looked upwards. It was that feeling again, rushing through me, as my heart raced. Tensed up, I clutched the side of my skirt with my sweaty palms. Trembling under his touch, I met his gaze as he withdrew his hands, exhaling.

"Your fever seems to have gone completely."

Then he smiled and leaned in, and my whole body came to a halt. He gazed at me with his eyes filled with wonder, and his smile grew into a grin.

"I'm off, see you clumsy," he muttered.

Tapping his index finger on my nose and whispered.

"Breathe, Mina."

Smirking as he walked away, I exhaled.

Leaning against the wall, trying to steady my breathing, wondering what had brought up the change in Joon's attitude. The sight of his smiling face stirred something within me. I shook off the thought and sank to the floor, running my hands through my hair. Then a pair of white name-brand trainers appeared before me.

"Yo, what are you doing on the floor?" Terry asked, and I leapt up instantly.

"Oh, nothing, let's get to class," I said.

Walking ahead, but he grabbed my arm, making me halt.

"What's wrong?" he muttered, frowning.

"What do you mean? Nothing's wrong," I said, pulling his arms off.

My mind reverted to Joon during our lesson. Terry waved his hands snapping me back to reality; I gave him a reassuring smile and tried focusing.

After school, I got home and finished my homework and prepared for study group; then I remembered I was supposed to get Joon to teach me some words in Korean, so I could make our sign boards for the concert, as Ji-won wasn't good at writing Hangul, I was tasked with making the request. I scrolled at the thought and made my way to Ji-won's flat.

Ji-won opened the door for me, still in her school uniform. We both headed into Joon's room after I said my greetings to her Mum and grandma. Joon seemed indifferent about what happened at school, his cold demeanour resurfacing as he focused on the lesson; he was back to normal. I exhaled going through the questions he gave, only getting three wrong this time.

"Wow, Mimi, you've improved a lot," Ji-won muttered.

Cheering, but Joon was silent. His timer went off and our lesson ended.

"Ji-won, come and set the table," her Mum called.

She rushed off, and I gathered my books, spotting my note.

"Joon Oppa," he turned to meet my gaze.

"I love you," I muttered.

His eyes widened, and then his brows narrowed.

"Could you teach me how to write that in Korean?" I asked, and he sighed.

Glaring at me intensely.

"What for?"

"I need it for our N.O. signs for the concert."

He smirked, shaking his head, and headed for the door.

"Oppa, please, I only need those three-letter words," I said.

As I trailed behind him, trying to state my case, he suddenly turned around, catching me off guard. I lost my balance and began to fall backwards, but he swiftly caught me, his arms wrapping around my waist in a horizontal dip.

We locked eyes, our breaths mingling, hearts racing, and time seemed to stand still. His gaze held a depth that drew me in, and I couldn't tear my eyes away from his. Our lips were tantalisingly close, aching for a taste, and our noses brushed against each other, our linked gaze unable to break away in fear of missing even a single moment.

"예쁘다(yeppeuda)," he said.

I blinked rapidly, trying to process his words. His hand gently grazed my cheeks, causing my breath to hitch and my body to tense. His touch trailed down to my lips, and I swallowed as his thumb brushed against them. Slowly, he leaned in, and I closed my eyes, surrendering to the moment.

"Oppa, it's time to eat."

Ji-won's voice called out from outside, breaking us out of our trance. My eyes sprung open, and he swiftly lifted me back up, releasing his grip, causing me to stumble slightly. He exited the room just as Ji-won entered.

"Oh, Mimi, you're still here?"

"Huh, oh erm, I'm leaving now."

I gathered my books, shoving them into my backpack.

"See you at school tomorrow," I said.

I bid my goodbyes, racing for the door, and shutting it. Leaning against the wall, my heart was beating out of my chest and my palms were sweaty. I sat on the stairwell, lost in thought, oblivious to the people passing by.

Torn between my buried feelings and the desire to attend the N.O. concert, spending time with Joon was becoming a challenge. I groaned, running my hands through my hair.

Buzz buzz.

It was a text from Mum. Checking the time, I gasped and hurried home. After placing my bag in my room, I joined the dinner table. We ate in silence, but I tousled my fork around my Jollof rice.

"Mina!" Mum called, making me jump.

"What are you deep in thought about? You've barely touched your food," Mum scolded, and I shook my head.

"Nothing, I'm just tired, that's all," I muttered, and Dina smirked.

"Mum, can I be excused? I just want to sleep," I said.

Mum nodded, and I headed for my room slumping into my bean bag chair, hugging my legs, and burying my face in my knees. My heart was stirring up new emotions or resurfacing buried ones.

Getting closer to him was becoming risky, and I couldn't afford further entanglement. If Dina found out, it would be chaotic, and Mum would likely prevent me from going to the concert. I wondered if I should quit the study sessions. But if I did, then I would expose myself for faking my grades. I sighed, torn for what to do.

Chapter Ten

I woke up abruptly, realising I had fallen asleep on the floor. My alarm had failed to wake me on time. I gasped seeing the little time I had left. Rushing through my morning routine, I quickly dressed and raced out the door. Ji-won was already waiting for me outside the estate, holding two apple juice boxes.

"Morning Mimi," she said.

Handing one over to me, I grinned, taking it. She seemed unaware of what happened between Joon and me yesterday. I exhaled, intertwining my hand with hers as we made our way up the hills.

"Ji-won."

All eyes were on Rachel who had dyed her hair ombre with a mixture of honey blond and brunette, wearing a mint green midi dress and over-the-knee black boots. Ji-won waved at her, and Rachel hastened her steps to join us.

"Woah, unnie, you look stunning."

Ji-won gushed, and Rachel turned tomato red.

"Thank you."

She said and turned to me.

"Hey Mina," she said.

"Hey Rachel," I responded, and we carried on walking.

"So, how's study group going, girls?" she asked, and I swallowed.

"It's going okay," Ji-won said, and I nodded.

"Unnie, why did you stop coming, Oppa wouldn't say?" Ji-won asked.

I lowered my head.

"Well, it was Joon's choice, not mine," she muttered.

Ji-won's eyes widened.

"But why?" she asked.

Rachel smirked, shaking her head.

"I guess he didn't like how hard I was on Mina," I gasped.

Biting down on my teeth as we all halted, and they both faced me.

"No way, I'm sure it had nothing to do with me," I said, and she smirked.

"Don't be so defensive, Mina," Rachel muttered.

I shook my head and spotted Dina and her friends approaching. So, I turned nudging Ji-won to change the subject.

"So unnie, where did you get those boots?" Ji-won muttered.

Rachel's gaze shifted towards Dina, and her eyes narrowed and glanced back at Ji-won and me. Dina passed by, rolling her eyes, and I exhaled.

"Mina isn't that your twin sister?" Rachel asked, and I nodded.

"Why did you guys change the topic when she passed by? Is there a reason why she shouldn't find out you're getting tutored by Joon?" she asked.

"She can't find out or everything will be ruined," Ji-won said.

Rachel's brows frowned.

"But why?" she asked.

"It's a long story," Ji-won muttered.

I raised my brows at Ji-won, and she bit her bottom lips, placing her hands over her mouth and I exhaled.

"We should get going. The bell will go off soon," Ji-won said.

Changing the subject, Rachel frowned but didn't pry any further.

"See you guys later," she said as we got to the school gate.

After our first two lessons, we met Emily for lunch. Joon was usually surrounded by juniors, including the one who asked Ji-won about me. Our eyes briefly met before I looked away.

"Erm Ji, I don't feel good. You guys go ahead. I'll head for the nurse's office," I muttered, and their eye narrowed.

"Why, is it your cramps again? I'll come with you," Ji-won said.

"No, it's nothing too serious. I'll text you," I muttered.

I retreated to my storeroom hideout; I hadn't been there since the day of the incident. Plugging in my headphones, I played "Home" by N.O., as the song played, flashes of Joon's face flooded my mind. His touch and the intense gaze in his eyes stirred up a mix of emotions.

I sighed pushing his thoughts away. I needed him out of my head. It was hard enough eight years ago. The bell rang after a while, and I headed to my next class in block E. Terry saved me a seat, and we were then given an unexpected quiz on the Cold War. Despite knowing all the answers, I deliberately answered a few questions incorrectly.

"Mina Adebayo," Mr Chapman called.

Whose uneven tan had everyone in constant fits of giggles, he fell asleep on the last day of his holiday in the Bahamas, leaving his sunglasses on whilst tanning.

"Yes sir," I responded.

Suppressing my laughter, he asked me to return the textbooks we used for the lesson back to the school library. Terry offered to help saying the books were too heavy for me to carry alone. I rolled my eyes, and he smirked. As we walked down the hallway, Terry made his unamusing knock-knock jokes. I tried resisting, but one caught me off guard and I busted out laughing.

"You laughed," he muttered.

Sounding proud of himself. We arrived at the maze-like structured library, divided into rows based on different themes. As we approached the reception desk, the librarian sipped her coffee before counting the books we returned. While we waited, I glanced around the unfamiliar territory. I forbade myself from entering. I swallowed spotting Joon, deeply engrossed in a book.

"Mina!" Terry called.

Everyone turned to us, and I gasped lowering my head.

"My bad," he murmured.

"Shhhhh."

The librarian whispered, giving Terry and me a sterned glare.

"Sorry," I muttered.

Turning around, I locked eyes with Joon who glared at me, then his eyes moved over to Terry.

"Let's go," Terry muttered.

Traced my eye view, and spotted Joon and his brows frowned.

"Yes, let's go," I muttered.

Terry grabbed my hands, and a faint smile swept his cheeks. Without resistance, I followed him, refraining from looking back as we exited the library and ascended the stairs. It was for the best. I needed to create a distance between Joon and me.

"Yo T, what's good, man?"

A friend of Terry's approached him, ending my train of thought.

"I'm cool, bro. It's been a minute," Terry said.

I waited for them to finish their conversation.

"In a bit, yeah," they both said their goodbyes.

"M," Terry called.

"Hmmm."

"Can we make one more stop?" he pleaded, and I sighed.

"Where to this time?"

"The boy's bathroom. I'm about to burst," I smirked.

"Go on your own. I'll meet you in class."

I turned to walk off, and he placed his hands on my shoulder.

"Don't be like that; if we don't go back to class together, I'll be in trouble, please," he said.

Giving me puppy dog eyes, and I sighed.

"Argh, fine! But hurry," he exhaled, grinning.

"I won't be long, I promise, let's go."

We reached the boys' restroom, and I stood outside, overlooking the school grounds from the balcony. A noise drew my attention to the first floor, where I spotted a group of boys holding a flowerpot. One of them removed his hoodie, and it was the same boy who had attacked Joon.

I spotted Joon obliviously walking towards their perimeter with headphones plugged in, so I waved my hands to catch his attention, with no success. So, I sprinted down the stairs, panting.

"Mina!" Terry called.

But I ignored him, racing down breathlessly. I got downstairs and Joon was getting closer to where they were positioned, but he didn't notice my frantic gestures. Eventually, he looked towards me but dismissed my warning and continued walking. I picked up my pace and finally reached him just in time, wrapping my arms around his shoulders and pulling him away. We both stumbled and fell onto the grass, narrowly avoiding the flowerpot that shattered on my leg.

"Ahhhh," I cried out.

Joon gasped, tightening his grip around me, and rolled over as another flowerpot crashed beside us.

"Let's go, let's go."

The boys muttered, running off. I squeezed my eyes shut as the pain in my leg increased, and Joon rose.

"Mina! Mina!" Joon called.

Joon glared at me breathlessly. I clenched my teeth as the pain in my leg intensified.

"Are you okay?" he asked.

I nodded, slowly lifting myself up.

"What about you, are you all right?" I asked.

His brows frowned, and his eyes darkened.

"Are you hurt?" I asked.

Checking his body to check for injuries, but he yanked my hands off.

"Mina!"

He yelled with his eyes burning with rage.

"How is that important right now, you reckless girl? Why did you intervene?" he said.

Then his eyes grew teary, and the veins in his neck became prominent as he squeezed his eyes shut and reopened them panting, my brows knitted together as I glared at him.

"Usually, people say thank you in situations like this. I don't get why you're so angry," I muttered.

"Why would you put yourself in danger like that?" he yelled.

My lips pressed into a hard line then I tried getting up.

"Ahhh," I yelped.

Feeling a sharp pain in my leg, Joon crouched down, examining my bleeding cut below the knees. His frowned brows deepened as he glared at it, then took out a powder-blue handkerchief from his pocket, folded it, and gently wrapped it around the wound.

"It must hurt a lot," he muttered softly.

I reached out my hand to pat his head but stopped halfway. I exhaled, seeing that he wasn't hurt.

"Mina!" Terry yelled.

We both looked up, and I pulled my hands away. He rushed over, pushing Joon to the side.

"Are you badly hurt?" he asked.

Looking down at my leg, then turned to Joon.

"How could you let this happen?" he yelled.

Glaring at Joon, who didn't react, then we heard footsteps coming from the side of the building, Joon looked over, and his face grew grim.

"Take care of her," Joon muttered.

Then ran off chasing after those boys.

"Oppa, don't go!" I murmured.

However, he didn't look back. I tried getting up to run after him, but Terry held me back.

"Where do you think you're going?" he asked.

Staring at me with his darkened expression.

"Can't you see you're hurt?"

He inhaled, squeezing his eyes shut, and then exhaled as he opened them again, lifting me in his arms, and I gasped.

"Terry, what are you doing? Put me down!" I said, but he did not respond.

"I can walk, put me down," I said, but he didn't.

"I'll put you down when we get to the nurse's office," he said.

I turned to check if I could see Joon, but he was nowhere in sight. What if they attacked him again? Why did he run after them alone? My head was spinning with multiple scenarios. We got to the nurse's office, and Terry laid me down on the bed.

She quickly set aside her jam doughnut, wiping off the sugar from her upper lip, and approached the bedside. Her dreads were neatly wrapped in a blue turban that matched her uniform. Leaning down, she carefully examined my injury.

"Could you wait outside?" she asked Terry.

He nodded leaving reluctantly.

"I'll be right outside, okay," he muttered and I gave him a forced smile.

"What's your name?" she asked.

As she took off the handkerchief.

"Miss, could I have that, please?" I asked.

Stretching my hands out, she handed it over. It had gone from blue to red, covered in blood.

"Ahhh," I yelped as she cleaned the wound.

"Your name?" she repeated.

"Mina!" I yelped.

"How did you get injured?" she asked.

I paused, recalling Joon's warning, but even if I reported it, things could get bad for me too, as the school would've called Mum, and if word got out and Dina found out, I'd been done for, I shook off the thought.

"I tripped and fell," I said.

She looked at me with her eyes narrowed, then sighed.

"It looks like something fell on your leg hard," she muttered.

I bit down on my lip and swallowed.

"Well luckily, no permanent damage was done," she said.

Then began wrapping a bandage around my leg and I exhaled.

"What are you doing here?"

I heard Terry yelling outside. I sat up, glaring at the door.

"Don't move. I'm not done yet," the nurse muttered.

I sat back down, squirming, glued to the door, but they suddenly went quiet. She taped down the end of the bandage, and I got on my feet but stumbled down to the ground.

"Ahhh," I yelped.

"Don't put pressure on your injured leg," she warned, and Terry came running in.

"Mina, are you all right?" he asked, helping me up.

"She needs to take it easy," the nurse warned.

I ignored them, stretching my neck out the door.

"I sent him away," Terry said.

Answering my unspoken question, my brows frowned.

"Why?" I sighed.

"Did he seem okay? Was he hurt?" I asked, but he didn't respond.

"Is there something I should know?" the nurse asked.

I bit my lip, forgetting she was present.

"No, it's nothing, thank you, miss," I said.

Limping my way out and Terry followed on. I looked around the hallway, but Joon was nowhere in sight.

"Was he hurt?" I asked, and his jaw clenched.

"He was walking just fine, unlike you are right now, so he must be fine."

I exhaled leaning on the wall, and the last bell ended the school day. The hallway flooded with students.

"Let's go get your bag," Terry muttered.

Grabbed my hands, wrapping them around his shoulders, and all eyes fell on us, so I pulled my hands off.

"It's fine. I can manage on my own. Thanks for your help today," I said.

Giving him a tight-lipped smile, and he grabbed my arm again.

"Just let me help."

I sighed but didn't resist further, as we turned the corner, we saw Dina and her friends. I pulled my arms off immediately and carried on walking on my own; Dina's frowned brows deepened as I walked past.

"Yo D, thank God you're here. Could you give her a hand? She's badly hurt," Terry said.

I halted, and Dina gasped.

"She seems to be doing just fine on her own," Dina replied.

Terry's eyes widened.

"Besides, she doesn't like people fussing when she's hurt, right Mina?"

She rolled her eyes at me, and then she turned back to Terry.

"Let's go. There's something I need to talk to you about," she said, pulling him away.

"Wait, what about Mina?" he asked.

Looking back at me as she pulled him off.

"She's fine, don't worry," Dina said.

I gave him a faint smile as they walked off, and limped my way back to class and grabbed my bag pack.

"Mimi, what happened to you," Ji-won came running.

"It's nothing. I just had a little accident," I said, and her face fell.

"It's not as bad as it looks, really."

She sighed, collected my bag pack, wearing it from the front, and wrapped my arm around her neck.

"You need to be more careful," she scolded, and I nodded.

We walked home, and as we approached our block, I spotted Joon lurking in the corner.

Ji-won and I entered the lift. We got to her floor, and I collected my bag and said goodbye. Then I headed back downstairs.

Joon stepped out from the shadows, walking in closer to me.

"Not here," I said.

Turned to lead the way to the nearby park.

"Don't worry. I didn't tell anyone," I muttered.

Then he suddenly pulled me into an embrace, squeezing me tightly. I gasped as my eyes widened.

"Mina," he called softly.

Making my heart melt into a million pieces.

"Didn't you promise to stay out of my affairs? You should have just let it hit me, instead of, instead of you…"

He stopped mid-sentence. He sounded like a wounded soldier defeated at war. He squeezed me tighter, sighing continuously. Then he slowly pulled out of our embrace, crouching down, lifting his hands to my injured leg, his eyes shut as he gasped, and his hands formed into a fist.

"It doesn't hurt that much," I said.

But his expression remained the same. Opening his eyes, he got up, leading me to the nearby bench, and we sat.

"I reported them," Joon muttered.

I gasped, turning to him, with my jaw dropped.

"I should have done it long ago. If I had, you wouldn't have gotten hurt," he muttered.

With his gaze fixed on my leg. I grabbed his trembling hand.

Chapter Eleven

"Don't worry. I made sure none of it would come back to you. There's a camera on the first floor where the boys were. That was enough evidence to have them suspended," he muttered.

"But why were they after you?" I asked, and he sighed.

"Their leader likes one of the juniors that always follows me around school," I gasped.

Thinking back to the girl that asked Ji-won about me. It must be her.

"So, it was all because of a girl?" I sighed.

He turned to face me.

"Mina, you were right to keep your distance away from me eight years ago and now," he muttered, and my brows frowned.

"Eight years ago?" I repeated, and he nodded.

"You also got hurt back then because of me," he said, as his head sank.

"I know being close to me back then made things hard for you," he said.

I turned to him as my eyes widened, wondering how he knew.

Joon grabbed my hands, meeting my gaze.

"Eight years after the incident at the swings, you started avoiding me, and I thought it was because of that," he sighed.

"Whenever I tried apologising you would run off. The last time I tried, as you ran, one of the books you were carrying fell, picking it up. I noticed my name on the open page."

I gasped, pulling my hands away from his, realising, he was talking about my diary. I squeezed hold of my skirt, clenching my teeth; did he read everything? He sighed, turning to me.

"I didn't mean to invade your privacy. I only read the open page with my name on it and gave it to Ji-won to return to you," he said.

"You wrote about keeping your distance from me to protect your sister," he looks down at his fingers.

"That day, I saw the aftermath of those girls harassing Dina mistaking her for you; however, I knew intervening would only make things worse, but I still selfishly wanted to hold on to you. However, after seeing your diary, I knew I had to let go," he swallowed.

"So, I created distance between us and stopped being friendly with the girls at school."

I turned to face him, lost for words, as tears built up in my eyes. It finally all made sense; he pushed me away to protect me. I'm the reason he became this way.

"But being around me has put you in danger once again. I'm sorry, Mina, I shouldn't have taken your hand that day by the staircase."

His words felt like daggers piercing my heart.

"Let's go back to the way things were. I'll stay away from you at school. We can continue our after-school lessons until exams start in two weeks."

And before I realised it, tears came falling down my cheeks. He gasped as his eyes widened.

"What's wrong? Is it your leg? Does it hurt?" he asked.

Staring at me wide-eyed, I shook my head.

"All this time, I thought, I thou…"

My words failed me. He sighed, lifting his hands to wipe my tears off one cheek at a time.

"I'm sorry to have hurt you in so many ways, and thank you for always protecting me," he said.

Making my tears fall even harder, he leaned in close, pulling me into an embrace, gently tapping my back, cradling me like a child. A while later, he pulled back.

"Feeling better?" he asked.

Wearing a sunken expression, making my heart ache even more, my phone buzzed, but I didn't check it.

"It's late. We should get going, also don't worry about today's lesson, just get some rest. I'll explain to Mum," he said.

Gave me a weary smile, and then he crouched in front of me.

"Get on," he said.

Memories of being on his back years ago flooded back. Not wanting to resist, I got on, and he stood up, wrapping his arms around my legs. And his warmth enveloped me. The scent of coconut from his hair filled my nostrils.

"You should eat more; you're too light," he nagged, making me smile.

Ignoring my better judgement, I cherished the fleeting joy of the moment as we approached our building. Leaning my head against his neck, I savoured the sound of his racing heart, yearning for time to stand still. In measured strides, we arrived at our destination. He gently released my embrace, and as I stumbled on my injured leg, he swiftly grasped my hands, restoring my balance.

"Clumsy," he chuckled, and I grinned.

Relishing the connection of our intertwined hands. He maintained his grasp, guiding us towards the lift. It felt like an electric current surged between us. He pressed the call button, and the lift arrived. I bit my bottom lip to steady my breath, and a group of people entered just before the doors shut.

I tried pulling my hands off, but he didn't let go. Instead, he linked our hands and turned, shielding me. As the others exited the lift on the fifth floor, Joon and I remained locked in our position, our hands intertwined, lost in each other's gaze. The doors closed, sealing us in.

"Sixth floor."

The lift announced, bringing me back to the present.

"Oppa," I called.

He blinked, looking down at our linked hands, hesitating to let go.

"I'll get you home first," he muttered, and I nodded.

His gaze remained fixated on our hands. As the lift reached the eighth floor, the doors opened, and I gently released my hand from his grasp, and he reluctantly let go. Stepping out of the lift, I turned back for one final glance, our eyes locked until the doors sealed our separation.

I sunk to the ground panting, tears streamed down my cheeks recalling Joon's actions were driven by a desire to protect me.

He had always been there for me, sacrificing himself to keep me safe. I grinned staring down at my injured leg, knowing I was able to return the favour just a little.

My phone buzzed again, and it was Mum asking where I was. I got up, wiped my face, and exhaled before heading inside. Dina and Mum were in the living room watching TV when I got in.

"Ḱi ló dé tí õ fi ṕe?" Mum asked why I was late in Yoruba.

Then she gasped as her eyes widened, spotting the bandage on my leg.

"What happened to your leg?" Mum asked franticly.

Then she glared at Dina, whose brows frowned.

"Why are you looking at me? It wasn't me," she said.

"But if you ask me, she got what she deserved," Dina added.

"Dina!" Mum yelled.

"What, why are you yelling at me because of her?" Dina muttered.

"Mum, Mum, I am okay, I just tripped a little. It's nothing serious," I said.

She turned to me as her face sank.

"You need to be more careful."

She scolded as she examined the bandage.

"Go and get changed, and I'll get your dinner ready," she muttered.

Mum's fix for everything was always food. Although it took me getting hurt again to gain her attention, I grinned, watching her prepare my dinner.

"You did this to get everyone's pity and attention right," Dina muttered, rolling her eyes.

"Pathetic as ever," she murmured.

I sighed and ignored her comment, retreating to my room. I emptied my pockets and took out Joon's handkerchief, heading to the bathroom to wash it. Joon's weakened expression replayed in my mind as the blood flowed down the drain. I shook off the thoughts and squeezed out the excess water. I laid it to dry on the radiator back in my room, noticing the embroidered initials: C.J.

After dinner, I got in bed, and played N.O.'s latest album, "Back to the Beginning." Looking at my hands, I recalled the electric pull between Joon, and me when we linked hands. I pushed the memory aside, keeping it buried in my heart as a sweet dream as I drifted into a slumber.

I opened my eyes to the start of a new day, and a clearer mind. The pain in my leg had subsided, allowing me to move more freely. After breakfast, I stepped outside, finding Ji-won waiting by the lift.

"Hey, Mimi, how are you feeling today?" she asked.

"It doesn't hurt as much," I said, grinning.

We got downstairs, and she linked arms with mine for support and we walked up the hill. I looked back constantly searching for Joon.

"What or who are you looking for, Mimi?" Ji-won asked.

"Nothing, no one," I responded.

We headed straight for the school hall for our weekly assembly. Our principal, Mr Callum, walked onto the stage, sweeping what was left of his front hair to the side. He struggled to fit his belly behind the podium, eventually standing beside it. Clearing his throat, he began his speech.

"We had some disturbing reports yesterday about an attack on a fellow student. This kind of behaviour will not be tolerated in our school," the principal said.

I fidgeted in my seat, biting my bottom lip as I listened.

"Omg, who could it be," Ji-won muttered.

Other students began to mumble, making guesses.

"The students involved have been expelled from school, so this is a warning to the rest of you to be on your best behaviour at all times," he said, turning the page on his script.

"Today will be the beginning of study week for those in Year Ten, Eleven and sixth formers, so make sure you revise as your upcoming exams will impact your grades. That's it for today. You are all dismissed," he said assertively.

We made our way out, and I spotted Joon, leaving the hall ahead of us. I felt a pit in my stomach, and my heart ached.

"Mina, what's wrong?" Ji-won asked.

I shook my head.

"Nothing, let's go," I said.

Our classes were silent. Everyone had their noses glued to their books. During lunch, Terry waited outside my classroom. Spotting my injured leg, his face fell as I stepped out.

"I'm okay," I muttered.

He sighed, continuously glaring at my leg.

So, I walked around, displaying my limp wasn't as bad anymore.

"See, it doesn't hurt as much," I said.

Pressing his lips together, he folded his arms and sighed, and I grinned.

"I am hungry. Let's go get lunch," I said, walking off.

"M," he called, and I halted.

"You should stay clear of that guy, or you will keep getting hurt," he said.

My smile faded, recalling I wouldn't be able to be around him anymore even if I wanted to, and that it was Joon who would get hurt if he stayed close to me. I exhaled and my shoulders dropped.

"Promise me," he said.

"You don't have to worry about that," I said, returning my plastered smile.

"And what's up with you and D? She behaved a bit odd yesterday. Did you guys get in a fight or something?" he asked, and I sighed, shaking my head.

"I am always getting injured. I think expecting a reaction from her every time will be unreasonable," I chuckled.

"Terry, I am hungry. Let's go."

I repeated, pulling his arm along.

"Don't get cute with me," he said, smirking.

We walked down the hall, giggling with our arms linked together. We entered the dining hall bumping into Joon and Rachel, our grin faded, and Joon's eyes travelled down to our linked arms, and I pulled mine out of Terry's.

"Hi, Mina," Rachel said.

"Hi," I responded.

Joon walked right past us, and Rachel grinned, placing her hands over her mouth.

"Well, I'll see you around," Rachel muttered.

Waving as she caught up with Joon.

"What a dickhead, who does he think he is?" Terry said and sighed.

Although I knew why Joon was keeping his distance. My heart ached more than I had anticipated. I exhaled, cracking a smile and linked arms with Terry again.

"Let's eat," I said, and we joined the line to get lunch.

After school, Ji-won, Emily, and I headed home, Ji-won went on about how her horoscope had been super accurate that day, then halted suddenly and gasped as her eyes widened.

"OMG, Mimi, big news," she muttered, out of breath.

"How could I have forgotten to tell you."

Her eyes beamed, ready to give me the full gist.

"Remember the junior that asked about Joon Oppa the other day."

I gasped, clenching my teeth. Could she have found out that I was involved in the incident? Did the whole school know? I swallowed, bracing myself.

"She's transferring schools," Ji-won said, and my eyes widened.

"Why?" I asked.

"Apparently, she was involved with the boys that got expelled, so her parents were called in," she added, and I exhaled.

"But how was she involved?" Emily asked.

"Not sure, but her parents wanted her to move schools, so the rumours don't affect her future," Ji-won added.

"Well, Mina, at least you finally can relax now that the leader of Joon Oppa's minions is moving schools. The rumours about you and Oppa falling out of the closet will die down now," she muttered.

Emily's jaw dropped, and I glared at Ji-won wide-eyed.

"OMG, Mina, that was you," Emily said in disbelief.

Ji-won covered her mouth, I sighed, and Emily smirked.

"Relax, Mina, I won't say anything," Emily said.

Although Emily was a good friend, we didn't share anything personal. Ji-won changed the topic by bringing up her horoscope again. We got down to the hill and waved Emily goodbye, and we headed to our estate.

"Sorry, Mina, I didn't mean to tell her," Ji-won said.

Biting her bottom lip, I smirked, shaking her.

"What am I going to do with you?" I muttered, and we both giggled.

After Dinner, I went downstairs to Ji-won's house while Dina was with her tutor and Mum was out grocery shopping. My palms grew sweaty as I stood outside the door. It was just Joon, I repeated to myself. Ji-won opened the door, and we headed to the living room.

"Mum and grandma are out for the evening," Ji-won said, and I nodded.

We headed to Joon's bedroom. He was immersed in the book he had in front of him. Ji-won and I sat opening our textbooks.

"I'll be giving you both a practice test today," Joon muttered avoiding eye contact.

My pen slipped out of my sweaty palms.

"Mimi, you okay?" Ji-won asked.

"Huh," I murmured, clearing my throat.

"You're all sweaty," she said.

I placed my hand on my forehead. It was covered in sweat. I used my hands to fan myself.

"Is it me, or is it boiling in here?" I muttered.

Fidgeting in my seat, Ji-won tilted her head, assessing the temperature.

"It feels okay to me," she mumbles.

Joon still didn't react, placing the test sheet in front of us.

"You may both begin," he said.

I took a deep breath, trying to calm my racing heart, and opened the test paper. The questions Joon had given me were at a much higher level than before. I glanced at Ji-won's paper, noticing it was different. As I looked back at Joon, his glare answered my unspoken question.

"I need the bathroom," I said, rushing out.

Entering I locked the door behind me, and sank to the ground, covering my face with my trembling hands. How long had he known? Had he always known? And why didn't he say anything? Memories of him seeing my blue notebook flooded my mind, and I sighed. He must have recognised my handwriting from my diary. Taking a deep breath, I gathered myself and made my way back to his room.

Returning to my seat, I resumed writing, aware of Joon's gaze on my answer sheet. I positioned my elbow to block his view. His alarm went off and he assessed Ji-won's paper, providing feedback before returning it. Then, he shifted his attention to mine, and his lips formed a hard line.

"Oppa, aren't you going to mark Mina's?" Ji-won asked.

"Ji-won, go to the living room for a moment. I need to speak to Mina privately," he said.

Her eyes narrowed. Still, she quietly got up and left.

"I think I should leave for today," I said, getting up.

"Mina, what do you think you're doing?" he asked.

I lifted my head to meet his sunken gaze.

"I don't know what you're talking about," I said, grabbing my bag.

"Your grades, Mina, I know you're failing on purpose. The book you dropped the other day, I know it's yours," he said.

I lowered my head, biting down on my teeth.

"How much longer will you go on pretending?" he asked.

I swallowed as my hands trembled.

"What's gotten into you suddenly? If you've known all along, why didn't you say anything, and why are you bringing it up now?" I asked, and he sighed.

"Because I can't bear to see it anymore. Do you have any idea how hard it's been to watch you slowly destroy yourself these past few years? At first, I thought it was because of me, but even after keeping my distance, you carried on killing off the things that made you, who you are," he said.

My heart constricted. I grabbed my bag, headed for the door, pulled on the handle, and then halted.

"You won't understand, Oppa," I muttered, pulling on the door handle.

"Then help me understand," he murmured.

Chapter Twelve

My hands fell off the door handle, and I turned to him.

"I did something unforgivable to Dina in the past. This is the only way I can think of to protect her from getting hurt again."

His brows frowned as he walked in closer to me.

"How does being yourself put her in harm's way?" he asked.

"Because of this," I said.

Pointing at my face with my trembling hands.

"Because we share this face, just the way those girls attacked her, thinking she was me, was the same way he…"

I stopped mid-sentence, squeezing my eyes shut, trying to erase the thought. Joon ran his hands through his hair and exhaled.

"Although I don't know what happened between you two in the past, the one thing I know for certain is that you would never hurt anyone intentionally," he said.

I turned, catching my reflection in his mirror.

"That's what makes it worse, even when it's unintentional. This face is like a ticking time bomb that could explode at any moment, destroying everything in its path, and the person who suffers the aftermath is Dina."

I lowered my head, biting my bottom lip to halt my tears.

"But what I don't get is why you're willing to give up everything else, but this? You've broken so many of your own rules just for a chance to go to the N.O. concert. Why is that?" he asked.

I gasped, turning to meet his gaze.

"Because N.O. is my life source, with them, I don't feel the weight of my sins, besides as a fangirl, I'm one of many, a speck of dust in the desert, invincible and unnoticed, all anyone will be looking at, all I will be looking at is N.O," I muttered.

Turned around and grabbed hold of the door handle.

"What about me?" he murmured, making my heart clench.

"Can't you look at me, Mina? The way I felt about you eight years ago hasn't changed. I never kept my distance because I gave up on those feelings. It was never meant to be forever. I've been waiting," he blurted out.

My eyes widened as I turned to meet his piercing gaze. He swallowed and continued.

"Waiting until you were ready to reach out your hands to me again. And you finally did that day at the stairs, so I thought we could…"

He walked in closer, and I took a step back.

"You thought we could go back to the way things used to be?" I asked.

Taking a deep breath, holding back an ocean of brimming tears.

"Oppa, that will never happen, the Mina you knew back then was a girl who thought she could find forgiveness and happiness regardless of her past mistakes. However, the Mina standing before you now knows better," I said.

Turning around, I pulled the door handle, racing out of the house.

"Mina, Mina," Ji-won called.

"I'll see you tomorrow," I yelled.

Getting outside, I looked down at my trembling hands, shutting my eyes, panting.

"Mina, you need to keep it together," I repeated.

I exhaled and began to walk up the stairs. As I got to our floor, the lift opened.

"Mina," Mum called. I grinned and collected the shopping bags in her hands.

"Coming back from your lesson?" she asked.

I nodded, lowering my head.

"ḱi lọ́ dé?" Mum asked what was wrong in Yoruba.

"Nothing," I muttered. Lifting my head to meet her gaze.

"Mum," I called.

"How would you feel if my grades improved?" I asked, and her brows furrowed.

"That's an odd question. Of course, I'd be glad. You used to get the best grades in the whole school before we moved to this area. I still remember the last award you received," she smiled, reminiscing.

I thought back to the day I received an award for solving a university-level math problem. Dad had just passed away, and Dina had developed PTSD from the traumatic incident that occurred a year earlier. Mum was focused on helping her heal, and I was filled with pain and guilt because it was my fault Dina was hurt. My only escape during those dark times was burying my nose in my books, especially solving math problems.

It helped pass the time. When my maths teacher saw my notebook filled with solutions, she was stunned that I had solved them all independently and showed them to other teachers. They couldn't believe it and asked me to solve them again, gathering around to watch. Then, the principal called Mum in and suggested having a reporter write an article about me for the local newspaper.

But Mum declined immediately, settling for an award at the school assembly, I recalled the grim look on Dina's face as she watched me on stage.

I sighed, remembering my conversation with Dina that night at bedtime.

"Mina," she called.

Her voice was buried under an abyss of sorrow. I got up and robbed the sleep off my eyes.

"Yes, Dina," I answered. She walked over to my bedside.

"I hate you," she muttered, and my brows narrowed, feeling chills run down my spine.

"I hate you so much. I hate that you look like me, I hate that we are compared, and I hate that only bad things happen to me while you enjoy all the glory."

Tears began streaming down our cheeks. Her words were like daggers piercing my heart. She then grabbed onto my shoulders.

"Don't you think you should be paying for what you did to me by living like a sinner seeking redemption," her eyes darkened.

"But instead, you're still going around seeking people's attention," I shook my head.

"Dina, that's not true," I said, as her grip on my shoulders tightened.

"Shut up," she said.

I lowered my head, as tears fell on my fingers.

"Because of what you caused to happen to me that day, Dad took on all the guilt, that led to his death. You killed him," she said.

Breathlessly squeezing hold of my collar.

"Do you think you deserved the award you received today," she gasped.

"If you truly want to pay for what you did, then you should live like a ghost, unnoticed by anyone. If you bring attention to yourself again like today, I will end both our misery," she warned.

Then she raised her right hand, hitting it on her chest repeatedly.

"Do you have any idea how much it hurts here, Mina?" she asked, and I gasped.

Then she moved her hands to her head, hitting it continuously.

"And here," she said, breathless.

"I can't forget his face. No matter how hard I try, his face is embedded in here," she said.

Falling to the ground, continuously hitting her head, and crying, I crouched down, holding her hands back.

"Dina, I'm sorry," I muttered.

Wrapping my arms around her, as we sobbed.

"I'm so sorry, Dina," I muttered repeatedly.

Then she suddenly rose her head, pushing me off.

"If you're sorry, then promise me you'll live the rest of your life like a ghost. Although nothing you do will ever make up for the things you've taken from me, it's the least you can do," she said, glaring at me wide-eyed.

"How I wish I could rip your face off," she muttered.

With bitterness in her voice as she gripped hold of my shirt again.

"Promise me, promise me you'll live like a ghost," she yelled.

She pushed me back and forth, demanding an answer. I nodded continuously, and then she finally let go and returned to bed. I stayed kneeling, sobbing through the night until I tired myself out and fell asleep. After we moved into a new neighbourhood and school, I saw the opportunity to start afresh. So, I began faking my grades in hopes to keep my promise to Dina.

But no matter how much I gave up, it was never enough. However, going to the N.O. concert was where I drew the line, hoping I wouldn't hurt Dina in the process.

"Sometimes I wonder if moving here was a good idea," Mum said, bringing me back to the present.

Then our door opened, and Dina walked her tutor out.

We exchanged greetings and we all waved him goodbye as he got on the lift.

“Why are you both together?” Dina asked with her brows frowning.

“We met by the lift. Mina, go and put the shopping away,” Mum said.

Stopping Dina’s questing.

“Where is she always off to these days,” Dina murmured.

“Let’s go inside,” Mum said.

After putting the shopping away, I entered my room and noticed Joon’s handkerchief on my desk. I stowed it in my drawer and collapsed into bed, squeezing my eyes shut, regretting extending my hands out to him that day. Everything felt messed up. Rolling over, I buried my face in the pillow and screamed into it.

Headed out to school the next day, Ji-won was by the lift waiting as usual.

“Why did you rush off yesterday? Was Oppa harsh with you?” she asked, and I shook my head.

“Just wasn’t feeling well,” I said.

Then she looked down at my legs.

“Your bandage is off,” she said, and I nodded.

“Yep, it’s all healed now,” I muttered, and she grinned.

We entered the lift and left for school. The next few days were repetitive, but I kept out of Dina’s radar. Everyone was focused on revision. Joon and I have barely interacted at school since our talk. During tutoring sessions, we only spoke when reviewing answer sheets. Everything seemed to have returned to normal.

"Mina!" Terry called.

"Time to eat," he said, and I nodded.

He had been glued to my side ever since the flowerpot incident.

Two weeks passed, and it was officially the end of study week. Everyone at school seemed worn out and sleep-deprived after revising until late.

"Let's meet at the amusement park," Ji-won said.

She suggested we go for some joy rides to let off some steam before our exams began.

"Mina let's just have some fun, regardless of the results we get," Ji-won said.

I nodded in agreement but still hadn't decided whether to go for a C or just give up on attending the N.O. concert. But I decided to make that decision on the day of our exam, Ji-won jumped with joy, giggling from ear to ear.

"But Ji, why can't we just go together?" I asked.

"I can't. Mum is dragging me along with her and Grandma to the hairdresser for a trim. My split ends have multiplied."

She rolled her eyes, running her hands through her hair.

"Don't get why mum has us going all the way to the other side of London for a haircut just because the salon owner is a friend," she pouted, folding her arms.

"Can't I wait until you return," I said, and she shook her head.

"No, Mina, think about it. It's Saturday tomorrow; it'll be packed with lots of people, so we need to get there before it gets too crowded. After my hair is done, I'll make my way down immediately."

I sighed, nodding, and we headed home.

"Ah, I completely forgot. Oppa said I should tell you that yesterday's lesson was our last," Ji-won said, and my brows narrowed.

"Wait, why?" I asked, perplexed, and Ji-won smirked.

"You sound disappointed? I thought you'd be happy to finally be free of my brother," she said.

I gasped, chuckling.

"It's nothing like that. It's just unlike him not to see something through, that's all," I muttered, and she grinned.

"Well, it was actually his idea for us to go to the amusement park," she muttered, and my eyes widened.

"He said all work and no play makes Jack a dull boy," she said, chuckling, and I sighed.

Finding out yesterday was our last session felt strange. If I had known yesterday was our last, I would have, I would have…

"Mimi," Ji-won called, bringing me out of my train of thought.

"Huh," I raised my head.

"What are you thinking of so deeply?" she asked.

"Oh, I was just thinking I agree with Joon Oppa for once," she nodded.

"Me too, I can't wait," she said, giggling, and then her grin faded, making my brows frown.

"Mina," she called, glaring deep into my eyes. I felt my breath halt as I listened.

"I know you don't like us speaking about your personal struggles, but it's been difficult for me to ignore the signs I see of you crumbling, especially of late. I usually try brightening the mood talking about horoscopes or N.O., but I want you to know that I am here for you always whenever you want to talk, as your best friend, I want you to know that I've got your back both in your good moments and bad and that I love you," she muttered and we both got teared up.

Ji-won always pulled me out of my darkness, but I had no idea she did so intentionally. I fought back my tears overwhelmed by her confession. She then shook her head and wiped off her tears wearing a grin.

"Okay, enough of that, let's plan out our day for tomorrow," she said, and I nodded, wiping off my tears too, and then we started listing out the rides we were looking forward to the most as we walked home.

The first majestic thing I saw was falling snow when I woke up. Rushing to my window, I admired the neighbourhood covered in a beautiful white blanket. After breakfast, I packed some leftover Jollof rice for Ji-won and me. Mum and Dina were out, and as I cleared my dishes, something seemed amiss, but I brushed it aside, determined to have a good day at the park.

I showered and got dressed and left a note for Mum. I headed to the amusement park, listening to N.O.'s "Good Time." Spotting my train approaching, I ran holding onto my beanie hat and caught the train before the doors shut, squeezing myself in.

As we rode, some people sang, babies walled, and conversations were exchanged between lovers, friends, and families. I turned up the volume on my MP3 player, then felt movements on my left side, but I could not turn to see what it was. Finally, we arrived at the amusement park, and everyone pushed their way out.

I headed to the blossom tree where Ji-won, and I had agreed to meet, but she was nowhere in sight, so I reached for my phone, but it was gone. I searched my pockets with no luck. I gasped as I recalled I felt movements in my pockets earlier. I crotched down drained of excitement. I paced back and forth, biting my finger.

Should I return to the train station to report my phone stolen? I shook my head, as I might miss Ji-won. I sighed, running my hands through my head, and then spotted a phone booth nearby. I called Ji-won, but her phone went to voicemail, so I left a message.

"Ji-won, it's Mina. My phone was stolen on the train, so I'm calling from a pay phone. I'm waiting under the blossom tree by the entrance."

I hung up and headed back to the blossom tree that was now stripped of its beautiful flowers and covered in snow. I rubbed my palms together. My ears twitched knowing Mum would nag about me losing my phone. I changed the song on my MP3 player selecting Snowfall by N.O. as I waited.

Five songs later, Ji-won was still nowhere in sight, and I bit my finger, wondering if she received my message. Pacing back and forth to keep warm, the sixth track, "My First Love" from N.O.'s first album, started playing. Suddenly, I spotted a familiar figure walking towards me.

Despite the distance and the face hat he wore, I knew it was him. My heart rate quickened as he approached.

As he got closer, I took steps back but tripped over my legs. He leaned in, catching me in an embrace. I looked up at him blinking.

"Are you okay?" he asked. I glared at him, speechless.

"Mina?" he called, shaking me.

I nodded blinking rapidly. Why was he here? I pressed my lips together, and he lifted me back upright. My heart rate rose. Was it because I was excited to see him, or because it was unexpected, I wondered, as we looked everywhere but at each other.

"Ji-won."

We both said as our eyes met and then his phone started ringing.

"Yes, I found her," he said, answering the call.

Then he stretched his hands out, handing his phone over to me.

"Hello," I muttered.

"OMG, Mina, I'm so sorry, I'm still stuck at the hair shop. Grandma's perm is taking longer than expected, so I asked Joon Oppa to come instead," she said.

I turned, walking a bit further away from him.

"Why, we could have just cancelled instead," I muttered.

"Mimi, we both know you need to let off some steam, so have fun, okay? It really sucks about your phone being stolen. Can't believe someone would do that."

She stopped mid-sentence "Ji-won," I heard her Mum calling in the background.

"Coming," she responded.

"Got to go, girl, have fun, okay, bye," she said, hanging up.

"Ji, Ji!" I called.

Then hesitantly walked back to Joon, handing his phone back, and we both stood fidgeting.

"Shall we go in," he said eventually.

I exhaled, nodding in response, and we headed inside.

Chapter Thirteen

The amusement park was bustling with families, friends, and couples queuing for rides. Joon and I walked in silence, passing by the roller coaster. My face lit up, but the queue was too long.

My head sank, and I turned to walk away, but Joon grabbed my hands, pulling me to the queue, and I felt butterflies in my stomach from our sudden skinship. As we waited, I embraced myself swaying from side to side as the temperature dropped, looking away from the couple in front of us, unable to keep their hands off each other.

"Here," Joon said.

Handing me his gloves and wrapped his scarf around my neck, then shook his head and sighed.

"Shouldn't you have worn warmer clothes," he nagged.

And my butterflies from earlier disappeared.

"I'm not cold, actually," I muttered.

Gave his scarf and gloves back to him, and his brows furrowed. As the queue moved, I walked ahead, leaving him behind. After forty-five minutes, we were next in line, but Joon seemed hesitant and fidgety. The ride arrived, and I took a seat.

"You can get on now," a staff said.

"Oppa, aren't you getting on?" I asked.

"Coming," he murmured, taking a seat next to me.

"Please make sure your seat belts are on as we are about to hit some turbulence," the Pilot warns, transporting me back to the present.

I was hoping for a smooth plane journey, but the storm coming our way had other plans. I tremble through every bump, but then I start grinning as I am reminded of that roller-coaster ride with Joon sending me back in time.

As the ride was about to take off, Joon turned to the side to look at how high up we were but squeezed his eyes shut instantly, and I chuckled.

"Oppa, are you scared of heights?" I asked, giggling, and his eyes widened, meeting my gaze.

"Who, me? No way," he mumbled.

The countdown began, Joon gripped the sidebars tightly, and we were off. The cold air on my face and being so high up was liberating. I raised my hands, screaming continuously. At the highest point, the ride halted. I turned to Joon, who was panting with his eyes shut. I smirked, watching him tremble. He looked so childlike. Then his eyes sprung open suddenly and I looked away. The ride resumed, and he gasped, screaming as we went down.

His screams set me off in fits of giggles, and then our eyes met, and my laughter faded, as my butterflies returned. The ride slowly ended, and a staff member came over to lift the safety bars up, making us break eye contact, and we got off. I picked up my lunch box and we headed to the exit room, where our pictures were displayed. Ours came up, and it was a shot of me giggling, while Joon gazed at me intensely.

"It's been years since I've seen you laugh like that," he muttered in astonishment.

I swallowed, turning away.

"You looked so beautiful," he blurted out.

I gasped, turning to meet his gaze taken aback by his unexpected compliment, and he grinned, making my heart rate spike.

"Would you like a copy?" a staff asked, making us break eye contact, and then Joon walked over to the counter.

"Yes, can I get two copies, please," he said.

Handing over a ten-pound note to the cashier.

"You guys look great together," the cashier said.

As she handed the pictures over to Joon.

"We're not together," I blurted out.

Louder than I intended, Joon smirked as he walked back to me, handing me a copy, but I contemplated taking it.

"Don't want one?" he asked.

Waving it in front of me, and I gasped, biting my bottom lips.

"Yes, please," I said, eventually stretching my hands out to take it.

He smirked, handing it to me and walked out. I exhaled joining him, tucking the photo safely in my pocket.

"What ride do you want to go on next?" he asked.

I stopped, and he turned to face me.

"Actually, can we stop to eat," I said.

As the rumbling in my belly got louder, he looked over at the lunch box in my hand.

"There is a spot right over there," I said.

Pointing to a sitting area nearby with a shade over it, we walked over and sat opposite each other.

"Erm, I'm not sure if you'll be able to handle the spice. I brought it because it's one of Ji-won's favourite Nigerian foods," I said.

Lifting the lead on the plate, and his eyes narrowed.

"It's called Jollof rice," I muttered.

He nodded picking up a spoon to dig in.

"It's really spicy," I warned.

He smirked, taking a scoop. I watched as he chewed, then he stopped suddenly, and his eyes widened.

"Are you okay?" I asked.

Trying to hold back my giggles, his hands formed into a fist, and his eyes got teary. I rushed to the nearby drink stand to get some milk.

"Here," I said.

I handed it over, and he gulped it down, making me giggle. His breathing quickened, and his face turned red. Then he left his mouth open letting air in. I sighed, then picked up my spoon and began eating. He exhaled and resumed eating too. I gasped, and held his hands firmly, making him halt.

"Oppa, stop. You don't have to eat it," I said.

He grinned, moving my hands away.

"Isn't it too spicy?" I asked, and he shook his head.

"It is, but it's really good," he said.

I smiled, watching him eat.

"Is this your first time trying African food?" I asked.

He nodded. I sighed, shaking my head, baffled by his determination and picked up my spoon, joining him. After we were done eating, we got on two more rides.

"Any more rides you would like to get on?" he asked, but I shook my head.

"Let's just walk through the stores and maybe play some games," I suggested, and he nodded.

The sky had already gone dark, but the twinkling lights from the stores gave off a magical atmosphere as we walked. We arrived at a stand for teddy bears, and I gawked at the huge panda on display.

"Do you want it?" Joon asked.

I shook my head and carried on walking.

"Can I pay for a round?"

Joon told the store owner, and I halted to watch him play. The storekeeper gave him three tennis balls, saying he needed to knock down five stacked rows of tins to win the panda. Joon aimed for the first stack, but missed. He sighed, shaking his head, then prepared for his next shot and threw it, hitting all the tins at once.

"Yessssss!" I yelled, cheering.

"Pick one," Joon said, and I grinned.

Pointing at the giant panda and Joon handed it over to me. My face beamed as I smiled from ear to ear. As we walked, our hands grazed from time to time. Each touch left an electric current cursing through my body.

"OMG, do you think they're together?"

A female voice muttered. We looked around and spotted two girls about the same age as Joon wearing Mickey Mouse hairbands by the candy floss stand glaring at us.

“What is an Asian guy doing with a black girl? What a weird combo.”

The taller girl said, and they both chuckled.

“Besides, isn’t he way out of her league?”

The other girl added, and they burst into fits of giggles. I lowered my head, and Joon’s hand formed into a fist as he glared at them, panting. We had been getting stares all day from people, but this was the first harsh comment we had received. I started walking off quickly, and Joon jogged stepping in front of me, making me halt. I lifted my head to meet his gaze, and he smiled, reaching down for my hand, and linking it with his.

“Leaving me behind?” he asked.

He waved at the girls, placing our linked hands in his pocket, and their jaws dropped. We continued walking, and my smile returned, feeling tingles down my spine. We got to a jewellery stand, and a necklace with a star pendant caught my eye. I stopped, picked it up, admired it for a moment, and then dropped it back.

“Let’s go,” I said, and Joon’s eyes narrowed.

We carried on walking, but then he stopped, letting go of my hand.

“Wait here, I’ll be right back,” he said.

Running into the distance, I stretched my neck to see where he went, but he had disappeared into the crowd of people. After a while, he reappeared, panting.

“Where did you go?” I asked.

But he just shook his head, smirking.

"We should start making our way home. The last train will be leaving soon," he said.

I nodded, and he reached down, taking my hands again, and placing them back in his pocket.

"Let's go," he muttered.

His cheeks turned tomato red, and I bit my lip to hide my smile. Exiting the park, we reached the station and boarded the last train. It was packed, but thankfully, Joon towered over me, shielding me with his body. But then the train stopped suddenly, squashing everyone in.

As the train jolted, I found myself pressed closer to Joon, my head resting against his chest. He held onto a safety bar with one hand and wrapped the other around my waist. I clung to his puffer jacket for balance with one hand and clutched my stuffed panda tightly with the other.

The train huddled again, bringing us even closer, and I could hear his heart beating rapidly, just like mine. Closing my eyes, I pressed my ears in to listen. Spending the day with Joon, free from fear or worries, in a place where no one knew us, was like a dream.

After exiting the train, we walked home slowly holding hands, knowing our dream-like day was about to end. Every step forward made my heart ache as the end drew nearer, but with each step, his grip tightened. I smiled, knowing he didn't want the night to end either. Finally, we stood in front of our building, hesitantly unlinking our hands, and he handed me my lunch box.

"I had fun today," he muttered.

I swallowed, lifting my head to meet his gaze. He truly was beautiful, especially when he smiled with his eyes, melting me like butter.

"You?" he asked.

Awaiting my response, I nodded, grinning, and then turned heading inside.

"Mina…" he called.

I turned to him, but he hesitated to speak.

"Joon," a familiar voice called.

We both turned, and it was Rachel walking out of our building. I stepped away from Joon, gripping my stuffed Panda, and his brows frowned. Rachel's smile faded as she walked glaring at the stuffed panda.

"What are you doing here?" Joon asked, and she smirked.

"Why? Am I not allowed to be here?" she muttered, wearing a forced smile.

"I came over to hang out and let off some steam before exams start on Monday, but Ji-won said you had gone out," Rachel muttered as a disdainful look swept her face.

"So, I spent the day with your family instead, but I was hoping to see you before leaving, so I stayed till late," she continued, turning her attention back to me.

"Hi Mina," she said hesitantly, and I swallowed.

"Hey, Rachel," I responded.

"So did you guys meet up on your way in?" she asked.

It seemed Ji-won didn't tell her Joon, and I were together.

"Yes, we did," I blurted out.

Joon's lips fell into a hard line.

"No, we went to an amusement park together," Joon said, and I gasped.

Why would he tell her that? I wondered, sighing, as I watched her face grow pale.

"Ahh, looks like you guys had fun," she muttered.

Wearing her plastered smile, doing her best to hold in her visible disdain as she glared at me with daggers.

"Joon, it's quite late. Could you walk me to the bus stop?" she asked.

He looked over at me, and I gave him a forced smile.

"All right, hold on, I'll go and grab my bike," he said.

Running into the building, then Rachel walked in closer leaning in.

"Mina, I get that you're not book smart, but I thought that you would at least know your place," she muttered.

My eyes widened, and she smirked.

"Still don't get it? Do I need to spell it out for you," she said.

Then grabbed onto the stuffed panda, pulling it to the ground.

"You should go for someone in your league and stop shamelessly throwing yourself at Joon," she added.

I bit down on my teeth, trembling, and she smirked again.

"Do you seriously think you and Joon make sense together," she chuckled.

Just as I was about to respond, we heard footsteps, and she bent to pick up the panda and shoved it back in my arm. I stood frozen, unable to comprehend what had happened and Joon reappeared with his bike in hand.

"Mina, why are you still here? It's cold out. You should go inside. I'm just going to walk Rachel to the bus stop," he said, and I nodded.

"Bye, Mina," she muttered, with a plastered smile.

Rolling her eyes, Rachel held onto Joon's arm. I got in the lift, dazed, unable to comprehend what had happened. The dream-like day was turning into a nightmare. Getting to the door, I turned in my key. Opening the door, a cushion came flying at my head.

"You selfish bitch," Dina yelled.

Throwing another cushion at me, but I placed my hands over my head for cover, my brows narrowed, taken back by her sudden outburst. Mum was sitting by the corner motionless, then I spotted a photo of Dad on the coffee table, and then it hit me. My hands grew weak, releasing my grip on the lunch box and panda. Dina walked in closer, grabbing me by the collar.

"How could a sinner like you forget a day like today?" she yelled.

"The least you could do is remember the day he died since you were the cause of his death," she added.

Pulling me back and forth, but I don't fight back or stop her.

"Dina, that's enough," Mum muttered.

And walked into her room, shutting the door, and Dina smirked.

"Enough! Enough? I haven't even started yet," she said.

Dragging me to the coffee table where Dad's photo was and pressed my head down on it.

"How could you forget the day you killed him, huh?" she yelled.

Tears rolled down my face, and I lifted my gaze to meet hers.

"What's with the pitiful look? Am I wrong? Aren't you a murderer? Wasn't it your thirst for fame that led to my path of endless misery and Dad's death?" she asked.

I lowered my head as my tears continued pouring. How could I have forgotten such an important day? Dad must resent me too. Dina's eyes fell on the stuffed Panda, and she gasped, walking over to pick it up.

"Well, seems like you had a good time today," she said.

Walking back towards me and began hitting me with it.

"You were out there having the time of your life while Mum and I went to visit Dad's grave, crying all day," she muttered.

Then threw the panda, panting.

"I can see right through your fake act, Mina. You knew exactly what today was but pretended not to remember. Isn't that why you had your phone switched off all day? You selfish bitch," she muttered.

I slowly lifted myself off the coffee table.

"Dina, that's not true," I murmured.

"Shut up!" she screamed.

"Just get out of my sight. I hate you, Mina. I hate the sight of you. You make me sick, so just go, get out," she yelled.

Pulling me up and dragging me towards the front door.

"Get out," she said.

After she threw me out and slammed the door, I leaned against it, sobbing as my heart ached. Suddenly feeling the urge to end it all, I got up and ran, going down the stairs and out of the estate building. I kept running, with tears streaming down my cheeks, with no destination in mind.

"Mina!"

I heard Joon call, but I didn't stop or respond. I just kept running. Then, he suddenly appeared beside me, following along on his bicycle.

"Mina, Mina, what's the matter?" he asked.

I still didn't respond. After a while, I began slowing down and eventually came to a stop, leaning on my knees, panting.

"Get on," Joon Muttered.

I looked over at him, breathless, as tears streamed down my cheeks. Joon was another person who had gotten hurt, too, just because I existed.

"Don't worry. I won't ask any questions. Just let me give you a ride, okay? You'll get hurt if you over-exert yourself," he warned, and I slowly rose.

"I promise not to ask you anything, Mina. So please get on," he pleaded.

I sighed and walked over to him. He placed the spare helmet on me and buckled the straps around my chin. I then walked over to the back of his bike and got on.

"Hold on," he said.

I wrapped my hands around his waist and began riding. Soon after, we hit a big bump, pushing us closer. I tightened my grip around his waist, and he picked up the pace. I inhaled the cold breeze blowing on my face, leaning against his back for comfort.

The image of Dad popped into my head, and tears came pouring again. The night air was cold, but Joon's back felt like a warm blanket. We rode for a while, only stopping when the traffic lights turned red. Joon remained silent as promised, turning occasionally to check on me. All cried out, my face was swollen, and my head was throbbing. Joon began slowing down until we eventually came to a stop.

Chapter Fourteen

"Shall we take a break?" he suggested.

I lifted my head from his back, smiling as I spotted Big Ben, we got off the bike, and he grabbed the bottle of water attached to his bicycle, handing it to me.

"Here, drink this," he said.

I gulped it down, almost emptying the bottle, then handed it back to him. He drank the rest and followed me with his bike. London Bridge was covered in twinkling lights, and I exhaled mesmerised by its breathtaking view. I had never been there so late at night.

"Isn't it beautiful?" Joon muttered, and I nodded.

"I usually come here when life gets too much," he murmured.

He walked in closer and pointed up at the sky.

"This is the best place to see the stars clearly," he said.

My eyes followed the direction of his hands.

"Back in South Korea, when my grandpa passed away, I had a tough time getting through it… he was my hero, my everything," he muttered.

"One day after crying non-stop, my dad took me outside, and we laid down on our outdoor bench watching the stars."

I turned to Joon as I listened, and he smiled, recalling the memory.

"Then he pointed at the brightest star in the sky and said it was my grandpa's star shining down on me, but that I needed to be at my happiest in order for him to continue shining bright, so the happier I become, the brighter grandpa's star will shine, dad said," Joon added grinning.

"Ever since we moved to London, I always come here whenever I'm struggling. To remind myself that my Grandpa only shines bright when I'm happiest," he added.

Then he leaned in, lifting my hand up to search through the sky until we found the brightest star.

"There he is," Joon muttered, smiling.

Tears streamed down my cheeks as I was unable to find Dad. His light must be deemed because of me. Everyone was unhappy because of me.

Joon turned to me, wiping my tears off, and then pulled me into his embrace.

"It breaks my heart to see you this way," he said.

Making me sob harder, and his grip tightened. After a while, he pulled out of the embrace and reached into his pocket.

"I was going to give this to you after exams, but I think you need it now," he said.

Pulling out a necklace with a star pendant, the one I admired at the amusement park, I gasped. He walked behind me, putting it on.

"Mina, never forget you're a living star who deserves to shine brightly," he said.

I sighed, caressing the pendant.

"I don't know what happened or what you're going through, but I'm sure you'll overcome it Mina," he said.

I rose my head to meet his gaze. His eyes were filled with certainty.

"Do you think I can overcome it?" I asked.

"I believe in you, Mina," he muttered, and my heart constricted.

I looked back at the stars, wondering if it was a sign from Dad telling me he was watching over me. I sighed at the thought.

"Oppa, I'm not who you think I am. I don't deserve to be happy," I said, looking down at my hands.

"That is not true, Mina."

He raised his finger, lifting my chin.

"How do I know that?" he muttered, and I looked up to meet his gaze.

"Because I see you, Mina, I see the real you, I see all of you, even the parts you try to hide desperately," he said.

My heart melted at his every word, and he pulled me into his embrace again, pathing me gently.

"Even if the world casts stones at you, just remember that I know who you are," he said, and I smiled.

His phone buzzed, and we pulled out of our embrace.

"Omma, I'm on my way back now. I decided to go on an impromptu ride around the city… Okay, see you soon," he said and hung up.

I wiped my face with my sleeves, clearing my throat.

"We should get back. Don't want you getting scolded because of me," I said.

Turning to leave, he pulled me back into his arms.

"Don't worry about me," he said, and I exhaled.

We remained that way for a while, then he slowly spun me around to face him.

"Feeling better?" he asked.

I exhaled and nodded.

"I am now, thank you," I muttered.

We got back on his bike and headed home. The ride back was smooth. I held on tightly to his waist, leaning on the wet patch I left on the back of his jacket with my tears. Joon was slowly becoming my safe place again. We arrived at our building and hesitated to get into the lift. Then Joon linked his hands with mine meeting my gaze.

"Let's go," he said.

I exhaled and followed him in, and we soon arrived at the eighth floor. The doors opened, and I turned to him.

"Will you be okay?" he asked.

I nodded, bracing myself, and stepped out of the lift, waving goodbye as the doors closed. Walking down the hall, I found my panda still on the floor outside. I picked it up and quietly opened the door. I exhaled finding the living room empty, then headed straight to my room. I jumped into my bed with my clothes on, pulling the covers over my head, ready in case Dina came to kick me out again.

I replayed the day's events; it had a mixture of the best and worst moments. A beautiful nightmare to be precise. Clutching the panda and the star pendant Joon gave me, wondering if I could overcome everything as he said.

Despite living like a sinner for the past few years, that day's unfortunate incident was not something I intended to cause. I wondered if Dina would ever see it that way. Although I could never fully understand her pain, had I not been punished enough? I sighed, shutting my eyes, and drifted off, escaping my tormenting thoughts.

I woke up to a silent Sunday morning, still dressed. I heard Dina and Mum moving around, putting me at ease and making me uneasy. I had been in bed all morning to avoid setting Dina off, but I was bursting to pee unable to hold it any longer. I quietly opened the door and snuck to the bathroom.

"Ahhhhhhh."

I blurted out, relieving myself. After washing my hands, I opened the door to leave.

"Oh my gosh," I yelped.

Placing my hands on my chest after finding Mum unexpectedly standing outside the door, I lowered my head to avoid her gloomy gaze.

"Aren't you going to eat?" she asked.

But I just stared down at my feet as my belly rumbled.

"Go get some breakfast. Don't worry. Dina's in her bedroom?" Mum said, and I lifted my head.

"Mum, I'm sorry about yesterday," I said, and she sighed and walked off.

I hurriedly made toast in the kitchen and rushed back to my room to eat. I stayed in my bedroom for the rest of the day, then prepared my school uniform for Monday. I was still unsure about the exam. As Joon said, I never intended to hurt anyone, but every choice I made to be happy always hurt the people around me, I wondered.

Shaking off the thought, I went on my computer to search for N.O.'s recent activities. I discovered that they had just released a surprise album as a gift to their fans before their Europe tour. I grinned from ear to ear, clicked on the announcement interview and pressed play on the attached video clip.

"What we want our fans to take from the new album is self-love. We also struggle with it daily, so we hope this would be a way to help us and our fans heal both the scars that are visible and invisible," the band leader, Kim Dong-min said.

I downloaded the album and plugged in my headphones to listen. This album was exactly what I needed; just like that, my mind was made up about the exam. I listened to every song until I dosed into a slumber.

Hand in hand, Ji-won and I walked to school, gushing about N.O.'s new album. Then Ji-won checked her horoscope and grinned, saying she had a good feeling all would go well. However, I was unconvinced.

They usually turned into a disaster whenever she said things would go well. The other students passing by also seemed on edge. In our form class, Mr Harris gave us a pep talk, about staying calm. Then the bell rang, and we headed to the exam hall. I spotted Joon Oppa from across the hallway, and we paused, exchanging glances.

"Mina, I believe in you."

I smiled reading his lips, and he grinned. The hall was crowded with students walking by, but we only saw each other. I held the pendant he gave me and mouthed the words.

"Thank you."

He read my lips and smiled, responding.

"You're welcome," he muttered.

Then headed down the hallway, I turned to find Terry standing in front of me with a grim expression. He grabbed my hands, pulling me into a classroom.

"What do you think you're doing?" he asked, and my brows frowned.

"What do you mean," I muttered, and his eyes widened.

"Wait, don't tell me you actually like that guy," he said.

"Wh... what!!! Like who?" I muttered.

Struggling to get my words out, and his face went from grim to horrified.

"M, are you crazy?"

I bit down on my teeth, and my hands formed into a fist.

"Crazy?" I asked.

"Do you really think that makes any sense, and how can you possibly believe he likes you back or takes you seriously," he added.

My jaw dropped, and my eyes widened.

"M, wake up. You're both from totally different cultures and races. How can that ever work? Besides, would you be able to handle the judgement you'd face from other people," he said.

"Terry, I think you should stop right there," I muttered, trembling.

"No, M. You need to hear this. I'm only saying this for your own good. Have you forgotten he was the reason you got hurt a few weeks ago," he said.

Walking in close, placing his hands on my shoulder.

"Mina! Please, come back to your senses before you get hurt."

My lips pressed into a hard line, and I pushed his hands off my shoulders.

"I must say, I'm truly disappointed in you, Terry. Even if I did like him, what has culture or race got to do with it? Why is any of that important, isn't the way we feel about each other all that matters," he smirked.

"You must be living in a bubble. Open your eyes, Mina. The world isn't as kind as you may think," he said.

"Tell me, have you seen a couple that looks like both of you on the street before?" he asked.

But I just glared at him, lost for words.

"Even if you both like each other, do you think his family will ever accept you," he gasped, and my eyes narrowed.

"They are not that kind of people," I said, and he chuckled.

"They are not that kind of people? You say, yes, they may be nice to you now because you're neighbours, but once they find out you like their son, that's when their demeanour will change. That's when they'll reveal who they really are, so stop this now before you end up getting hurt. Besides, it seems to me like he only sees you like a little sister and nothing more," he said.

Running his hands through his head.

"One more thing, haven't you seen that gorgeous senior with whom he always hangs out? They don't look like they are just friends to me," he sighed.

Placing his hands on my shoulders again, leaning down to meet my gaze.

"M, be honest with yourself. Do you truly believe he would skip over a girl like that and choose you? They are both well-suited, from the same country, similar in age and intelligence, and from what I heard from Ji-won, she is also a childhood family friend, and her parents are loaded. It's a no-brainer," he said, and I gasped.

Lowering my shoulder, making his arm fall off, I picked up my bag and headed for the door.

"I am not saying you're not good enough or pretty enough. I'm just saying you should go where you belong. We need to stick to our own people, so learn to love yourself," he added.

I spun around, glaring at him.

"So does liking someone outside my race mean I hate myself or my race?" I asked, walking back towards him.

"Do you really think so little of me? For your information, I could care less about the colour of anyone's skin or race. All that matters is what's inside," I muttered.

"Do you think I'm friends with you because we are both black? No," I murmured.

Squeezing my eyes shut, and opened them back up.

"It's because I thought we shared similar views about the world. But I guess I had you all wrong. At first, I was disappointed in you, but now I'm downright ashamed," I said.

Turned to leave, but he grabbed my hands.

"M, can't you read between the lines? Do you not get why I'm saying all this?" he muttered, and I yanked my hands off.

"I don't care what your reasons are," I said.

"It's because I have feelings for you, M."

He blurted out, and my eyes widened at his sudden confession.

I turned to face him, and he swallowed, awaiting my response.

"Terry," I said.

Then I lowered my head and sighed, lost for what to say.

"I'm sorry."

Was all I could mutter, his eyes widened, and he moved to speak.

"What are you both still doing here?" Mr Harris said.

"Coming, sir," I exhaled.

Then grabbed my bag and raced for the door, processing the things Terry said, recalling Rachel said something similar that night, but they both made no sense to me and why would Terry have feelings for me? I wondered.

I had also unintentionally hurt Terry; he had been a dear friend, but things had gotten complicated. I finally got to the hall and rushed in finding my seat, pushing the conversation with Terry out of my mind and taking a deep breath.

"You may now begin," the exam Invigilator announced.

I started writing, still getting a few answers wrong to avoid being flagged. Our time was up, and I handed in my paper, satisfied with the choice I made. Pushing away thoughts of the consequences. Outside the hall, I saw Rachel with her friends, and our eyes met briefly, but I quickly turned away.

"Mina," she called, and I halted.

I turned to find her wearing a plastered smile.

"How did you find the exam? It must have been difficult for someone with your brain capability, right?" she muttered, and I gasped.

"Well, I hope you at least get a C. That way, those N.O. tickets won't go to waste," she smirked.

I bit down on my teeth, squeezing the side of my skirt.

"I think I managed," I muttered, and she chuckled.

Then her laughter faded, and she moved to speak, but something caught her attention from behind me then her fake smile returned, and I turned to see what it was.

"Mina," she called, stopping me midway, so I turned back to face her.

"I guess you're right. Having a great tutor like Joon would surely help improve your grade. You're a true N.O. fan. You went through all that trouble just for a chance to meet them in person," she said.

Looking to the side again, my brows frowned, I turned to see who it was, I gasped, and my jaw dropped. I took a step back, and then Rachel walked off barging me.

Chapter Fifteen

Her eyes were burning with fury, making my hands tremble, but other students surrounded us, so she pulled my arm and dragged me away.

"Ouch, Dina, you're hurting me," I said, as her grip tightened.

But she didn't respond. We got to a quiet corner, and she pushed me against the wall, grabbing my collar with both hands and squeezing them around my neck tightly.

"What the hell was that girl talking about? You've been getting tutored by who?" she gasped.

"I see you forgot my warning," she said.

Tightening her grip made it hard for me to breathe, I pushed her off and fell to the ground, panting, and began crawling away.

"Where do you think you're going?" she said.

She grabbed the back of my collar, pulled me back, and lifted her hands to strike. I raised my hands for cover, but nothing happened. Lifting my gaze and someone was holding Dina's hand mid-air and I gasped, spotting his baseball jacket.

Dina pulled her arm from his hold, and pushed me against the wall, pulling me by the collar again.

"What do you think you're doing? Let her go," Joon yelled.

Yanking off her hands and I fell to the ground panting. Joon leaned down, placing his hands on my shoulders.

"Mina, are you all right? Breathe, Mina, breathe," he said.

I glared at him breathlessly, why did he have to see that? I squeezed my teary eyes shut, turning away from him, wishing I could disappear.

"Move out of my way," Dina said.

Trying to push past Joon to come at me again.

"What is wrong with you? Are you trying to kill your sister?" Joon yelled, and she smirked.

"This is between us, so move," she said.

But he ignored her, shielding me, and Dina gasped.

"I see you got yourself a guard," she muttered, chuckling.

"Well, he can't protect you forever. I'll see you at home," she said.

Rolling her eyes and walked off.

"Mina! Are you okay?" he asked, pulling me up.

But I pushed him away and started running.

"Mina!" he called out.

Running after me, I entered the nearest bathroom, getting into the last stall and locked the door. I sat down hugging my knees, feeling numb, unable to cry or scream as it all seemed pointless.

Dina was certainly not going to let it go. I braced myself for what was to come, but had no regrets, feeling a weight had lifted. But then the image of Joon crossed my mind.

I sighed, squeezing my eyes shut. The look in his eyes made my heart ache. I stayed in the bathroom until the last bell went off, then I stepped out, walked into the empty hallway and exhaled.

"Are you okay?"

I stalled, hearing Joon's voice from behind, making me quiver.

Still, I didn't turn and carried on walking.

"Don't worry. I won't run after you. I just wanted to make sure you were okay," he sighed deeply.

"Perhaps you should stay at our house tonight. I'm worried she might attack you again," he said, and I exhaled, lowering my head.

"Don't worry about me. Besides, I don't think she'll kill me," I muttered.

"But still," he muttered.

"My Mum will be home, so she won't be able to hurt me," I lied.

I carried on walking, and Joon didn't follow me as promised. I didn't want him to get involved in my mess. Every step I took led to my doom, but I was prepared to face it. Although seeing N.O. live would have been nice, I just wasn't meant to have anything that brought me joy. I got in front of our estate and walked up the stairs. I smiled recalling the memories I shared with Joon there.

Finally, I arrived at the door and heard things breaking inside. My heart raced, and my hands trembled, but I took a deep breath and unlocked the door. It was still midday, so Mum wasn't home yet. I took off my shoes and walked in.

Dina threw a mug at me, but I didn't dodge it. The mug hit the wall, shattering into pieces, and a shard cut my left cheek, causing blood to drip down my face. She glared at me, panting, then dragged me into my room and shoved me to the ground.

She began tearing down my N.O. posters, smashed my computer, ripped up my books, and grabbed scissors, cutting my clothes. Then walked towards me panting.

"Didn't I warn you to live like a ghost, or I'd kill you and kill myself?" she muttered.

"Did you think I wouldn't do it?" she asked.

"Answer me!" she screamed.

But I remained unreactive. She then pull me up, and her eyes darkened as her pupils dilated. She then placed her hands on my neck and squeezed my throat, pushing my head back against the wall.

"Don't you think you should pay for what he did to me? It was all your fault after all," she muttered as her grip tightened.

Gasping for breath, looking into her tormented eyes. I tapped her hands, continuously, but she didn't let go. Tears streamed down my cheeks as I shut my eyes, and surrendered ending both our suffering.

Everyone would be better off without me, I thought. Dina was right. I should be the one who paid the price. But suddenly, she released her grip, and I fell to the ground, choking. Dina sunk to the ground, staring at her hands in disbelief.

"How did I? How did I become such a monster," she muttered.

Glaring at her trembling hands.

"I just wanted to forget his face, and forget what he did to me," she looked up at me.

"If dad hadn't found me if he hadn't found me, then that man would have, he would have…" she muttered.

Unable to finish her sentence, and broke down in tears.

"Although Dad found me before anything happened, the thought of the possibility of what could have happened still drives me crazy. I still have nightmares about it," she added, and my eyes widened at her confession.

It was the first time I'd heard what happened from Dina. I couldn't imagine how scary it must have been for a seven-year-old to go through such a traumatic ordeal. Tears streamed down my cheeks uncontrollably.

Back when I was a child actress, Dad had brought Dina to set to visit me, but while he grabbed the flowers he bought from the back seat, a stalker tried kidnapping Dina, mistaking her for me. Luckily, Dad stepped in before it was too late.

"I know you didn't mean for me to get hurt, but I was filled with so much anger and resentment with nowhere else to channel them but at you," she murmured.

Dina looked so fragile, like a helpless child.

"But every time I'd hurt you, my heart ached ten times more, and I became reliant on that pain. Whenever guilt overcame me from hurting you, it helped me forget. I just wanted to forget," she added.

Then she placed her hands on her chest, squeezing tightly with her eyes shut and continued sobbing, and I crawled to her.

"I'm sorry, Dina, I'm so sorry," I said.

Placing my hands on her shoulders, sobbing. This time, she didn't push me away but lifted her gaze to meet mine.

"I'm sorry for hurting you. As your older sister, I should have been the one protecting you, but instead, I've been hurting you to make myself feel better. I'm so sorry, Mina," she muttered.

I embraced her, and we both sobbed continuously, apologising to each other. It'd been years since we last hugged. We remained that way for a while, neither wanting to let go. It was like reuniting with a family member I had not seen in years.

"What in the world happened here," we heard Mum's voice from outside.

Then she stormed into my room, frantic and found Dina and me sobbing in an embrace.

"Mum!"

We both called out and she crouched down, wrapping her arms around us, sobbing.

"What's the matter? What happened?" she asked.

Unable to respond, we just continued crying hysterically.

"Oh, my babies. It's all right, it's okay. Mummy's here now," she said, patting our backs.

All cried out. Mum guided me to bed and helped Dina to her room. I was still in disbelief at how the night unfolded. I never anticipated that reaching a breaking point and nearly losing my life would lead to a heart-to-heart with Dina. Seeing her release all the pent-up anger was surreal.

I woke up the next morning to find my bedroom clear of last night's mess. My head was throbbing, and my whole body ached. The walls in my room looked bare and unfamiliar without my N.O. posters. I checked my closet to see if I still had any unripped clothes, then made a list of the things I needed to replace.

I walked past my broken mirror and saw the cut on my cheek. Strangely, I didn't feel resentment towards my reflection for the first time. I applied a flesh-toned plaster and headed to the kitchen. Mum had made fried plantain and eggs for breakfast. Dina was at the table wearing a tortured expression, but she gave me a faint smile when our eyes met, and I reciprocated.

"Are you okay? Did you sleep well?" she asked.

I froze, hearing those words coming from her was strange.

"Yes, I did, how about you? Did you sleep well?" I asked.

My voice was more high-pitched than intended, and she nodded. I walked to the dining area, sitting beside her. Mum brought over our plates, grinning from ear to ear.

"Since you both are done with your exams, I called the school to let them know you won't be coming in today," Mum said.

Then leaned in assessing my face, but I placed my hands over my cheeks.

"Don't we need to get that checked out?" she asked.

I shook my head, and Dina lowered hers.

"Mum, it's fine, honestly, really," I muttered.

"Dina and I will go shopping to replace some stuff around the house. You should stay home and get some rest. Mina, just make a list of the things you need, and we'll get them," Mum said.

"Just a second," I muttered.

Then handed over the list I made earlier, and they left. I began clearing out my closet and putting up the leftover

N.O. posters on my wall. Then heard knocking. I checked the pigeonhole and gasped when I saw him.

"Mina, I know you're inside, open the door," he said.

I paced around, biting my finger hoping he'd leave, but he didn't. Finally, I decided to open the door but kept the latch on hiding my face.

"Mina, are you okay? Why didn't you come to school today?" he asked, poking his head around.

"Oppa, I'm okay; I'm just not feeling too well," I said.

"Are you ill? Have you gone to see the GP?" he asked.

"No need; I'm feeling much better now. I'll be back to school tomorrow," I said.

He went quiet, and I peeked through the door, unable to see him clearly. Then I spotted Dina coming up the stairs. What if she saw Joon, I thought, then all the progress we made would have been in vain. So, I took off the larch, and pulled Joon inside, leading him to my two-door closet.

"What's going on, Mina?" he asked.

"Shhh," I murmured.

Dina entered while Joon and I fiddled around to get comfortable. The lack of clothing inside gave us more room.

"Mum, where did you say you put your wallet?" Dina asked.

And the sound of her footsteps moved down the hall to Mum's room.

"Mina, why are we hiding?" Joon asked.

"Shhh," I murmured.

Pressing my fingers against his lips, my heart was pounding, and I broke out in sweats.

"Found it. I'll head back down now," Dina muttered.

I bit my bottom lip, waiting for her to leave, and then I heard my bedroom door opening and froze.

"Mina," she called.

I squeezed my eyes shut. My heart was beating uncontrollably.

"Where did she go? Mina?" she called again.

I squeezed hold of my jumper with my trembling hands.

"Why are we…"

Joon attempted to speak again so I quickly covered his mouth with my hand and locked eyes with him, silently urging him to stay quiet. The light from my window reflected into the closet door that was left slightly ajar. His eyes narrowed, but he remained quiet.

Dina approached the closet door, and I held my breath, praying she wouldn't open it. As she reached for the handle, my heart clenched, unable to watch. I squeezed my eyes shut and then her phone started ringing, giving us both a fright.

"Hello, Mum, yes I'm coming now," she said, leaving the house.

I exhaled, turning to face Joon, then gasped realising I still had my hands over his lips. As I took them off my fingers brushed past his lips, sending an electric wave through my body. Meeting his intense gaze, I swallowed reaching for the closet handle to escape but he placed his hands over mine.

I locked eyes with him, and my heart rate spiked squirming under his intense gaze. My head told me to run, but my heart kept me frozen in place. His eyes were filled with wonder, eluding a mixture of fear and fascination. I bit my bottom lip to contain myself, unable to break away from his mesmerising gaze.

The sound of our heartbeats filled the closet, and Joon's gaze intensified, making their way to my lips, and giving me butterflies. He leaned in even closer, gently caressing my cheeks, and I trembled under his touch.

Joon's fingers travelled down to my bottom lips, making me gasp. He gently tugged at them, and my mouth went dry. It felt strange yet familiar. Suddenly, I lost my balance and began falling out of the closet, but Joon quickly wrapped his arm around my waist, pulling me into his embrace, and sending tingles down my spine.

"Clumsy," he muttered, grinning.

Our breathing quickened and the magnetic pull between us intensified. His grip around my waist tightened, drawing me closer. I tried looking away, but he gently lifted my chin, locking my gaze back onto his, and at that moment, I knew there was no escape.

He leaned in slowly pressing his lips against mine. I gasped, feeling a tremor of energy pass between us. Our lips intertwined, and the wall I had built crumbled. I surrendered to the moment, savouring the softness and tenderness of his lips. He tasted like banana milk, and every part of me longed for more as my hands trembled with anticipation.

We both surrendered to the moment, and our worries faded away. He linked our fingers together, sending electric waves down my spine.

A moan escaped his lips when our tongues intertwined, playing thug of war, barely coming up for air. I was spellbound by the flame of passion that coursed through my veins and a teardrop escaped my eyes. All I knew about kissing was what I'd read or seen on TV, but this was far beyond anything I'd imagined.

We finally began slowing down, pulling out of our embrace and panting, I opened the closet beside me, letting in some light, and then his eyes narrowed, and I gasped covering my bandage. He leaned in, examining my face and his lips fell into a hard line, bursting our magical bubble.

He opened the door beside him for a better view and reached for my cheek. I swallowed, moving my face away from his palm.

"What… what happened to your face, Mina?" he asked.

Sounding like a wounded puppy.

"It's nothing," I said.

Stepping out of the closet, he followed me out, turning me to face him.

"Did she do this to you?" he yelled, panting.

"Oppa, calm down. It's not what you think," I murmured.

His brows frowned, and he ran his hands through his hair.

"Then tell me what happened to your face because this wasn't there yesterday," he muttered.

His frown deepened as he scanned my bedroom walls, then he spotted my broken computer, along with the basket filled with my torn clothes. He then walked up to my desk, picking up broken pieces from my keyboard.

"Are you going to keep insisting nothing happened?" he asked, trembling.

Then he reached into his pocket, took out his phone and started dialling 999. I snatched his phone ending the call.

"This is abuse, Mina. You can't keep living this way," he muttered.

I sighed, giving him a faded smile.

"Oppa, remember how you said you always could tell how I was feeling even without me saying a word?" I asked.

He gasped with his lips pressed together and nodded.

"Then look into my eyes, and believe me when I say I'm okay," I said with a faint smile.

"Yesterday was probably the best day of my life. Dina and I finally had a breakthrough. Although a few things were broken in the process," I muttered, grinning as I reminisced.

"For the first time in years, we felt like sisters again," I added.

Without breaking eye contact with him, I lifted my hands to my injured cheek.

"And this was just an accident. I guess you could call it a battle scar," I chuckled, and he sighed.

"Oppaaaaa," I called, softly.

He chuckled, giving him puppy dog eyes, failing at my attempt to do aegyo.

"Don't try to be cute with me," he said.

Then he opened his arms, inviting me in, and I happily obliged, walking into his embrace.

"Be careful next time? I can't bear to see you hurt," he murmured.

Swaying me, then I caught a glimpse at the clock and gasped pulling out of his embrace.

"Oppa, school, you're going to get in trouble."

I pulled his arm, leading him to the front door.

"I was waiting for you downstairs before school, but you never showed, so when I saw your Mum and sister leaving, I came up to check on you," he said, and I smiled.

"Well, as you can see, I'm okay. Oppa hurry, you're already so late," I murmured, pushing him out the door.

He walked to the lift but stopped midway, turning.

"What's the matter? Did you forget something?" I asked.

He grinned and nodded, walking towards me, then leaned in and lifted my chin, pressing his lips against my forehead, making my knees weak, and then he pulled back, wearing a mischievous smile.

"That's what I forgot," he muttered, smirking, and I smiled.

The lift arrived, and he got on, waving as the doors closed. My smile faded to tears. Knowing I would eventually have to let him go. My feelings for Joon were undeniable, but I couldn't risk jeopardising the progress I made with Dina. He was always a dream beyond my reach. I sighed deeply, wiping away my tears before closing the door.

Chapter Sixteen

After a few hours, Mum and Dina returned, and I helped them unpack the shopping.

"Did you go out? I came back to get Mum's purse, but I couldn't find you anywhere?" Dina asked.

I swallowed as my eyes widened.

"Ooh, ermmm, just went out for some air," I muttered.

She nodded, giving me a faint smile, I was still in disbelief that Dina and I were having a casual conversation or exchanging pleasantries.

The next morning, I hit snooze twice before finally getting up. After showering and dressing, I headed to the kitchen approaching the fridge, I gasped finding Dina at the dining table, having breakfast with an extra plate.

"It's yours," she muttered.

Pointing at the plate next to hers, I swallowed.

"I made toast and sunny side up," she said.

"Well, it was your favourite when we were younger," she added.

"It's still my favourite," I muttered, and she grinned.

I sat beside her, staring down at my plate, teary-eyed.

"I'm not sure it's any good," she said.

She gawked at me with her lips parted as she watched me take a bite. I grinned as I chewed, giving her a thumbs up. She made it just how I liked it. She smiled softly and carried on eating her breakfast.

After we were done, I took our dishes to the sink, and we left for school.

We stood by the lift, looking everywhere but at each other. The lift finally arrived, and we both entered bumping into each other.

"Sorry," we both said, then we looked at each other busting out laughing.

"This is really awkward, isn't it?" Dina said.

I nodded, and we giggled again.

When we reached downstairs, Ji-won smiled as she saw me approaching, but turned away when Dina walked out behind me.

"Ji," I called.

She hesitantly turned, glaring at the both of us, puzzled.

"Hey, Ji-won," Dina said, waving.

Ji-won's eyes narrowed, waving back, fidgeting. It was the first time Dina had ever acknowledged her.

"I'll see you at school," Dina said, walking ahead of us.

Ji-won pulled me in, linking arms with mine.

"Mimi, did your sister really just say hi to me or was I hallucinating?" she asked.

Shaking her head in disbelief, she gasped, suddenly coming to a halt.

"Pinch me," she muttered, and I obliged.

"Ahhh," she cried out, and I giggled.

"Come on, spill, did something happen? Was that why you weren't at school yesterday?" she asked.

"I couldn't call because your phone was stolen, and I didn't want to go over to your house in case that got you in more trouble," she said as her face sank.

"I'm okay, just had a bit of an accident," I said.

Holding onto my cheek, she pulled my hands off.

"Oh my gosh, Mina, what happened to your face?" she asked.

Spotting the plaster, I covered it again forcing on a smile.

"Oh, this, it's nothing; besides it doesn't hurt anymore," I muttered, linking our arms again.

"We need to hurry, or we will be late," I said, pulling her along.

Terry stood outside our classroom. I gasped halting. I'd completely forgotten about our last conversation. So much had happened since then. His brows frowned spotting my cheek, and I covered it. I stepped back as he reached out his hands.

"It's nothing serious," I said. Answering his unspoken question.

"Why weren't you in yesterday? I was worried, I tried calling, but your phone was off," he said.

"Oh, that, my phone was stolen on Saturday," I responded, and his eyes widened.

"What, how, where, have you reported it?" he asked in a breath.

"Wooaw, wooaw, slow down, I decided on just getting a new one," I said.

"But?" he muttered. Then the bell rang, cutting him off.

"We should go inside," I suggested.

Walking into the classroom, his lips pressed into a hard line as he followed on.

"Mina," he called, and I turned to him hesitantly.

"About Monday," he muttered.

Then Mr Harris walked in.

"Quiet everyone, get your books out," he said, Terry sighed, and I exhaled.

With ten minutes left in the lesson. I pleaded with Mr Harris to let me go to the bathroom, and he agreed, so I quickly grabbed my bag, and hurried out. Terry's face fell, but I played coy.

I went to my hideout, but the door was left ajar. I poked my head in slightly to get a closer look at who was inside but suddenly got pulled in with my back against the wall, and I gasped meeting his gaze.

"What are you doing here," I murmured.

"Shhh," he murmured, grinning.

Seeing him smile, made my heart ache. Then he leaned in making my heart race.

"I thought we could come back to the scene of the crime," he whispered, and I grinned, recalling the last time we were there.

So much had changed since then. My smile began to fade knowing our end was drawing near. I couldn't continue delaying it.

"What's wrong?" Joon asked.

Lifting his hands to caress my injured cheek.

"Does it still hurt?" he asked.

I moved my face, fighting back my tears, and his eyes widened.

"Mina," he murmured.

Holding onto my arms, I raised my head to meet his gaze, folding my trembling hands into a fist.

"Oppa, I think we should go back to the way things were," I muttered.

His brows frowned, and he released my arm.

"What do you mean?" he murmured.

"Let's go back to the way things were before we fell out of this closet," I muttered.

His frowned brows deepened, and his eyes searched mine.

"Why? Did something happen? Is this because of your sister?" he asked.

I bit down on my teeth and swallowed.

"This has nothing to do with her. It's what I want," I said.

Not breaking eye contact, barely blinking, hoping he wouldn't read into my lies.

"How can you say that so easily after all that's happened ever since? How can we go back?" he asked.

"We both knew this would come to an end eventually. I don't want a target on my back. If anyone at school were to find out about us getting close, the past will repeat itself," I added.

My heart clenched as I uttered each word. I turned to leave before the bells went off, but he grabbed my arm.

"Then what about yesterday? Was it just me who felt the magic we shared?" he asked.

I squeezed my eyes shut and sighed, opening them again and pulling my arm out of his hold.

"I only played along because I thought it would have been embarrassing to push you away. You seemed happy, and I didn't want to burst your bubble," I said.

He spun me around to face him, with his eyes burning with fury.

"Mina, do you think I don't know what you're doing, or have you forgotten that I can read you like a book," he said.

I bit down on my teeth, trying to stop my built-up tears.

"Why are you really doing this?" he asked.

Searching my eyes for clues, I moved his hand off again.

"Do I need to spell it out? This is me rejecting you, Oppa. I get that it isn't something you're used to, as most girls throw themselves at you, but please get it into your head. I want nothing more to do with you," I muttered.

I walked out as the bell rang, the hallway filled with students, and the tears I had been holding back came pouring down. I didn't look back, afraid of running into his arms. Once I reached the school grounds, my legs felt like jelly, and I struggled to keep my balance.

"What are you doing over here?" Terry asked, suddenly appearing.

I covered my face, and he sighed. Then he took my hands, led me to a nearby bench, and handed me a pack of tissue. I collected it, wiping my face, and we sat in silence. But the aching in my heart made it hard to breathe, and my untameable tears came rushing back down.

"I didn't realise you liked him that much," Terry said.

I turned to him, and his head sank.

"I'm sorry about what I said on Monday. You were right. I should know better than to make such ignorant comments, and using jealousy as an excuse was cowardice," he said.

Hearing his apology set me off again, and he sighed, leaning in close, patting my back gently as I carried on sobbing.

"But I don't get it. If you like him so much, why not tell him how you feel?" he asked.

I sighed, sitting up.

"Don't worry. You don't have to say anything. I'm sure you have your reasons," Terry said, getting up.

"I won't stop you from sulking, but you can't skip lunch," he said, reaching out his hand.

"Let's go," he said.

When we entered the dining hall, Rachel and Joon were leaving. Joon glared at me, and I squeezed hold of my skirt, with my trembling hands. He then looked over at Terry, and his lips fell into a hard line. Rachel rolled her eyes, and turned to Joon.

"Let's go," she said.

But he didn't move or take his eyes off mine. I turned away from his gaze, linking my arms with Terry.

"Let's go, I'm hungry," I said, grinning.

Terry blinked rapidly but caught on to my act.

"Sure," he muttered.

But Joon walked out first, and Rachel followed him, barging into me. I unlinked my arms with Terry, and then I turned around, losing my appetite.

After school, Ji-won, and I made our way home.

"What's wrong?" she asked.

"Huh, nothing," I responded.

"Is it about our upcoming exam results? Don't worry so much. I'm sure you did well. Besides, regardless of our grades, I think Mum would still let us go considering how much effort we put in," Ji-won said and I nodded.

We reached our building, and I spotted Joon hiding in the shadows, but I blanked him. Ji-won entered the lift first, and before I could follow, Joon grabbed my arm. I tried pulling away, but his grip tightened.

"Ji… Umm, I forgot that I needed to get something from the corner shop. I'll see you tomorrow," I muttered.

She stared at me wide-eyed, but the lift closed before she could respond. He led me to the nearby park and then released my arm with his back turned. We remained in silence for a while. Finally, he turned to face me.

"Mina, did you really mean what you said at school today?" he swallowed.

I tucked my trembling hands in my coat pocket. His piercing gaze awaited my response. Then he exhaled, placing both hands on my shoulders.

"Answer me," he said.

My heart was beating out of control, I tried stepping away, but his firm grip made it impossible. Seeing him that way was unbearable, but I couldn't lose Dina again, I raised my head to meet his gaze.

"I think I made things clear enough at the dinner hall. Terry and I have decided to be more than friends," I muttered, and he smirked.

"Who? The boy that's always hovering around you," he muttered.

"Well, he asked me out and I said yes," his smirk faded, and his face grew grim.

"Do you expect me to believe that?" he asked, and I swallowed.

"Well, I don't care if you believe it or not, just stay away from me," I said.

Pulling his hands off my shoulders and turned to leave.

"Why won't you ever choose yourself, Mina?" he said, and I halted.

"You're still wearing the necklace I gave you," he said.

I raised my hands, grabbed hold of the star pendant, and sighed, biting down on my teeth.

"Mina, why won't you let me in? Can't you share your burden with me?" he asked, reaching his hands out to me.

I began reaching my breaking point, as my pent-up tears were about to fall.

Before his hands could reach me, I rushed off. If I had stayed for even a second longer, I would have succumbed to his will. I got in front of our estate building but froze when I saw Dina waiting by the lift. I turned immediately, wiping off my tears.

"Mina," she called.

I faced her with a plastered smile, and her face fell.

"What's wrong? Were you crying?" she asked, and I shook my head.

"No," I said, chuckling.

"No, I just had something stuck in my eyes," I muttered.

She leaned in to take a closer look, and I stepped back.

"Don't worry. It's out now," I muttered.

We entered the lift, and as the doors closed, Joon appeared but didn't stop the doors from shutting. I gasped, tightly gripping my jacket, our eyes remained locked in until the doors shut, and I exhaled. We arrived home, and Mum was preparing dinner.

"How was school?" Mum asked.

"Fine," we both responded, and I lowered my head.

"Mina, are you sure you're, okay?" Dina asked. I smiled.

"I'm fine, just hungry," I said.

"Well, dinner is almost ready," Mum muttered.

She made pounded yam and efó, one of my favourite Nigerian dishes. We changed and then joined Mum for dinner.

Afterwards, we watched some late-night shows. Dina peeked at me occasionally, and I wore a forced smile. I tried to turn in early, but the aching in my heart kept me awake all night. I tossed and turned, and before I knew it, morning had arrived. I walked up to my window, gazing at the heavy dark clouds, sighing deeply.

Our results were due, and I was likely to get a C, but I was still unsure about attending the N.O. concert. I headed to the kitchen after getting dressed, and Dina made breakfast again, and we ate quietly.

"I hope you get an excellent grade today," she muttered, and my eyes widened.

Although I was relieved by her comment, I was more apprehensive about running into Joon at school. We got to class to collect our results, and just as I thought, I got a C, and so did Ji-won. She jumped for joy, grabbing onto my shoulders.

"We did it, Mimi, we did it," she muttered, grinning from ear to ear.

Her joy was infectious, so I joined her to celebrate. After school, we made our way home, and Ji-won suddenly took off running, so I turned to see where she was headed.

"Oppa, we did it. Mina and I got a C," she said.

Wrapping him in an embrace.

"Congratulations, girls," Rachel muttered, wearing her plastered smile.

"Mina," Ji-won called.

I hesitantly walked over to join them. Joon lowered his gaze to my neckline, and his eyes softened as he noticed I still had the necklace on.

"Congratulations, Mina," he said.

I swallowed, taken aback by his cheerful tone.

"It's all thanks to you," I said, smiling faintly.

"See you at home. Well done, kiddo," he said.

Patting Ji-won's hair before walking off with Rachel. I exhaled, and as they left, Joon seemed to have come to terms with my request, which left me feeling bittersweet.

"Mina," Ji-won called out, waving her hands.

"What were you thinking about so deeply?" she asked.

"Nothing," I said.

"I still can't believe we get to meet N.O. in person after the concert. I'm so excited," she gushed.

Mum danced with joy seeing our results, but Dina smiled faintly. After dinner, I struggled to fall asleep, unable to get Joon out of my head. He seemed different from yesterday, and I wondered why. Did he figure out it was all an act, or was it because Ji-won and Rachel were present? I sighed, running my hands through my hair.

Knock knock.

"It's me," Dina said. I sat up.

"Come in," I muttered.

She walked in, sitting at the edge of my bed.

"So, I've decided to start going to therapy again. Would you come to a few sessions with me?" she asked, and I nodded.

"Of course," I said, wrapping my hands around hers.

"But Mina, are you sure you're, okay?" she asked, and I lowered my head.

"You can talk to me. You don't have to hide your true emotions from me anymore," she added.

Tilting her head to the side, she tried reading my expression.

"I'm fine, truly," I said, and she looked down at her fingers.

"Is it because of your grade? Are you worried I might get upset?" she asked.

I shook my head, tapping our linked hands.

"Of course, not Di," I muttered.

She went quiet for a while, then looked up at me.

"Then, is it because of him?" she asked.

I gasped and my lips pressed together.

"It's fine, Mina. You can tell me," she insisted.

I stared at her, lost for words. She sighed.

"You like him, don't you," she said.

I started choking, so she ran out of the room, returned with a glass of water, and handed it to me.

"I'll leave you to get some rest," she said, heading for the door.

"Ah, Mum said I should remind you to pack for our trip to aunt Amira's house this weekend," she said, and my eyes widened.

I'd completely forgotten about our yearly visits to our aunt Amira's house. I bit my bottom lip trying to figure out what to do about the concert, and Dina chuckled.

"Don't worry, we'll be back on Saturday before the concert starts," she added, and I exhaled, nodding.

"Goodnight," she said, shutting the door.

It was the last day of school before the holidays. I sat on the school bench thinking of how it had been a truly memorable term. So much had changed, and my relationships had evolved, some for the better, others the latter. While I no longer had to live like a ghost, letting go was bittersweet.

"What are you thinking of so deeply?" Terry muttered, bringing me out of my daze.

"It's nothing. Let's go," I said, heading to our last lesson.

Thankfully, things with Terry were going back to normal. As we walked down the hall, I spotted Rachel and her friends, then looked around to see if Joon was nearby, but he wasn't. Rachel spotted me, and smirked, walking up to us.

"Hey, Mina," she muttered.

Nudging Terry to leave us.

"I'll see you in class," I said, and Terry's brows frowned.

"Will you be okay?" he asked, glaring at Rachel.

"I'll just be a moment," I muttered.

"Okay," he sighed, walking off hesitantly.

"Were you looking for him?" she smirked.

"Well, he seems to have finally woken up to reality," she said as the look in her eyes turned grim.

"But it seems you are yet to get a grip of yourself," she said.

I bit down my teeth, and my hands formed a fist.

"That's between Joon and me," I said, and she chuckled.

"What did you just say?" she said, stepping in closer.

Chapter Seventeen

"Mina," Dina called, rushing over to me, and Rachel stepped aside.

"Are you okay?" she asked.

"Is there a problem?" Dina asked, glaring at Rachel, and she gasped.

"Problem, there is no problem here," she looked over at me, raising her brows.

"We were just talking, isn't that right, Mina?" she asked.

My frowned brows deepened, and the second bell went off.

"Well, I don't want to be late for class. I'll see you around, Mina," she muttered, walking off.

"Are you sure you're okay?" Dina asked. I sighed and nodded.

"What is her problem?" she asked.

Then her eyes widened when a thought crossed her mind.

"Wait, is she being like this because of him?" she asked, and I bit my bottom lip.

"We'll be late for class. Talk later," I said, cutting her off.

At dinner time, I picked up my food.

"Are you excited about the concert?" Mum asked.

I smiled, nodding, doing my best not to raise any alarms.

"Mum, can I go out for a walk after dinner? I need some air," I said.

"Do you want me to come with you," Dina offered, and I shook my head.

"I just need some alone time," I said, and her expression grew grim, but she nodded.

"Take my phone. It's already dark out. Your new phone doesn't arrive until we get back from our trip," Mum said, and I nodded, collecting it.

Putting on my jacket, I left, taking a bus to London Bridge. When I arrived, I looked up at the stars wrapping my arms around my body against the cold wind. Tears streamed down my cheeks recalling that night. I grabbed hold of my star pendant, yanking it off.

Squeezing my eyes shut, I lifted my hands to throw the necklace. I swung my hands towards the river but was unable to let go, as throwing it was like throwing my heart away.

My hands hung in the air as I sobbed uncontrollably, and then someone grabbed hold of my hand, gently lowering it. I turned around and saw Joon, unable to halt my tears, unsure if it was a dream or reality. Holding back the urge to hide in his embrace. He watched me with a gentle gaze and sighed.

"I guess you can't seem to let go either," he said.

Slowly letting go of my hand, walking over to stand beside me, facing the water. Our twisted fate had once again led us to each other. I pressed my lips together and turned to walk off.

"Mina," he called.

I halted, turning to him, and he lifted my chin with his fingers, smiling as our eyes met, taking my breath away.

"It's okay," he said.

He opened my hands, took out the necklace, and leaned in, wrapping it around my neck. I stood frozen, as tears continued streaming down my cheeks. Unable to push him away, I inhaled his sweet scent, still powerless against him.

"Breathe, Mina," he whispered.

I finally let go, exhaling deeply. he lifted his fingers, gently wiping my tears away, and then his hands made their way down to my star pendant, picking it up and caressing it.

"I'll wait," he muttered. I lifted my head to meet his gaze.

"I won't pester you to tell me what's going on or why you are so determined to break things off," he sighed, grabbing my hands.

"Right now, your words don't match with your true emotions, but none of that matters. What truly matters is that I know how you truly feel. Even if you don't utter a word, I can hear you loud and clear. Besides, it wouldn't be the first time I've had to wait for you."

After hearing those words, I became undone and began sobbing out loud. Then he pulled me into his embrace, leaning my head against his heartbeat, patting my back gently.

"Mina," his voice echoed.

"I love you. I've loved you for a long time, although I had no idea what these feelings were back then," he gasped.

I tightened my grip around him, as my body melted into his.

"So, I'll wait until your words match what you truly feel inside." I lifted my head out of his embrace.

"Why won't you just lash out and get angry at me instead," I yelled.

Joon smiled, shaking his head.

"You're already doing enough of that to yourself, Mina. I don't want to see you hurt. That for me is unbearable."

At that moment, I was sure I loved him too.

"But keep this," he said, staring at my necklace.

"That way, I can stay close to your heart."

He gently released himself from our embrace and turned away, walking off. I took a step towards him but halted as Mum's phone vibrated. It was a call from Dina.

In that moment, I was reminded why I had to let him go. I sighed, watching him walk into the distance.

"Oppa, wait a little while longer. I'll come running to you once things improve between Dina and me." I whispered to myself, wiping away my tears and answering the call.

"I'm on my way back," I said and caught the next bus.

I returned home and began packing for our trip to Glossop. After breakfast the next morning, we were packed and ready to leave. Ji-won was waiting by the parking lot.

"Don't worry. I'll be back before the concert, okay?" I muttered.

She nodded, hugging me. I looked around, hoping to get a glimpse of Joon before leaving.

"Are you waiting for someone?" Ji-won asked.

"No, it's nothing," I said.

"Mina, we need to leave now to beat traffic," Mum said.

"Coming," I muttered.

I got in and we drove out. I spotted Joon hovering from behind a tree as we drove away. I turned, glancing at him until he faded into the distance. Although we were only away for a week, my heart ached to be parted from him.

"Shall we play some music?" Dina suggested.

I joined in the fun, ignoring the pit in my stomach. We sang during the seven-hour drive to Glossop, making a few stops for bathroom breaks and food. When we arrived, Aunt Amira grinned, glaring at my hair in astonishment.

"Mina darling, I love your new look," she said, grinning, revealing her gold tooth, and hugged us.

Aunt Amira, dressed in her typical bohemian-style outfit, and her brown-dyed dreads against her golden-brown complexion. As we entered her home, the familiar wholesome feeling enveloped us. The magnolia walls were adorned by exquisite paintings and the comforting warmth of the fireplace was accompanied by the scent of burning sage. We made our way into the living room to join the rest of the family.

Uncle Martin was sitting on his favourite lazy boy couch, stroking his grey beard, and the living room light glistened against his bald head. He grinned as we walked in.

"Aunty, still no cell phone services?" Dina asked, pouting, and everyone laughed.

During dinner, all eyes were on Dina and me. Dina offered me food constantly, ensuring I could reach every dish. Aunt Amira beamed cheerfully as she observed. After the meal, our cousins Temi and Tayo excitedly took us to their room upstairs, showing off their new clothes from a thrift store. They asked us to share stories about life in London, as not much happened in their small town.

Temi, our older daughter, had grown taller, a perfect copy of Aunty Amira, but Tayo, the younger daughter, looked like Uncle Martin and disliked inheriting his wide nose. Despite being close in age to Dina and me, she still held the title of the baby of the house due to her childlike mannerisms.

We spent the night playing games and exchanging stories. I looked over at Dina as she grinned, carefree, which gave me the reassurance I had made the right decision.

When everyone was asleep, I climbed up to the roof through the attic with my mp3 player and played "Missing You" by N.O. and laid back, gazing at the stars, permitting myself to miss him until the song ended.

In the following days, we took walks on the mountain, fed animals at nearby farms, and went shopping at thrift stores. Despite the fun, the pit in my stomach remained prominent. We went into town, and I tried calling Ji-won on a pay phone, but her phone was out of service, which left me on edge. I brushed it off, but something seemed amiss.

We sat down for breakfast on Friday morning and all I could think of was getting back to London the following day to check on Joon and Ji-won. After breakfast, Dina and I were on dish duty.

"Want to go for a walk, after, just us?" Dina asked, and I nodded.

Since arriving, we hadn't had any alone time. After finishing the dishes, we put on our coats and headed out. The smell of cow manure disrupted the scenery. Dina and I couldn't help but giggle, covering our noses. Reaching the top of the hill, we sat on a bench nearby.

"You miss him, don't you?" she asked.

I gasped, turning to her wide-eyed, and she grinned.

"You don't have to be so surprised; I've seen how you both look at each other," she sighed.

"I know that look all too well. It's the same one I have when I see Terry," she muttered, taking my hands into hers.

"Although you've been smiling a lot lately, I see the pain hidden behind your smile," she sighed.

"Mina, you don't have to live your life giving up your happiness for me anymore," she muttered, and we both began to tear up.

"Every time I think of the horrible things I put you through," she paused.

Squeezing her eyes shut and opening them back.

"It breaks my heart," she said.

Tears began streaming down both our cheeks, and I shook my head.

"I'm sorry, Mina, I'm so sorry."

We held each other, sobbing.

"You have nothing to be sorry about, Di," she shook her head, pulling out of our embrace.

"Yes, I do, so promise me that from this moment on, you'll stop giving up the things or people that make you happy for me or anyone else, and start putting yourself first."

I lowered my head, unable to respond, and she placed her hand on my shoulder.

"Mina, look at me," she said.

I lifted my head to meet her gaze.

"Promise me. That way, I can start forgiving myself."

I stared back at her, blinking through my teary eyes, then exhaled, nodding, and she grinned, wiping her tears and mine. I suddenly yearned to see him.

"Dina," I called.

"Yeah," she responded, but I couldn't get my words out.

"You want to go to him, don't you," she said, and my tears returned, as I nodded.

"Let's go," she said, smiling, and my eyes widened.

"What about Mum? We're supposed to leave tomorrow," I muttered, and she smirked.

"Don't worry about that I'll handle Mum," she said, reaching her hands out to me.

"Let's go," she repeated.

I smiled as I placed my hand in hers, and we began running down the hill, giggling, and we were back to the house in no time.

"Get changed and we'll take the next train back. I'll go speak to Mum," she said, and I nodded.

I got back down shortly after, and Dina had changed her shoes, ready to go.

"What did Mum say?" I asked.

"It's all taken care of. Let's go," Dina said, and Mum came into the hallway.

"Make sure you call me when you get to London," Mum said.

The rest of the family came out to wave us goodbye and we ran to catch the bus heading for the train station.

We got on the train headed to London, and I was unable to sit still, tapping my feet and biting my fingers, wishing the train would move faster. Even music was no help, my mind constantly drifted off, so Dina placed her hands over my trembling hands, squeezing and I exhaled.

"Don't worry so much. I'm sure everything's okay," she said.

But I sighed, unable to shake off my uneasy hunch.

"By the way, how did you get Mum to allow us to go back alone?" I asked, and she smiled.

"I told her I had an opportunity to make up for being such a horrible sister to you, and she agreed without hesitation," she said, and I smiled.

"Mina, Mina," I heard Dina calling, and slowly opened my eyes.

"We're here," she muttered.

I jumped up immediately, looking around, dazed, wondering when I had fallen asleep.

"We need to get off," she said, and I nodded.

We hurried out of the train and down the hill, reaching our building, I raced to Ji-won's flat, panting. Taking a moment to compose myself, I knocked but there was no response. Pressing my ear against the door, it was unusually quiet. I knocked again, but still, no answer.

"Maybe they went out," Dina said, my brows furrowed.

I used Dina's phone to call Ji-won again, but it was switched off.

"Don't you have his number?" she asked, and I shook my head and sighed.

"Ah, Mum, I think she's got Ji-won's Mum's number."

Dina called Mum and collected Ji-won's Mum's number, and we called her, but her phone was also out of service. I crouched down, panting.

"They probably went somewhere overnight. Let's go home for now and try again tomorrow morning," Dina suggested.

Wrapping her arms around my shoulders and leading me upstairs, we ordered Chinese takeout for dinner, but I had no appetite and spent the night turning and tossing. I grabbed hold of my star pendant, praying in hopes nothing bad had happened. Picking up my MP3 player as a last resort, I played "Always With You" by N.O. and drifted off slowly.

I opened my eyes, squinting at the bright lights from my window, then leapt up, dressed as fast as possible, and headed out.

"Mina," I heard Dina call, but I didn't stop or respond.

I got to Ji-won's door, and it was wide open. I paused as my heart rate spiked, and then the doors to the lift opened.

"Excuse me, young lady, could you please move out of the way."

It was a man I had not seen before, carrying a box. I stepped aside, and he walked into Ji-won's house, and I gasped as my eyes widened and then he walked back out.

"Excuse me, what are you doing in this house?" I asked.

He glared at me with his brows furrowed.

"What does it look like? I'm moving into my new flat."

My knees grew weak, and my hands trembled, unable to fathom what he said. Then Dina appeared, pulling his arm.

"What do you mean by that, sir? What about the family that lives here?" she asked.

I met his gaze, awaiting his response and he sighed.

"I'm not sure. They sold the flat in a hurry as they needed the money urgently. That's what I heard from the housing agent," he muttered. I leapt up grabbing his other arm.

"Money for what? What did they need the money for?" I asked.

His lips pressed into a hard line, and he yanked both of our hands off his arms.

"Let go of me, listen, girls, I'm not sure about the details. All I heard was that the father who was back home had a heart attack after a failed business deal had gone burst and got hospitalised, but that's all I know. If you'll excuse me, I still have a lot of things to move, and you're both in my way," he said.

Then got on the lift, and as the doors shut, my heart went numb.

"Mina, are you okay?" Dina asked.

Feeling light-headed and breathless, I sank to the ground, unable to make sense of what he said. Ji-won probably couldn't reach me because I'd lost my phone.

I couldn't imagine how hard it must have been for them, then I gasped recalling it was the day of the N.O. concert, and Rachel might be there too, so I leapt up and started running, with no clear plan on how to get in.

"Mina," Dina called.

But I didn't stop or respond, so she ran after me. We got off the train and headed for the concert venue. I rushed over to the V.I.P. entrance, but security blocked us from entering.

"Pass please," one of the bouncers said.

I gasped, searching my pockets, looking for a pass, then recalled Ji-won had them. I pressed my lips together, trying to figure out a way in.

"Please sir, I just need to go in and look for someone quickly," I said.

Trying to push my way in, but the bouncers held me back.

"We can't let you in without a pass, miss," I sighed.

"Please, sir, it's extremely important."

I walked towards the doors again, but Dina held me back as I pleaded with them.

"Fine, can you call Rachel out here, please? Her Dad is the C.E.O of underground entertainment," I said, and they all chuckled.

Then the head bouncer asked for us to be escorted out of the premises, so they pulled us out of the queue. I dropped to the ground as my body went numb. I was out of ideas on what to do or where to look.

The uncertainty of never seeing Joon Oppa and Ji-won again weighed on my heart. I imagined the turmoil they must be facing after their sudden upheaval. Then I gasped thinking of one more place I could check and got back up, heading for the train station.

"Mina, Mina, where are you going," Dina called out.

Dina followed me onto the train, and we both got off at London Bridge station. I rushed towards the bridge, reaching the spot where Joon and I had stood together. Memories of that moment flooded my mind, his words, his gaze, and his touch. Tears streamed down my cheeks as I relived that moment, praying it wouldn't be the last time I'd feel his touch. I collapsed to the ground, crying uncontrollably.

"Mina, you've been like this for hours. Let's get going. You'll get sick if you stay here any longer," Dina said.

She pulled me up, leading me away. I turned to look back at the stars as their sparkle faded, filled with regrets, wishing I'd been honest with him about how I felt, wishing I'd never pushed him away, then I halted joining my hands together.

"God, I know it's been a while since we spoke, but please let Joon's dad be okay."

I prayed as that was all I could do.

Chapter Eighteen

Getting home, I was so drained that I passed out when I laid my head on my bed. The weekend passed quickly, and I spent most of it in bed, crying relentlessly.

Mum and Dina tried to persuade me to eat, but I could only manage a few bites. I eagerly awaited Monday to return to school and find Rachel to inquire about Ji-won and Joon Oppa.

Monday arrived, and I was already at the school gates by 6 am, I kept a close eye on every passing student. Three hours later, the bell rang, but there was no sign of her. I was unable to focus during lessons with Ji-won's empty seat beside me. During lunch, I recalled some of Rachel's friends were in the debate club, so I rushed there and spotted one of them with bright red hair, who always wore similar designer brands as Rachel.

"Hi," I said.

She turned to me, puzzled, then turned back around.

"Please, do you know where I could find Rachel?" I asked.

She turned again, and her brows furrowed.

"And you are?" she asked.

"A friend of a friend," I muttered.

"Last I heard, she decided to move back to Korea suddenly."

My eyes widened as I lost my balance. Just like that, my last string of hope was gone. I grabbed hold of her hands.

"Please, do you know of a way to contact her? Any means of communication would be very helpful," I pleaded, and she yanked my hands off and smirked.

"What's your problem?" she asked, stepping back.

"I need to find her. It's a matter of urgency," I said, and she chuckled.

"Look, Rachel and I weren't that close. I only hung out with her because she comes from money, so I wasn't that interested in keeping in touch when I heard she was leaving," she muttered and walked off.

I sunk to the ground, and buried my face in my hands, lost for where else to turn. Hours, days, weeks, and months went by, and I was still trapped in my memories of Joon and Ji-won and haunted by regrets over things I left unsaid. I tried to bury those emotions, safely hidden within me. Believing that one day we'd meet again.

When we were finally off to college, I took one last lap around the school grounds, saying my goodbyes to all the memories Joon and I made there, lastly, I went to London Bridge to let go of the past and embraced the start of a new beginning.

"We are now ready for landing," the pilot announces.

Jolting me back to the present, I must have slept through the journey. The pilot welcomes us to the Incheon airport in South Korea. It's all starting to feel real. After trying and failing to get an internship at Underground Entertainment, three years later, I finally got accepted but was only given two weeks to prepare, which wasn't nearly enough time.

But it was an opportunity I couldn't pass by and although the fan girl in me is excited to finally meet and work with N.O., which is a dream come true, my main goal for joining the company is for a chance to meet Rachel, she's my only hope in finding Ji-won and Joon.

Coming all the way here doesn't guarantee I will find them, but I'm hoping Rachel will have some information. I've wondered about them often curious about how they're doing or how much they've changed, if Joon still remembers or thinks about me, or if he is still waiting for me as he promised. I shake my head, ridding myself of such expectations.

It had been ten years since I last saw him, but he still held a special place in my heart. Although I'd been on a few blind dates, none of them could ever compare. The last date I went on was with a tall, handsome guy from a well-established family, but he was arrogant and full of himself. He thought taking me to the Shard in his luxury car and buying me expensive food would compensate for his bad attitude. But when the bill arrived, I insisted on paying for my own bill, which bruised his ego. And as a result, he cancelled our plans for drinks after and that was the last I heard from him.

During freshers' week in university, I met Michael. We stayed up late one night to finish a project, and I accidentally fell asleep. When I woke up, he was leaning in to kiss me, and I pushed him away, causing him to hurt his ribs. After that incident, he never partnered with me again on any project. I sighed, shaking off the thought.

I clasp my star pendant tightly and exhaled. It had been a great source of comfort over the years. As the economy class passengers begin to disembark, I grab my hand luggage and join the line. The airport is captivating. It looks more like an art gallery. The architectural designs and artistic ceilings make it a stunning sight to behold. Even the sitting area is a work of art.

After getting my bag, I explore the stores, enamoured by everything. South Korea already captivates me. I sit in the greenery-themed area with an iced Americano, before heading for the arrivals exit.

"Miss Mina, Miss Mina."

I hear my name being called and spot a man in a navy blue shirt and blue jeans, hoping to get my attention. Perhaps he recognises me from the photo on my CV. I walk over to him with my suitcase in hand.

"Miss Mina, right?" he asks.

"Hello, I'm Mina Adebayo. Nice to meet you," I respond in Korean, and his eyes widen.

"Yes, nice to meet you too. My name is Park Tae-yung. I'm the production runner at Underground Entertainment."

We shake hands as we both bow slightly, customary in Korean culture.

"Wow, I'm lost for words. Your Korean is good," he says in Korean, and I smile.

"I studied the Korean language in university," I say, and he nods.

"Ahh, I see. I think you will fit in just fine then," I smile at his warm welcome.

"Please take good care of me," I say, and he nods.

He takes my luggage and leads me to his car. The drive out of the airport offers a breathtaking view, with tall sculptures depicting a man and woman holding a suitcase. I look out the window, mesmerised by the city of Seoul; the only downside was the fine dust in the air.

"There would be a lot of fine dust today, so please make sure you keep your facemask on at all times," he says.

Handing me a few face masks from his gloves box as we reach a traffic stop, I nod, collecting them. Mr Park doesn't seem like much of a talker, so we listen to the radio as we drive on, and soon arrive at the apartment I'll be staying in.

"This is Itaewon. There are lots of foreigners around here, so I think you will like it here," Mr Park says.

He grabs my suitcase from the booth, and we head upstairs to the rooftop. It's much bigger than I was expecting. I thought it'd be the size of a shoe box from the look of the pictures I was sent. It's painted green with a brown outdoor bench and some drying lines. I grin, feeling like I have walked onto a Korean drama film set.

"I'll leave you to get settled in. Here are the things you will need to set up your phone," he hands me a bag.

"And this here is your T-money card. Do you know how it works, or would you like me to walk you through it?" he asks, and I shake my head.

"I've watched a few videos on how to use them, so I think I'll be fine," I say, and he smiles.

"Excellent, we have topped it up for you. There should be enough for you to use for at least two weeks, but if you need anything or have any questions, here is my card. Just give me a call," he says.

I collect it and bow slightly.

"Thank you so much for your help," I say, and he reciprocates before leaving.

I walk up to the wooden door, turn in my key, and walk in. It's a medium-sized room with minimal furniture, a wardrobe, a coffee table, a single bed, and some cushions to sit on. There's a small kitchen area with all the essentials and an ensuite bathroom. The walls are painted blue with heated brown flooring. I dive onto the bed, exhaling, finding it hard to believe I'm truly in Seoul.

The day passes quickly as I unpack and arrange my belongings. When I finally open the curtains, it was already dark outside—I had lost track of time. My belly rumbles so I head downstairs with my wallet in hand. I take a leisurely walk around the neighbourhood, searching for a place to eat. Itaewon's urban and cultural atmosphere captivates me—it's truly a beautiful and unique place.

I spot a ramen restaurant and decide to try it. The ramen tastes better than I imagined. After my meal, I walk back home. Despite the late hour, the streets feel safe. Once on the rooftop, I lay down on the outdoor bench, using my arm as a headrest. The cool night air is soothing, but being in a new country alone is still strange.

Recalling I haven't called home to let them know I arrived safely, I run inside to grab the bag Mr Park gave me to set up my phone. First, I check the time in London, then dial Mum's number, and she picks up on the first ring.

"Hi Mum."

"Mina, do you realise how long I've waited for your call," she yells.

"Sorry Mum I lost track of time, but I arrived safely, and I'm all settled in," I say, and she exhales.

"Have you eaten?" she asks.

"Yes, I have. I hope everything ended well at the wedding. I feel horrible for leaving early," I muttered.

"Don't worry, everything went well. They left for their honeymoon a few hours ago," she yawns.

"Mum, you must be exhausted. Go get some rest. I'll call you tomorrow," she sighs.

"All right darling, talk soon and make sure you lock your doors and windows," she warns.

"I will, talk soon, I love you," I say.

"Love you too, baby. Good night."

After the call, I shower, brush my teeth, and get into bed. The next day, a peaceful Sunday in Seoul, I explore the city, do some shopping, and return home. As I arrive, I notice an elderly woman with silver grey hair wearing a flower print dress sitting on a bench in front of the building.

"Annyeonghaseyo."

I greet her, and she smiles.

"You speak Korean well, and you're so beautiful," she mutters, and I give her a slight bow.

"Thank you, I'm your new neighbour. I moved into the rooftop upstairs," I say.

"Oh, I see. Well, it's great to have you here. You have nothing to worry about. This area is very safe and quiet. I'm sure you'll like it," she says, and I grin.

"See you around halmeoni," I say.

After reaching upstairs, I call Mum and Dina, then prepare my clothes for my first day at work. I'm ecstatic about meeting N.O., but a little saddened that the line-up no longer includes

Kim Dong-min. However, I hope I still get to see him around the company.

My alarm goes off at 6:30 pm, and I get ready for work. I head for the subway, smiling as I'm reminded of home. The subway system is easy to navigate, even for non-Korean speakers. I notice a few empty seats, but I'm puzzled why some people remain standing. I sit, and everyone stares at me wide-eyed, making me fidget. I wonder if the seat has a problem or if it's because they've never seen a black foreigner before. I try to ignore their stares, but it's hard. At the next stop, an elderly man's eyes meet mine, and his brows frown.

"Why are you sitting there," he yells in Korean, and I leap up instantly.

"Don't you see the sign indicating these seats are only for specific people?"

I lower my head, biting my lip. How did I not notice the sign? I hear a few giggles, but I keep my head down, plugging in my headphones and turning up the volume, wishing I could just disappear. We arrive at my stop, and I burst out the open doors.

I follow the directions on my map and reach the company building. It's much bigger than the pictures online, with its dazzling glass high-rise reflecting the sun. The entrance is crowded with fans and reporters hoping to see celebrities. Some pose for pictures in front of the underground entertainment landmark sculpture. I stand there, mesmerised by the scene, taking a deep breath, and reflect on the long journey that brought me to this moment.

"Miss Mina."

I hear a familiar voice calling. I turn to find Mr Park.

"Over here," he says.

I walk towards the entrance with him, and he helps me through security before we head inside. The interior of the company is even more breathtaking, but I can't fully appreciate it as I'm distracted by famous artists and movie stars casually walking by. I look around, hoping to spot Rachel, but no luck so far. Instead, I get distracted by Kim Soo-young, the king of romance, and I stand in awe, mouth wide open.

"It's a lot to take in, right?" Mr Park says, and I nod, and he chuckles.

"Don't worry, you'll get used to it or maybe not," he smirks.

"Let's head up to meet the director and the rest of the team," he says, leading me to the elevator.

When we arrive at the eighteenth floor, we walk in, and everyone's preoccupied, either answering phone calls, making phone calls, or busy on their computer. It's an open-plan office with only one closed-door room, and the see-through window lets in lots of light, giving it a very vibrant feel. Mr Park leads me to the office at the back of the room and knocks before entering, and I follow him in.

"She's here, sir," Mr Park says.

The director gets up from his seat, walks over and shakes my hands, smiling warmly, wearing a powder brown three-piece suit and black dress shoes. His eyes are warm and welcoming.

"Welcome aboard, Miss Mina. We are all excited to work with you. My name is Lee Jung Woo, and I'm the director of the production team," he says.

"No sir, thank you for having me," I mutter.

"This way, I'll introduce you to the rest of the team," he says, leading us out, then claps his hands, grabbing everyone's attention.

"I know you are all busy planning for the upcoming drama, but I need your attention for a moment. There's someone I'd like you all to meet," I swallowed as all eyes fell on me.

"Introduce yourself," Mr Lee says, and I bow my head.

"Hello, my name is Mina Adebayo. I'm twenty-five years old and from London, England. For as long as I can remember, it has been my dream to work here at Underground Entertainment, so it's an absolute pleasure to meet you all, and I look forward to working with you. Please take care of me," I say and bow again.

All their jaws drop, and their eyes widen.

Chapter Nineteen

"Wow, how do you speak Korean so well, Miss Mina?" A guy wearing a grey and yellow stripe tie says. They all await my response, and I smile.

"I studied Korean as one of my university majors," I say, and they all nod, grinning.

"Woow, very impressive," he responds.

"I hope you all make Miss Mina feel welcome and help her get settled in," Mr Lee says.

"Welcome, Miss Mina. We are happy to have you," a lady with a pixie cut and thick-framed glasses mutters.

They warmly welcome me and introduce themselves along with their positions in the department. There are seven of them in total, all older except one intern who's a year younger and recently started.

"To welcome you properly, we will go for a company-paid dinner tonight," Mr Lee says, and they all begin to cheer.

"Miss Soo-jin."

Mr Lee calls the younger female staff; she walks over and bows her head.

"Could you show Miss Mina around the company and help her get settled in," he says, and she smiles in response.

"Yes, sir," she mutters.

"Well, I shall leave her in your hands," he says.

Then headed back to his office, I'm glad Soo-jin will be the one showing me around as we're similar in age.

"Miss Mina," she calls.

Urging me to follow her, we head to a desk at the far-end corner.

"This will be your desk and editing station. It's right next to mine, so if you need anything, just let me know," she says, and I nod in response.

"It's small but has everything you'll need. It's the desk I used when I first started too."

Miss Soo-jin says, and I grin filled with glee.

"It's perfect," I say.

I sweep my hands through the desk. It's all beginning to feel real. I can't believe I'm a member of staff at Underground Entertainment.

"First things first, we need to get your badge made. Come with me," Miss Soo-jin says.

I nod, following her to the elevator, going up to the twenty-fifth floor for a quick photo session for my new badge. Within minutes, I have my badge. I grin, gawking at it like a lottery ticket. We then head back down to the eighteenth floor.

"Miss Soo-jin," I call, and she turns to face me.

"I've seen quite a few idols around the company but I'm yet to see N.O. or Go Ae-ra," I say.

"Tomorrow, you'll be officially introduced to N.O., and Miss Go Ae-ra, is currently in Japan for a photo shoot. She'll be back tomorrow," she says, and I nod.

Although the thought of meeting N.O. gives me butterflies, I'm more eager to meet Rachel.

"Miss Mina," Miss Soo-jin calls, and I turn to her.

"Make sure you keep your professionalism whenever you're around the idols because how you act reflects on our department as a whole. I hope you'll keep that in mind," she says.

Her tone grows cold, sending chills down my spine, and then she wears a plastered smile that doesn't reach her eyes.

"I'm sure you'll do just fine," she adds.

The doors to the lift open, and she walks out. I hesitate to step out, taken back by her change of tone.

"Aren't you coming?" she asks, and I rush out to join her.

Back at the office, Mrs Kim-Sun-ah, the production team leader with the pixie cut, calls me over and assigns my first task. I then go around to each person, asking what errands they need me to run. As the newest member, everyone else is my senior, including Soo-jin. My tasks include making photocopies, returning clothing items to the styling department, and taking notes during meetings.

It's noon now, and I'm on a coffee run for the whole team. Though not the first day I imagined, I'm grateful to be part of the team and company. On my way back from the coffee shop, I notice a cleaner struggling with the back door while holding a few bean bags. I rush over and use my leg to hold the door for her to pass through.

"Thank you," she mutters.

She places the bean bags onto a cart and drives off. Deciding to take the back door instead of going back around, though I'm not entirely familiar with the route back to the office. But I stop in my tracks when I hear a rattling sound coming from outside.

I wonder if it's the cleaner, as I approach the door, the rattling sound continues. Suddenly, the door pushes open, hitting my cheeks, and I fall back, spilling coffee on my white blouse.

"Argh," I yelp.

"I'm so sorry," a familiar voice says.

I look up and gasp as my hands start trembling. He's wearing a black face mask, dark sunglasses, and a black hoodie.

"Are you okay?" he asks.

Shaking my shoulders, then I spot a small black gun in his hands, and start screaming, pulling away from him. He must be a stalker or a crazy fan.

"Calm down," he says.

Placing his hands over my mouth, and my heart rate spikes.

"Who are you?" I ask, trying to wiggle my way out of his hold.

"I'm not trying to hurt you," he says.

I take a deep breath, raise my head, and head-butt him, making him fall.

"Argh," he yelps.

Holding onto his head, I get up immediately, running to the nearest door, and then he grasps my ankle.

"Hold on a moment," he says.

Then he lets go and slowly takes off his glasses. I raise my eyebrows; he looks familiar, but I still can't tell where I've seen him before. Then he pulls off his mask and takes off his hoodie. I gasp, stumbling backwards, and my eyes widen.

"Argh," he yelps.

Rubbing his now swollen forehead, I place both hands over my mouth.

"Ki, Kim Dong-min," I blurt out, in disbelief. He looks just as dreamy in person.

Then rush over helping him get back up.

"Are you okay?"

I ask, squeezing my trembling hands, then lowering my head into a bow.

"I am so sorry; I had no idea it was you."

I squeeze my eyes shut, biting my bottom lips. How can this be the way I meet him for the first time? What if I get fired for this? Or worse, what if he calls the police and reports me for assault? I began to fidget, and my palms get sweaty. I pinch myself hard, wishing this is all a dream.

"Ouch," I yelp.

"Are you okay? Sorry for frightening you," he says.

Placing the gun in his pocket, I step back, and he raises his brows and chuckles.

"Don't worry, it's not real," he says.

Pulling it back out, pointing it upwards, and pulling the trigger, I shut my eyes, placing my hands over my ears, but nothing happens. I slowly open my eyes to find the gun lit with fire and sigh. He chuckles again.

"It's just a lighter, Miss," he says, placing it in his pocket.

He looks down at my coffee-stained blouse, and gasps, walking in close.

"Are you okay? Was it hot? Did you get burnt?" he asks.

Searching my eyes for answers, I shake my head.

"No, no, I'm fine. It was iced coffee," I say.

Attempting to reassure him to no avail.

"This will not do," he says.

Then he suddenly starts taking off his shirt.

"Oh my gosh, what are you doing?" I ask, turning immediately to face the wall.

"Here," he says.

I turn around, and he hands over his black t-shirt. I swallow as I stare at his muscular arms. He waves his hands to grab my attention, and I shake my head, changing my train of thought.

"You really don't have to. I'm okay," I say, pushing his shirt away.

"But I'm not okay, so please take it and give me your account details so I can pay for your dry cleaning," he offers, and my eyes widen.

"Oh no, no, there's absolutely no need for that. I'll just take the top if that puts you at ease," I say.

Grabbing the top from him and heading for the door, but then I stop, turning as he puts on his hoodie.

"But why were you coming in that way?" I ask, and he sighs.

"Well can I trust you to keep my secret?" he asks, and I nod.

"I went out for a smoke. As you know, smoking is frowned upon for idols, but it's the only thing that helps relieve my stress, so to avoid getting caught by fans, the press, or the company, I come this way for a quick cigarette," he says.

I nod slightly, then turn back, heading out.

"Why do you look disappointed?" he asks, and I shake my head.

"Not disappointed, just worried for your health," I say.

"Miss Mina," he calls.

I freeze with my eyes widening. How does he know my name? I turn around and exhale when I see him holding my I.D. badge. I look down at my neck. I didn't notice it coming off. I walk up to collect it, but he pulls his hands away.

"Your Korean is impressive, here," he says, handing over my badge and grins.

"See you around," he mutters, leaving the room.

I exhale, crouching down, panting. He's even more breathtaking in person and a complete gentleman. I grin and wiggle as the fan girl in me celebrates.

I consider sharing my encounter in the fangirl group chat but hesitate, fearing it could create false rumours and controversies. Instead, I savour the moment, holding his shirt tightly in circles. I inhale it, and the scent of roses and cigarettes fills my nostrils, and then my phone starts buzzing.

"Oh crap," I yelp.

Finally, coming back to my senses. The team must be waiting for their coffee.

"Miss Mina, where are you?" Miss Soo-jin asks.

"I ran into some trouble. I'll explain later, but can you please meet me outside the office?" I ask.

"Why, is something wrong?" she mutters.

I hesitate to answer, and she sighs.

"Okay, I'm coming," she says, hanging up.

I quickly grab the coffees that are still intact and race for the elevator, getting to the eighteenth floor, Soo-jin is already waiting by the door. Her eyes widen as she spots me coming out.

"What happened?" she asks.

"I had a bit of an accident. Could you please take these in, so I can go get changed," I say, handing over the coffees to her.

"Don't worry about getting any more. Just get change and come back to the office. I'll explain to the team," she says.

I nod and make my way to the bathroom.

"Do you have a change of clothes?" she asks.

I look down at the shirt Kim Dong-min gave me and smile.

"Yes, I do," I say.

She looks at me puzzled, before going inside, I quickly enter a toilet stall, remove my stained blouse, and hold K.D.M.'s shirt in disbelief. I let out a silent scream, put on the shirt, and returned to the office with my stained blouse. As I walk in, all eyes are on me. I swallow and then bow.

"I'm so sorry," I say.

They all stare at me, looking more stunned, and then the team leader stands up.

"Are you okay? You're not hurt, are you?" she asks, seemingly overreacting.

"Not at all. I'm fine," I say, and my brows frown.

I look over to Soo-jin, wondering what exactly she told them. She looks back at me with a grim smile.

"Miss Soo-jin said you tripped and fell on the staircase, and coffee spilt all over your blouse."

I look down at my fingers. It's not entirely a lie, but it also isn't the whole truth. Soo-jin must have said that to help me, but it doesn't sit right. What if they discover the truth later? It could give them the wrong impression of me, I thought.

"Are you able to carry on working? You must have been startled," she says, I shake my head.

"No, honestly, I'm okay. Thanks for your concern," I say.

She nods hesitantly before returning to her seat, and I head back to mine. Soo-jin grins, perhaps expecting my gratitude for her white lie; however, I just continue with my work, ignoring her. At 6 pm, the department director, Mr Lee, comes out of his office, announcing my welcome dinner. Everyone cheers in anticipation.

We make our way out, and as we arrive at the reception, I realise I have left my blouse under my desk.

"I'll meet you guys at the restaurant. I forgot something upstairs," I say.

"Okay, I'll text you the address. It's just around the corner," Soo-jin says.

I get back in the lift, heading upstairs. I rush into the office, grab the bag with my blouse, and return to the lift. On the way down, I receive a text from Soo-jin with the address and put it on my map. Then the doors open, and I rush out, walking in headfirst, and hitting my head on someone's chest.

"Argh," I yelp.

Lifting my head to check whom I hit, silently praying it isn't an idol, I gasp when our eyes meet. Stepping back, I lose my balance, tripping over my legs and begin to fall backwards. It all happens so fast but plays very slowly in my head.

He leans in, catching me mid-way, wrapping his hands around my waist. Our eyes lock, and I gasp. He looks just as breathtaking as they say. Liam Choi, who, up close, indeed has a face worthy of being described as the national treasure of South Korea.

I'm spellbound by the sparkle in his caramel-brown eyes as he blinks through his long lashes. I'm left speechless, breathless, and unable to move, captivated by his presence, his overgrown fringe unravels sculpting his face. My eyes are drawn to his soft and tender cherry lips.

However, something about his gaze feels familiar, so I lean in closer, searching his eyes for answers. His expression mirrors mine. He stares as though he's seen a ghost. His eyes widen, tracing down my neck, and he gasps when his gaze falls on my star pendant.

I see tears building up in his eyes as a smile escapes his lips. Suddenly, his smile fades, and his lips press into a hard line. He sniffs my shirt and sighs, lifting me back up and pulling away. Then, he clears his throat.

"Don't you know that smoking is bad for your health?" he says.

My brows frown, puzzled at his comment, and then I look down at my shirt and gasp, I forgot about the cigarette smell on K.D.M.'s shirt.

"And next time, watch where you're going," he says, walking out of the lift.

"No, it's not what you think."

I try to explain, but the doors shut before I finish, and I roll my eyes. He's just as cold and arrogant as they say. I must have been momentarily hypnotised earlier. I kick the lift door, picturing his face.

"Ahhhh," I yelp.

As the pain in my foot sinks in, then the image of his eyes pops back into my head, unable to shake off their familiarity. My phone starts buzzing, and it's a text from Soo-jin.

"Oh, crap."

I completely forgot that they were waiting for me. I head out following the directions on the map and soon arrive at the restaurant.

"Mina, over here," Soo-jin calls out.

I head over to the table to find a lot of hungry faces.

"Sorry I'm late," I say with a bow,

"It's okay, take a seat," Mr Lee says.

I head over to the empty spot next to Soo-jin and Mr Lee.

"Let me pour you a drink," Mr Lee says.

So, I raise my glass with both hands as it's respectful to do so when someone senior pours a drink.

"Oh, Miss Mina, I'm impressed you know how to receive a drink well."

He mutters grinning as he pours me a glass of soju, I turn to the opposite side to drink, but when I turn back to face everyone, they all stare at me with their mouths open.

"Where did you learn Korean drinking etiquette?" the team leader Mrs Kim asks, and I smile.

"It's a secret," I say, and they all laugh.

"From tomorrow you and Miss Soo-jin will be in charge of filming the behind-the-scenes for Liam Choi's upcoming drama alongside Miss Go Ae-ra. I am relying on you both to do a good job," Mr Lee says.

We both bow our heads in response, but I squirm, recalling my earlier encounter with Liam Choi. The fact that he already has the wrong impression about me makes things even worse.

"You both better brace yourselves if you're going to be working with those two," the team leader says, chuckling.

She seems to have had one too many drinks, so Mr Lee urges her to stop talking.

"They should know what to expect if they will be working with them," she continues.

"Let's be honest, I can't tell if they are filming a drama or a reality show," she says, giggling.

"Mr Lee, stop stepping on my foot," she yells.

He turns red as the whole table goes quiet.

"Come closer," she urges us to lean in.

"There will be a surprise announcement tomorrow."

"Now that's enough now," Mr Lee interrupts her.

"Why, they will find out tomorrow anyway," she says, smirking.

He retreats, leaving her to carry on.

"As I was saying, Kim Dong-min, will join the cast tomorrow," the whole table gasps.

"He'll be playing the second lead in the love triangle between Go Ae-ra and Liam Choi."

She stops and takes a shot of soju, and we all eagerly wait for her to continue.

"But what makes this hilarious is the fact that, in reality, they are involved in a real love triangle. Go Ae-ra has a one-sided crush on Liam, but he isn't interested in her romantically. From what I heard, they have been friends for years now, but nothing romantic. Kim Dong-min has had a crush on Go Ae-ra since their trainee days. However, she only has eyes for Liam, which is why he hates Liam." She takes another sip.

"To make things worse, Liam was his replacement in N.O. after he was forced out of the group and made to go solo due to his many scandals as the company did not want the other members of the group to get affected," she says before passing out on the table.

Chapter Twenty

Mr Lee shakes his head and sighs.

"I think we should call it a night," Mr Lee says.

Then walks over to Mrs Kim and wraps her arm around his shoulder, and my eyes widen.

"They are married," Soo-jin whispers, noticing my stunned expression.

"Ahh, I see," I nod.

Soo-jin and I wait for all the senior staff members to either grab a taxi or wait for their replacement drivers.

"Well done. It must have been a tough first day for you," Soo-jin says.

"It was okay. I'll see you tomorrow," I say.

After bowing, we go our separate ways. Waiting for my bus, I think about the love triangle between the idols. Given his cold and arrogant attitude, I can't understand what Rachel sees in Liam Choi. Looking at the stars, I wonder about Joon Oppa and how much he's changed over the years.

As my bus arrives, I notice a massive poster of Liam Choi's face promoting a skincare product. His popularity has risen, particularly among younger audiences, despite joining N.O. only a few years ago. I roll my eyes before boarding the bus.

I get home, reminiscing about meeting Kim Dong-min, looking down at the shirt he gave me, despite the disastrous first meeting. Grinning, I head inside, take off my shoes, collapse into bed, and soon doze off.

After yesterday's train debacle, I opt for the bus to work today, sitting at the back near the window. The bus ride is pleasant, and I hope for a smooth day as I step into the office.

"Good morning, everyone," I say, getting weak responses.

They appear to be recovering from last night. Mrs Kim tries hiding her face behind her computer, then Mr Lee enters the room, and the atmosphere shifts, as everyone straightens up.

"Morning everyone, as you all know, production for the drama 'Meet You at Sunset' is set to start filming today. Miss Mina and Miss Soo-jin will oversee the filming of behind-the-scenes footage. Mr Park," he calls the production runner.

"Yes sir," he responds.

"Take them up to meet Liam Choi and the other boys from N.O. as they will be making a cameo in today's scene," he nods.

"Yes sir, this way ladies," Mr Park says.

Leading us outside, we head to the thirteenth floor. Once we arrive, my eyes widen; it's like we've entered a whole new building. The interior here is on another level, with teal blue painted walls and mesmerising artwork on each wall. Even the couch in the reception area looks like an art piece that shouldn't be sat on. As we walk by, I glimpse at the door to the C.E.O.'s office at the end of the hall.

"Wait here," Mr Park mutters before walking into another room.

"Is this the great acting opportunity you said you had for me?" We hear yelling from the C.E.O.'s office.

"Why the hell would you put me in a drama with him," I raise my brows, hearing a familiar voice.

"Calm down. It's all for your benefit," a deeper-sounding voice says.

"How the hell will this benefit me? First, you remove me from a band that I put my blood, sweat and tears into growing, forcing me to go solo and now what? You want me to be the second lead in a drama with my replacement?"

Soo-jin and I look at each other after realising who it is speaking to the C.E.O. Then we suddenly hear slamming, giving us both a fright.

"Dong-min! Being in a drama with Liam and Ae-ra, who are scandal-free, will help clean up your reputation and reflect positively on you. You have no idea what strings I had to pull to get you into this drama? Because of your scandals, no one in the industry wants to work with you anymore," the C.E.O. says, then the room grows quiet.

"Dong-min, I still have faith in you and your talents. This is the best way for you to make a comeback before releasing your solo album. First, we need to get people to see you in a positive light, okay."

Soo-jin and I avoid making eye contact for unintentionally listening. We exhale when Mr Park returns.

"Let's go," he says.

Leading us to a room with N.O. written on the door, we get inside, and it's a dance studio, with a resting area on the other side where the boys are sitting. My heart is unable to contain itself. I can't believe it's finally happening; fifteen-year-old me would have fainted at this opportunity.

"Boys, these ladies will be following you around to film the behind-the-scenes from today's cameo and for you Liam, they will do so throughout."

Soo-jin and I bow our heads before introducing ourselves.

"Hello, my name is Yoo Soo-jin," she says.

"Hello, my name is Mina Adebayo," I say.

Hiding my trembling hands, it's as though they've stepped out of my bedroom poster. They haven't aged these past few years. I look up to find their eyes dancing with curiosity.

"Wow, Miss Mina, you speak Korean?"

The youngest band Member, Jin Tae-hee, gushes.

"Yes, I do," I say.

"Ahhhh, what country are you from, if you don't mind me asking," the dance leader, Lee Min-woo asks.

"I was born in Nigeria but moved to London with my family when I was two," I say.

"Oh, that's cool."

The lead singer, Park Sung-mo says in English, and they all chuckle.

"Is that the only English you know? That's all you ever say?" Jin Tae-hee says.

And they all begin teasing him. I look over to the left, where Liam Choi is sitting unresponsive and seemingly disinterested.

"Liam, you lived in London too, right," Jin Tae-hee says, and my eyes widen.

Liam glares fiercely at Tae-hee. Is he from London? The only information online says that he once lived in a foreign country when he was younger, perhaps that is why he seems familiar. Maybe I should ask what part of London he's from. But before I can, the door opens, and Kim Dong-min walks in. The boys get up, running over to him, except Liam.

"Hyung, we just heard you're going to be in the drama too. Congratulations."

They all say, and he smirks, looking at Liam.

"Well, someone had to be there to make the drama worth watching," Kim Dong-min says.

But Liam doesn't react. Then he turns towards Soo-jin and me, raising his brows, and I lower my head.

"Uh, hey friend, what are you doing here?" Dong-min asks.

Then walks over to me, grinning, and everyone in the room stares at us wide-eyed, and I bite my bottom lip, squeezing my eye shut.

"Hyung, you know her?" Tae-hee asks.

I gasp and lift my head, silently pleading with my eyes to keep our encounter a secret; Liam's also glaring at me from the corner of my eyes, seemingly awaiting my answer to Tae-hee's question.

"Of course, she's a friend," he says, smirking.

He then wraps his arms around my shoulder. I gasp, while their eyes widen.

"Ooh, friends," the boys say, smirking.

"So sorry about your blouse. I hope the shirt I gave you fitted well," Dong-min added.

I bite my lip harder looking down at my fingers, wishing I could disappear. Why would he mention that, knowing it would only create misunderstandings?

"Ohh, what blouse are you talking about? Wait, are you sure you guys are just friends?" Min-woo asks, and I gasp.

"No, no, it's nothing like that," I say.

Moving Dong-min's hands off my shoulders, Mr Park and Soo-jin's brows frown. I turn to escape their glares, facing Liam Choi, who gives me a disdainful glare. I swallow, lowering my head, and he sighs, getting up.

"What's with all the chit-chat? Shouldn't we get going," Liam says.

Walking out of the room, barging into Kim Dong-min on his way out.

"Hey!" Dong-min yells.

But Liam ignores him, slamming the door behind him. Dong-min attempts to follow him out, but Sung-mo holds him back.

"Hyung, just leave him. When will Liam ever manage that temper of his," Sung-mo mutters.

The rest of the boys walk over talking him down.

"Bye Hyung," the boys say before making their way out.

"See you later," Kim Dong-min says.

"We need to get going, too," Mr Park says, and we make our way out.

"See you around, friend," Dong-min says and winks.

I sigh, lowering my head, closing the door behind me, and avoid eye contact with Soo-jin and Mr Park in the hallway.

"Both of you head downstairs and grab your equipment, then wait for the rest of the crew by the production van. I need to print out today's filming schedule," Mr Park says, and Soo-jin and I head down.

"What exactly happened between you and Kim Dong-min?" Soo-jin asks.

"It's not what you think. He was the one I had the coffee incident with yesterday, so he gave me his shirt to change into, that's all," I say, but she doesn't seem satisfied with my explanation.

"Be more careful next time. Don't you know rumours travel fast in this industry?" she says.

And I nod, feeling like an errant child. We head downstairs to the production van, load up our equipment and head out to the location. We soon arrive and it's bigger than I imagined. The sets are well-built and have an eclectic range within them. We're told to be quiet as several other shows are also being filmed here.

"This way," Mr Park says.

Directing us to where we will be filming today. The first scene is set in a school hallway, where the two lead characters meet for the first time.

"Mina, can you hand out the shooting schedule to the cast and crew," Mr Park says, handing me the printouts.

"Soo-jin, can you start filming the boys in hair and makeup."

We both nod, heading off to do our assigned tasks. My fingers slip, making the printouts drop to the floor. I bend to pick them up and six-inch heels appear before me.

"Unnie, when was a foreigner hired into the company? I don't think I've seen her before," the lady in heels says.

Then another pair of sneakers appear next to her.

"Who are you?" the lady in sneakers asks.

After bowing to greet them, I raise my head to introduce myself.

"Hello, my name is......"

But I stop mid-sentence when I recognise the lady in heels. It's her. It's really her. My eyes widen, and my hands tremble. I walk in closer to her, grabbing her hands tearing up.

"Rachel, I can't believe it's really you."

"Excuse me, what do you think you're doing?" the lady in sneakers with a mushroom haircut asks.

Rachel's eyes widen as she stares back at me.

"Mina?"

She says, and I nod continuously as tears begin to stream down my cheeks.

"Rachel, is it really you? I can't believe I've finally found you," I say.

She gasps, staring at me in disbelief.

I hold onto her hands tightly, making sure I don't lose sight of her again.

"But how, how are you here?" she asks.

Then looks around searching for someone or something.

"Rachel, please tell me you know the whereabouts of Ji-won and Joon Oppa. I've been searching and searching for years now with no luck."

I squeeze her hands tighter, awaiting her response, but she doesn't speak.

"What's wrong?" I ask, but she keeps looking around.

"Whom are you looking for," then I gasp as the thought crosses my mind.

"Are they here right now by any chance?" I ask, tracing her gaze.

She turns me to face her.

"Wh wha what do you mean? she asks, shaking me.

Then I spot N.O. approaching with Liam in front of them, Rachel lets go of my shoulders, turning to see whom I'm looking at, and I bow to greet them as they walk by.

"OMG, he's so good-looking."

The staff members whisper as all eyes fall on the boys. Rachel stands frozen as she stares at Liam Choi wide-eyed and then back at me.

"Go Ae-ra, Nuna."

The N.O. boys chant, except Liam Choi, who walks off. Rachel exhales and puts on a smile as she exchanges greetings with the boys before they head off to set. I roll my eyes at Liam Choi's passive attitude.

"What a rude jerk," I say under my breath.

"What, who's a jerk," Rachel asks eagerly.

"Oh, no one," I say.

"Who, Liam Choi?" she asks, almost sounding amused.

"He's kind of arrogant," I say, and she swallows as her eyes widen.

"So, you've met him already?" she asks.

"Yes, unfortunately," I say, and her frown grows into a grin.

"So, you don't know who that is?" she asks, and my brows frown.

"Of course, I do. Doesn't everyone know who the arrogant Liam Choi is?"

She exhales, and I grab hold of her hands again.

"Rachel, please tell me; do you know where Ji-won and Joon Oppa are?" I ask.

She spaces out, staring at something or someone behind me. I turn to look, and it's Liam. They stare at each other intensely as seemingly talking with their eyes, and then Rachel moves her gaze back to me, pulling my hands off.

"I don't know where they are. I haven't seen them since they left London," she says.

I stumble backwards as my knees grow weak, and tears fall down my cheeks.

"Can we have Miss Go Ae-ra, on set, please," the director calls.

"I've got to go; can we catch up later?" she says with a massive smile on her face before walking off.

I stand frozen, unable to move, biting on my bottom lip to stop myself from crying out loud.

"Miss Mina, what are you doing over there? We need to start filming?" Soo-jin says, bringing me back to my senses.

I join Soo-jin as Liam and the N.O. boys get ready for the scene, while Rachel receives instructions from the director. But I'm unable to concentrate. Finding Rachel was my last hope of tracking them down. But it's hard to believe that Rachel hasn't kept in touch with them all these years. She left for South Korea around the same time they did. I sigh, glaring at her through my camera lens.

I try finding an opportunity to speak to Rachel again throughout the day to no avail, as she's always surrounded by others, and Soo-jin has her eyes on me, making it impossible to slip away. After we're done filming, the crew is packing up.

After putting our equipment away, I head straight to Rachel's dressing room; I knock, opening the door to find the room empty and sigh. Although I knew I might hit another brick wall, I didn't want to give up. I must do all I can to find them.

I walk out spotting a sign for a rooftop upstairs. I make my way up taken aback by the breathtaking view. The rooftop is like a greenhouse, adorned with beautiful flowers and roses. Fairy lights surround all the plants and trees, creating a magical atmosphere. I gaze up at the night sky. The stars shine brightly. Walking up to the edge, I catch a glimpse of the city below.

The city looks even more beautiful under the night sky, reminding me of the day Joon and I watched the stars together. I clasp my pendant tightly, tears flood down again. I gasp, hearing someone clearing their throat from behind. I turn to find a figure standing behind one of the big trees. His face is partly hidden by branches, so I get closer and gasp when I see Liam Choi.

"I'm sorry, I didn't realise anyone else was here," I say.

Wiping off my tears with my hands then turn to leave.

"It's fine. I was about to leave anyway," he says.

Walking towards me and I step back.

"Here," he says.

Handing me a handkerchief, I stare back at him, blinking through my teary eyes. He waves it, urging me to take it.

"Thank you," I say.

I collect it with a slight bow afterwards. As he walks off, I stare back at the handkerchief wide-eyed. Perhaps I had him all wrong. Is this who he is when no one's watching, I wonder. The cloth looks handmade, washed, and neatly ironed. It seems like a keepsake, too precious for my unworthy tears, but why would he give this to me?

My phone buzzes with a text from Soo-jin, saying the production van is ready to leave. I wipe my tears with my sleeves, unable to use the handkerchief. I rush to board the van, and on the ride back, I rack my brain for another solution to find Ji-won and Joon.

After arriving home, I take out the handkerchief. It has the initials "C.S.J" embroidered on it. I wonder if it's his Korean name. Memories of Joon's handkerchief and the flowerpot incident flood my mind, and I sigh.

Then I recall Liam's tortured expression as he handed it to me, but I push thoughts of him away, jumping straight into bed, and dozing off. Today's ride to work is smooth, but everyone seems on edge on set as this scene involves Liam, Dong-min, and Rachel.

After setting up, Soo-jin and I head to Liam's changing room to film behind-the-scenes footage. As we walk in, I see Liam sitting with his eyes closed while the makeup artist works on his face.

As I set up for close-ups, Liam suddenly opens his eyes making me jump, and I drop my camera. Soo-jin scolds me silently and I swallow, picking it up. After his hair and makeup are done, we follow him from behind. Crew members greet him, but he doesn't respond. I roll my eyes. He's back to being cold again. Perhaps he's only friendly when no one's watching.

"Liam?" Rachel calls.

She is dressed in character, wearing a grey and white school uniform.

"Wait up," she says.

Liam ignores her and walks on. She jogs ahead, linking arms with him, but he pulls away, looking towards me, and then walks off. Rachel rolls her eyes at me before chasing after Liam. Dong-min appears in front of Rachel making her halt, but she pushes him out of the way and keeps chasing Liam.

It appears the rumours about their love triangle are true. But they all seem unhappy. Dong-min and I exchange glances, but he quickly hides his frown and smiles, waving at me. I bow, then run catching up with Soo-jin. On set, Liam and Rachel get into character portraying lovers. Watching Rachel, I find it hard to believe someone who cared about Joon's family so much would give up on finding them so quickly. She even warned me to stay away from Joon.

But seeing the way she stares at Liam, she has the same look of longing she used to have when she gazed at Joon.

Chapter Twenty One

Rehearsals begin, but as Kim Dong-min's character walks in, the director yells cut!

"Dong-min, your character doesn't interfere. He just watches them from a distance," the Director says.

Dong-min's hand forms into a fist, then nods, returning to his mark.

"Action," the director yells, but he yells cut again soon after.

"Dong-min, don't look so angry; your character loves her, but instead of feeling anger or jealousy, he's torn because all he truly wants is her happiness," he says and Dong-min sighs.

"How does that make any sense," Dong-min says.

"What do you mean," the director asks.

"Why wouldn't he be angry? She's ignoring the one who loves her sincerely for a wanna-be bad boy who doesn't care, but what? He wishes her happiness? How can she be happy with such a jerk." Dong-min yells and Rachel rolls her eyes.

"Hey, Dong-min, can you stop being difficult and just do as you're told," she says.

He glares at her clenching his jaw.

"Does the script make sense to you?" he asks.

Throwing the script, Liam gets up and walks off.

"Hey, where do you think you're going," Dong-min yells, and Liam halts, turning.

"Why should I sit here and watch you waste everyone's time," Liam says.

"What did you just say?" Dong-min asks.

Then, he charges towards Liam, but the director steps in front of him.

"Call me when the issue is resolved," Liam says as he walks off.

"Yes, of course. You go get some rest," the director says.

Then glares at Dong-min, clenching his teeth. Soo-jin and I run after Liam with our cameras. After some convincing and a few changes, the scene is filmed, and we start packing our equipment.

"I'll be right back," I say.

Heading to Liam's changing room to return his handkerchief, I get in front of the door but hesitate to knock. Then I exhale, raising my hands to knock, but the door opens unexpectedly, and I gasp, falling to the ground. I look up, and our eyes meet. Liam smirks then reaches out his hands to help me up.

I hesitantly accept it, but he suddenly lets go, causing me to fall back to the ground. His attention seems to shift to something behind me. I turn and see Rachel glaring. Then the door to Dong-min's room opens. I try getting up but stumble. Dong-min rushes over, reaching out his hands.

"Need a hand, friend?" he says.

I notice Liam's hand forming into a fist, then Rachel walks over, linking arms with his and Dong-min's face falls. Taking a deep breath, I take Dong-min's hands.

"Let's go," he says, lifting me up.

Soo-jin appears from the corner of the hallway.

"Can I borrow her?" Dong-min asks.

Soo-jin stares at us blankly, as he pulls me into the lift. I glare at our linked hands in disbelief, we exit the lift, and he turns to me.

"Facemask on," he says.

Then pulls out another hat from his backpack and puts it on me.

"Miss Mina," he calls, and I meet his gaze.

"I'm craving a cigarette right now, but someone told me it was bad for my health, so I've decided to turn to other ways to relieve my stress."

I stare back at him with my brows raised.

"And since you're that someone, you need to take responsibility," he says, and my eyes widen.

"Take responsibility?" I ask, and he nods.

"But how," I ask.

He grins, tightening his grip on my hands.

"Let's go," he says.

He starts running, pulling me along, we head to the back of the film studio, where a track field set is located. Dong-min's eyes sparkle with each step, as if reliving a joyful memory from his past. He looks carefree yet trapped at the same time, a feeling I understand too well. He reminds me of my past self. As the wind brushes against my face, I feel alive and awaken, and then suddenly, rain starts drizzling down.

We stop, Dong-min removes his face mask, embracing the pouring rain with a smile mixed with sadness. He spins around, as the rain starts to subside and eventually stops. He collapses to the ground, breathless, eyes closed. I crouch down beside him.

"Aren't you worried about catching a cold?" I ask.

He opens his eyes, gazing at me, then pulls me to lay beside him.

"It's the middle of summer Miss Mina. I think I'll be fine," he says, chuckling.

"Mina," he calls, and I turn to face him.

"When was the last time you cried?" he asks, and my brows frown.

"Why?" I ask, and he smirks.

"I haven't allowed myself to cry since I was a kid," I gasp.

"No way, not even when you're alone?" I ask, and he shakes his head.

"I come from a poor family, you see, so growing up, I'd always go to my dad crying whenever he couldn't afford to buy me the things other kids at school had," he sighs.

Recalling what seems like a painful memory.

"For years, he'd let me cry. Until one day, he came home after losing his job. I ran to him, crying about not having a bicycle like my friends, and he grabbed my shoulders and yelled, Dong-min! Stop wasting your tears on such trivial matters. If little things like that make you cry, you'll never survive the harsh reality of this world," he sighed.

"I'd never seen that look in my dad's eyes before," he adds. My eyes widen as I listen to him.

"Before walking off, he said something I've never forgotten, Kim Dong-min. Save your tears for the day you'd truly need them," Dong-min sighs deeply.

"Ever since that day, I haven't cried, even after my dad died, or when I got kicked off the band, having to start all over again as a solo artist or watching someone I lov…" he stops mid-sentence and chuckles again.

My heart aches as I listen. Outwardly, he seems bright, confident, and outgoing, but on the inside, he's holding on to so much pain, unable to let them out, worried he would cry if he did.

"That's why I love it when it rains; when it does, it feels like the sky is crying for me instead."

He looks back up at the clear sky and smiles. Then turns to me.

"I don't know why I just told you all that," he sighs.

"But for some reason, I feel like I can trust you," he smirks.

"Ahhhh, I feel so much better," he says, stretching his arm.

I sit up, and he joins me suddenly leaning in close, making me blink rapidly as my eyes widen.

"What's your secret, Miss Mina? I don't feel the urge to smoke anymore. You're like my stress relief," he says, smiling, and then he gets up.

"That's what I'm going to call you from now on, stress relief," he laughs, and I gasp.

"What, stress relief?" I ask.

As my brows frown, he reaches his hands out to me.

"Let's go," he says.

I take his hands, and he pulls me up. I stare at him, unable to find words of comfort to say.

"Don't give me that pitiful look. You don't have to feel bad for me. That's not why I shared that story with you."

I put on a forced smile.

"That's more like it," he says.

Then we head to his car, a beat-up old Beetle, which makes me chuckle. The more I get to know him, the more unpredictable he seems.

"Don't laugh. It still works just fine," he says.

Unable to hold back his own laughter.

"Don't let her hurt your feelings, babe," he says, caressing his car, setting me off in fits of giggles.

He unlocks the car, but as he pulls the door handle, it wouldn't open.

"O baby, don't do this," he mutters.

Struggling to open the door, I cover my mouth to hide my laughter. Eventually, it opens, and he gestures for me to enter.

"What's your address?" he asks, and I fidget.

"Hurry up," he says. I look down at my fingers.

"You can drop me at the nearest subway station," I say, and he hisses.

"Why, don't you want me to know where you live?" he says.

I scratch the back of my head.

"You must be tired. Shouldn't you go straight home and get some rest?" I say, and he smirks.

"I'm okay," he says.

I bite my bottom lip and sigh giving in, telling him my address, he puts the radio on, and we set off.

"This is the first car I bought using the money I saved working part-time jobs, before getting a record deal."

A bittersweet smile sweeps across his face.

"A lot of people wonder why I don't just buy a new car now that my circumstances have changed, but I'm going to keep it until the day it stops moving," he says.

"Why," I ask, and he turns to me.

"Because it reminds me of who I am, which keeps me grounded. This industry can really bring out the ugliest parts of people, but whenever I get into my car, I think of what it took to get here and what my goal was when I first bought it, and that's what keeps me going," he says.

"The more time I spend with you, the more you surprise me, Mr Dong-min," I say, and he chuckles.

"Hey, why are you still calling me Mr Dong-min? We are friends now, aren't we? Just call me Dong-min Oppa when we are alone," my eyes widen, and he smirks.

"Why do you look so shocked? Aren't we friends?" he asks, raising his brows.

"Well, I'm not too sure about that. I mean, how can I call you by your name."

I shake my head at the thought of it.

"What's wrong with that? We can be formal at work, but when it's just us, you can call me Dong-min Oppa."

I bite on my bottom lip as I look down at my fingers.

"Okay?" he mutters.

I give him a slight nod in response. Finally, we get to my building, and he puts on his face mask and hat.

"You don't have to come out," I say.

But he ignores me, walking out, and then runs, opening the door that is now stuck again, making me giggle. He finally manages to get it open, and I step out.

"Well, as you can see, I needed to help you with the door," he says, and I grin.

"Thank you for the ride, oo, oo, Oppa," I say, and he smiles.

"That's more like it, and it's me who's thankful, 'stress relief,' bye," he says, waving and I gasp.

"Are you really going to keep calling me that?" I ask, he nods and chuckles.

Then gets back in his car acting like a mischievous teenager. I giggle watching him drive off. Heading upstairs, I see the neighbourhood lady sitting on a bench outside.

"Good evening, Halmeoni," I say.

"Welcome home," she says. Waving her hand, gesturing that I come close.

"Was that your boyfriend?" she asks, teasing.

"Halmeoni, he's not," I say as my eyes widen.

"Ayyyy, you can tell me, is he handsome? I couldn't see his face," I shake my head continuously.

"Halmeoni, he's not my boyfriend, just someone I work with."

"He didn't seem like just a friend," she Mumbles.

"Halmeoni, I'll see you later," I say, rushing off.

"Okay, get some rest," she yells out.

How could she think Kim Dong-min is my boyfriend? I shrug off the thought and search for my keys finding Liam's handkerchief. I sigh, recalling how he let me fall. I wonder which is his true face. Finding my keys, I head in, take a shower, and make Ramen for dinner.

I set the table with kimchi and seaweed as side dishes. I love Korean food but miss Mum's pounded yam and Ogbono soup. Just thinking about it makes my mouth water. Soo-jin mentioned some African restaurants in Yongsan-gu, and I plan to check them out soon.

I slowly open my eyes to the bright morning light streaming through the windows. I stretch, feeling aches all over. It must be from running with Dong-min Oppa yesterday. I get into the office, and see Soo-jin waiting by the lift.

"Good morning," I say.

She glares at me as though holding back her annoyance. I gasp, as I recall leaving before helping her load up the equipment yesterday.

"I'm so sorry about yesterday, Miss Soo-jin. Did you get back okay," I ask as the doors to the lift open.

"I managed just fine by myself," she responds, sounding bitter.

She doesn't seem ready to accept my apology, and I can't blame her.

"I'll take the next lift," I say. The doors close and I exhale, and get on the next lift.

"Hold the door," I hear a voice calling out, and Rachel and her manager walk in.

"Good morning," I say.

Greeting them both, Rachel is wearing designer sunglasses with her hair tied up, a red blazer over her shoulder, a white midi dress, and red six-inch heels. She looks picture-perfect, and then I recall our last conversation.

"Rachel, erm, sorry, Miss Go Ae-ra," I rephrase after getting a death stare from her manager.

"Can I please speak to you for a moment?" I ask, as the lift opens.

"Maybe later," Rachel says as they walk out.

I follow them out, and Rachel stops turning to me.

"Mina," she calls.

"Huh," she walks in closer, taking off her glasses.

"How do you know Kim Dong-min? You guys seemed awfully close," she says, and my eyes widen.

"Oh, erm, we met here at the company coincidentally," I say, and she chuckles.

"Wow, you never cease to amaze me with that skill of yours," she says, and my brows frown.

"Our relationship is strictly professional," I say as my hands form into a fist.

"You don't have to explain yourself to me. I don't really care what goes on between you two. I was just surprised to see Dong-min so close with a staff member, that's all," she says.

Turning to leave but halts again, tilting her head towards me.

"By the way, who placed you on Liam Choi's team," she asks, my brows frown deeper.

"Mr Lee," I say. Her lips press into a hard line.

"Why do you ask," I say.

She sighs and walks off without responding. Soo-jin and I load our equipment onto the production van, and we head to the location for today's shoot. Upon arrival, we find the entrance blocked by N.O. and Go Ae-ra fans eager to catch a glimpse of them. It seems the press leaked the location. As we wait for security to clear the way, I look out the window at the overwhelming crowd. It must be challenging to always be watched and followed by so many people. For a moment, I find myself worrying about Liam Choi.

I quickly dismiss the thought; we enter the building finally and begin filming. After Liam's hair is done, we head for the changing room.

"My battery is low. I'll be right back; I left the spare battery in the van. I'll just grab it and meet you back at the changing room," Soo-jin says before heading off.

"Mr Choi, I'll walk ahead to ensure everything is ready," Liam's manager says, leaving. This is my window of opportunity to give him back the handkerchief. I take a deep breath pausing the camera.

"Excuse me," I say.

He turns suddenly, and I collide with him, hitting my head on his chest and stumbling backwards. He catches me, holding my waist. I squeeze my eyes shut, not again. Why do I always become clumsy whenever I'm around him?

"You're still as clumsy as ever," Liam says as he smirks.

I open my eyes, meeting his gaze, and we lock eyes. His smile is breathtaking, and I bite my lip, trembling under his gaze.

"Liam?" someone calls.

He lifts me back up immediately and lets go clearing his throat. Rachel walks in closer, glaring at us, and then grabs Liam's arm.

"What's going on here?" she asks.

But he doesn't respond, pulling his arm off and heading for the changing room.

"Maybe you can tell me what you were just doing with Liam?" she asks, with her eyes burning with fury, crossing her arms.

"Nothing, I was just…"

Before I can complete my sentence, Soo-jin arrives with the spare battery, and Rachel leans in.

"I don't know what game you're trying to play, but I won't let you get in my way this time," she says, barging into me as she walks off.

"What's wrong? Did you make a mistake?" Soo-jin asks, and I sigh, shaking my head.

"It's nothing. Let's go," I say.

We enter Liam's changing room and start filming. He avoids eye contact with me. After Liam's done getting into character, we head for the set.

"Mina," Rachel calls.

Soo-jin frowns, nudging me to go. I leave my camera on the stand and walk over to her; she's sitting on a couch beside Liam.

"I left my purse in my car. Can you go get it?" she asks, smirking.

Liam's lips press into a hard line, but he doesn't say anything.

"Ae-ra, I'll go get it," her manager insists, but she shakes her head.

"Unnie, I need you here. She can go get it, right Mina?" she asks.

I bite down my teeth and sigh, giving a slight bow before heading to the car. I get back with her purse and hand it to her, and she frowns.

"How stupid are you? Can't you follow a simple instruction? I said bring me my purse. Does this cheap crap look like something I would own," she says.

Throwing the bag at me. The whole room goes quiet as everyone stares at us. Her manager rushes over and picks up the bag.

"Oh, this is mine," she says, turning to Rachel.

"I'll get it for you Ae-ra. Please calm down, everyone's watching," her manager says.

"Mina, what are you still doing here? Get my bag now and get the right one this time."

Liam's hand forms a fist, but he doesn't interfere. I give her a slight bow and turn to leave, and find Kim Dong-min standing behind me, with his eyes burning with fury, and his lips pressed into a hard line. I bow, saying my greetings, turning to walk off, but he grabs my hand stopping me.

"You don't have to go," he says.

Chapter Twenty Two

"What do you think you're doing," Rachel asks getting up.

"That's what I'd like to ask, Ae-Ra, what the hell do you think you're doing," he says, then turns to Liam.

"And you, why aren't you saying anything? Isn't she one of the people on your team?" he asks.

Liam glares at him with his lips pressed into a hard line but doesn't respond.

"Mr Dong-min, please stop," I say.

Pulling my hands out of his, but his grip tightens, and he pulls me along, leading me off set.

"Where do you think you're going?" Rachel asks.

But he doesn't stop or respond. I lower my head, as everyone stares, we get to the hallway, and I pull my hands off his hold.

"Why? Why did you get involved and make things worse," I say, and his brows frown.

"I don't want to lose my job here, so I'd appreciate it if you don't get involved regardless of how anyone treats me. Doing so will only make things harder for me, don't you see that?" I say, before walking off.

Returning to Rachel's car, I continue searching and finally find her red designer bag in the booth. While walking back, my heart sinks for snapping at Dong-min. I know he meant well, but being involved with me would only jeopardise his career further.

They'd already started filming upon returning to the set, so I hand Rachel's bag to her manager. Then, I resume filming with my camera. Lunchtime arrives, and Soo-jin sits with her friends from the fashion department, while I find an empty table in the corner of the break room.

"Stress relief."

Dong-min approaches with his lunch tray, and I lower my head as the cast and crew watch us. He sits opposite me, but I keep my head down, squirming in my chair.

"Stress relief, why are you hiding? Just ignore them and eat your food comfortably," he says, and I sigh.

He grabs a piece of chicken from his plate, adding it to mine, I raise my head to meet his gaze, and he grins.

"About this morning, I'm sorry for making things difficult for you. I was only trying to help but made things worse. So, it won't happen again," he says, giving me a reassuring nudge.

"I'm sorry too. I know you were only trying to help, but don't worry about me. I'm fine," I say, and he exhales.

"Oh, thank goodness, I was so worried you'd still be mad at me," he says grinning.

"Enjoy your lunch," he says.

I nod in response, but I keep my head low.

"Just eat comfortably. You'll get indigestion," he scolds, and I sigh.

Lifting my head, we dig into our food.

"So, what are you doing after work? Want to go for drinks?" he asks.

I begin to choke. Dong-min gets up to pat my back as I cough.

"Are you okay?" he asks. I move his hands away as everyone stares.

"I'm okay," I say.

He heads back to his seat, but the cafeteria begins to echo with whispers.

"I can't get drinks with you," I whisper.

"Why not? We agreed you'd take responsibility for relieving my stress," he says.

"I don't remember agreeing to that; besides, isn't drinking just as bad as smoking," I say, rolling my eyes, and he chuckles.

"Don't mind if I join, do you?"

It's Rachel and Liam, Dong-min's brows frown, but I nudge him to back down. He sighs, moving his tray to sit next to me. Liam tries walking off, but Rachel pulls his arm to sit beside her with their trays in hand.

"Liam let's sit here," she insists.

Rachel sits facing me, while Liam faces Dong-min, the stares become more intense, and I lose my appetite.

"You both look good together, don't they, Liam?" she asks, turning to him.

But he doesn't respond. Instead, he glares at me with the most chilling expression.

"As I told you this morning, nothing is going on between us," I say.

Dong-min places his hands over mine, I turn to him, and he shakes his head.

"You don't have to explain yourself Mina," then he turns to Rachel.

"Ae-ra, that's enough," he says, and she chuckles.

"Well, you're right. She doesn't have to explain, but anyone can guess what's going on between you two, so be careful Dong-min; you can't handle any more scandals," she says, and he glares at her.

"Hey, give it a rest," he says.

She places her hands over her mouth.

"Oops, did I strike a nerve? Well, then, let's talk about something else. How about something Mina would like to know," she says.

All eyes fall on me.

"What did you want to ask this morning? I'm guessing it's about Joon, right," she says.

I lower my head, hiding my trembling hands underneath the table. This isn't a conversation I want to have in front of others.

"Who's Joon?" Dong-min asks.

Rachel is all too eager to respond.

"Mina's unrequited high school crush back in London."

Dong-min's eyes widen, and I swallow as my brows frown.

"Rachel, that's enough," Liam says, glaring at her as his hands form a fist.

"You both went to the same school in London?" Dong-min asks, stunned.

"I don't think this is a conversation we should be having here," I say.

"Well, it's now or never. This is my only free time, as you can see."

I squeeze my hands together as they stare at me, awaiting my response.

"Fine, I'll ask you a question then," she says, and I meet her gaze.

"If you were to see Joon right now, would you be able to recognise him right away?"

My brows frown at her silly question.

"Of course, I would," I say, and she chuckles.

"You would recognise him?" she repeats.

"Why wouldn't I? No matter how much he's changed over the years, I would still recognise him," I say.

She continues laughing, and Liam slams his chopsticks on the table, making us jump. Then he takes a sip of his water as his eyes burn with fury. Seemingly irritated by Rachel's line of questioning.

"That's enough," he says.

Suddenly, the thought crosses my mind, perhaps Rachel knows more about Joon than she's letting on.

"Rachel, do you really not know where they are?" I ask.

"What if I did? Do you think he'd want to see you again," she says, and my heart sinks.

"Rachel," Liam yells, getting up abruptly.

"Stop saying useless things," he mutters and walks off, but I ignore his outburst.

"Rachel, please, if you know anything, tell me. I just want to know if they're okay, that's all," I plead.

"I'll say this in English to save you from further embarrassment—your right. I'm still in contact with Joon," she says.

My heart drops, and my hands begin to tremble.

"Are you okay? What's wrong?" Dong-min asks, noticing my change in demeanour.

"What did you say to her?" he asks Rachel, as he doesn't understand English, and Rachel smirks.

"I'm fine," I tell Dong-min.

"Go on, Rachel, I'm listening," I murmur.

"Are you sure you want to hear more? It might hurt more than you think," she says.

I squeeze the napkin in my hand, bracing myself.

"It's fine. I've spent years looking for them. I would like to know," I say, and she nods.

"Honestly, when I first saw you, I was taken aback. Who would have guessed we'd meet again here in Seoul, let alone at my dad's company? So, when you asked about Joon and his family, I was flustered, so I lied," she pauses for a while, then continues.

"So that evening, I called Joon, saying I ran into you, and asked if he wanted to see you. I even offered to arrange for you guys to meet," she stops and sighs.

"But to my surprise, he said no, that he wanted nothing to do with you."

My eyes widen, and my lips press together fighting back my tears, as my whole world crumble. He must still hate me for leaving him back then. I wouldn't want to see me either if the roles were reversed.

"Stress relief, what's the matter?" Dong-min asks, unable to keep up with our conversation in English.

"Well, my break time's over. See you around," Rachel says.

Getting up to leave, then halts, turning to face me,

"Mina, Joon and his family are doing great. He's even got a girlfriend now. They've been seeing each other for a few years and are very happy, so don't worry about them anymore and move on with your own life," she says, walking off.

"Hey, Ae-ra, what did you say to her," Dong-min yells.

But she ignores him and carries on walking, my held-back tears come streaming down my cheeks.

"Here, drink this," Dong-min says, handing me a cup of water, and I take a sip.

Lunchtime is up, and we all make our way back to set.

"Mr Dong-min, can you please excuse me for a moment? I need the washroom," I say.

But stumbling as my legs grow numb, Dong-min grabs my shoulder, helping me steady myself.

"It's fine. I'm okay," I say.

I head to the bathroom, and sit, hugging my knees and sobbing. I can't believe Joon Oppa doesn't want to see me. I try to stifle my tears when I hear someone enter the bathroom.

This is the price I pay for leaving ten years ago. What was I expecting? That he would have waited for me all these years? I must be crazy, my phone vibrates again, and I see six missed calls from Soo-jin, with a text message.

"Where are you? Get here now."

I quickly compose myself and return to the set. Rachel's insouciant between takes, but I remain pusillanimous. I turn my lens to Dong-min, and his gaze is fixed on me, and I read his lips.

"Are you okay?" he murmurs. I force a smile and nod in response.

In hindsight, I'm relieved that Joon and his family are doing well. After we're done filming, Soo-jin and I pack up our equipment.

"Stress relief," Dong-min calls, waiting by his car.

He walks over, and I keep my head down. I just want to go home and hide under my blanket. Dong-min gasps, placing his hands on my shoulders.

"How about we switch roles today," he says, and I raise my brows.

He takes my hand and guides me to his car, playfully struggling to open the door, which makes me giggle. After a few more pretend struggles, he finally opens the car door, and we drive away. To avoid being recognised by Dong-min's fans or reporters, I lower my seat as we approach the gate.

"Where are we going?" I ask, and he chuckles.

"Just trust and follow my lead. Today, I'll be your stress relief," he says, grinning.

We drive for a while then he stops by a convenience store.

"Wait here. I'll be right back," he says.

Dong-min puts on his hat and facemask and heads into the store. After a while, he returns holding bags, placing them in the back. We drive a while longer and eventually arrive at a forest. He grabs the bags, and we exit the car.

"What's in the bag?" I ask.

He opens it up to show me, and I smirk.

"You bought alcohol," I say.

He nods, and I shake my head.

"I got it for your sake, not mine," he says, smirking.

He grabs a blanket from the booth, handing it to me.

"Let's go," he says.

We venture into the woods, following a path adorned with big trees, each tagged with names and wrapped in fairy lights. Dong-min walks ahead, clearing the way by moving rocks. The forest feels enchanted, but there's a hint of despair lingering, but I resist the urge to ask where we're going. As we pass each tree, I notice flowers beside them, suggesting it might be a memorial ground.

"There he is."

Dong-min says as he halts, placing the drinks beside a tree.

"Who is it?" I ask.

He grins, facing a tree-tagged Kim Yoo-jung.

"It's my drinking buddy, my dad," he says.

I froze, staring at the tree wide-eyed, and exhale walking in closer and placing my hands on it.

"He's real steady, isn't he," Dong-min says, and I nod in response.

"Yes, he is," I say, then step back and bow.

"Hello, Mr Kim. It's an honour to meet you," I say.

"Dad, how lucky are you to have such a beautiful lady visit you," he says.

I gasp at his comment, and he chuckles. Dong-min collects the blanket, laying it beside the tree.

"Here," he says.

Handing me a glass, he opens a bottle of Soju and fills my glass, then his.

"Cheers," he says.

I take my shot in one go, feeling the burn in my chest. Then I scan the area to ensure no one is nearby to take our picture, but it looks like we're the only ones here.

"Don't worry, it's usually empty at night, so relax," he says.

"Ahhh," I nod in response.

I take another sip, as thoughts of Dad fill my mind. I hold onto my star pendant recalling the night I forgot Dad's death anniversary. I lie down on the blanket, gazing at the stars, just like Joon and I did that day.

"Do you miss him?" Dong-min asks.

Lying next to me, I turn to face him.

"Joon… the person Ae-ra was talking about, is he the reason your sad?" he asks.

I sigh as tears begin to build up.

"Well, I've spent the last few years looking for him. He's also part of the reason why I came to South Korea."

I stop to catch my breath as the aching in my heart worsens.

"But he said he doesn't want to see me. I've finally found him, after searching for the last ten years, but he wants nothing to do with me," I say.

My tears start falling non-stop, Dong-min sits up.

"What an asshole. Why are you crying over a jerk like that?" he asks, and I sit up.

"No, it's me who's the jerk. I understand why he wouldn't want to see me again," I say, grabbing a can of beer, drinking it halfway.

"Go easy. You'll get drunk," he says, and I sigh.

"The last time I saw him, I hurt him really bad due to a misunderstanding," I say.

"But still, he should've at least given you a chance to explain," he says.

I gasp, chugging down the rest of the beer, then pick up another can.

"Slow down," Dong-min says.

After chugging through a few drinks, I start feeling numb.

"I think you've had enough now; the replacement driver is waiting by the car. Let's get going," he says.

But I struggle to get up, and after stumbling a few times, I finally get on my feet.

"Mr Kim, it was nice to meet you," I mumble.

Bowing, but lose my balance stumbling, and Dong-min grabs my arm for support.

"Can you walk?" he asks.

I nod, but I stumble again and Dong-min sighs, then grabs my hands.

"This won't do," he says.

Then leans down in front of me, pulling my hands, and I land on his back.

"You don't have to carry me; I can walk," I protest, swinging my feet and urging him to put me down.

"No way. If I let you walk, we won't leave this place until dawn."

I don't resist any further. His back feels warm and comforting, bringing back memories of Joon's back as we rode on his bike. Tears begin streaming down my cheeks again.

"Joon Oppa, I'm here," I murmur, sobbing.

"Joon Oppa, I'm sorry… I'm so sorry," I say, slowly drifting off.

"Stress relief, stress relief, wake up."

I hear Dong-min call out. I open my eyes and look around.

"Wake up, we're at your place," he helps me out of the car.

"What happened? How did we get here?" I ask, feeling more alert.

"You're one sleepy drunk," he says.

Giving me a cheeky smile, I cover my face as I flush, and he gently moves my hands away.

"No need to be embarrassed. I think we're past that now," he says.

I keep my head down, unable to face him.

"I hope I didn't make any mistake," I say.

"Not at all, so don't worry. Do you need help getting upstairs?" he asks. I shake my head.

"No, no, I'll be fine. Ahhh!" I yelp, feeling dizzy from shaking my head a bit too fast.

"Are you okay," he reaches out his hands.

"I'm okay. I'm so sorry for being a burden," I say, and he grins.

"You're not silly. Good night, get some rest," he says.

"Good night," I respond, bowing.

I head upstairs, he waves as I look back, and then he drives away. I go straight to bed, grateful that the alcohol helps me forget today's events as I doze off.

My alarm goes off, and I hit the snooze button for the third time. My head is throbbing, and I have the worst hangover.

After getting ready, I rush to the bus stop but get caught in the drizzle without an umbrella. On the bus, I check Liam's handkerchief and exhale, finding it unscathed. The rain stops by the time I reach my stop. At the office, everyone is busy preparing for today's shoot.

"Good morning," I greet.

"Oh, Mina, you're soaked. Shouldn't you get changed first," Mrs Kim says.

"It's fine, I'll dry up soon. I don't want to be the reason we end up late," I mutter.

"But what if you catch a cold?" she asks, and I shake my head.

"It's just summer showers. The sun will dry me up soon; there's no need to worry," I say, and she nods hesitantly.

Today, the number of fans waiting has doubled, holding Liam Choi, Kim Dong-min, and Go Ae-ra posters. We finally get in and I set up my camera in the makeup room, while Soo-jin heads off to bring the rest of our equipment.

I take out the handkerchief from my backpack and approach Liam, who is sitting on the makeup chair wearing headphones, so I stretch my hands before him. He lifts his head, gaping at me, unplugging his headphones.

"Here, thank you for lending it to me."

He glares at the handkerchief and my wet clothes, but he doesn't take it. So, I press it into his hand, just as we hear approaching footsteps. His face grows grim, but he pockets it, plugging back his headphones, and I head back to my position. Soo-jin and the makeup team arrive, and we start filming.

There's a knock on the door, and I open it to find Kim Dong-min.

"Hey, stress relief," he says.

All eyes are on us. I bite my bottom lip, lowering my head.

"What's up with your clothes? They're completely damp," he says.

Then takes off his jumper, wrapping it around me. My eyes widen, lifting my hand to remove it, but he holds me still.

"Just wear it. What if you catch a cold and get sick," he says.

"Are we done here," Liam yells, seemingly agitated.

Chapter Twenty Three

"Yes," the makeup artist says.

He storms out of the room, and Soo-jin and I quickly follow. Despite his fast pace, we managed to keep up. As we walk, we encounter Rachel and her manager. She smiles when she sees Liam, but her expression turns sour seeing me.

"Mina!" she calls.

Then Liam suddenly turns, facing Soo-jin and me, giving me a stern look that sends chills down my spine.

"You!" he says.

"Aren't you a runner and a production assistant on my team?" he asks, and I nod, blinking rapidly.

"Yes, I am," I say, and he tilts his head and folds his arms.

"Then, shouldn't you focus on your job instead of fooling around running other people's errands? You need to stay focused on me to do your job properly," he scolds, and I nod profusely.

I lower my head and clench my fists. What has come over him suddenly?

"I'm sorr…" he cuts me off.

"I guess I need to make better use of you since you can't seem to focus on what you've been hired to do," he says.

I do my best to fight back my tears, as I listen.

"I need you to run some errands," he says.

I catch a glimpse of Rachel trying but failing to hide her amusement, but I don't let them get to me. So, I muster up enough courage to force a smile.

"What would you like me to do, Mr Choi?" I ask.

Sounding as enthusiastic as I could manage, he clears his throat,

"First, I'm thirsty. Go get me some water but ensure it's at room temperature."

I nod and head to the break room, grab a water bottle, and return to set. When the director says cut, I take the water to Liam.

"Here it is," I say.

Handing him the bottle, he touches the bottle and pushes it back.

"I asked for room temperature, not lukewarm. Take it back, and bring the right one," he says, and Rachel chuckles.

I touch the bottle and it is at room temperature. I glare at Liam wide-eyed, clenching my teeth to stay composed.

"I'm sorry, I'll get another one," I say, with a slight bow.

I grab another bottle, aiming for a cooler temperature and pass it to him, but he rejects it. I clench my teeth, exhale, and head off again. Looking back, a tortured look sweeps his face as he sighs deeply.

Rachel gapes at him with her lips falling into a hard line, and my brows frown. I'm the one being tortured. Why does he look haunted? I shake off the thought and return with a new bottle, as Dong-min arrives to film his scene.

"Is it so hard to get a simple task, right?" Liam asks, and I shake my head.

"I'm sorry," I say.

I take deep breaths, feeling myself reach my limit.

"Go back and get what I asked for," he says.

Dong-min approaches, but I shake my head, silently urging him to stay out of it. He stops, exhaling and gives me a stern glare.

"I'll get another one," I say, hopping off.

Liam's demands and eccentricities persist for a day and throughout the week. I find myself doing various odd tasks, from collecting his dry cleaning to acting as a personal hand fan during his breaks on set.

Yesterday, he presented me with a large bag of Skittles, insisting I separate out the green ones. Work is becoming far from what I had anticipated. And today, I'm roped into practising lines with him during breaks in filming.

"Miss Mina, Miss Mina," he calls, bringing me out of my thoughts.

"Yes, Mr Choi."

"It's your turn," he says, asking me to say my lines.

"You promised that we would recognise each other's hearts, but when you saw me, you walked right past me. I was right in front of you, right before your eyes, but you walked right past me."

I recite my lines, awaiting Liam's response, but he stays quiet. I lift my gaze from the script and see his intense, pained stare as if he's suppressing tears. My heart aches as I watch him. A strange feeling stares within me as I watch him.

"Are you okay?" I ask.

He breaks eye contact with me and turns away.

"That's enough for today," he says.

Slamming the script on the table and walking off, I head to the break room for water.

"Stress relief," Dong-min calls, waving.

I wave back but start coughing. It's been a few days now, and my cough won't go.

"Are you okay? Sounds like you're coming down with something," he says, handing me a bottle of water.

"Thank you," I mutter.

"Where have you been lately? I haven't seen you around?" he asks.

"Working hard," I say.

His brows frown, attempting to protest but holding back.

"Hey, love birds," Rachel mutters, smirking.

"Are you sure nothing is going on between you guys?" she asks, crossing her arms.

"Ae-ra, give it a rest already," Dong-min mutters and I sigh.

"Mina, I need a favour, seeing as you have nothing better to do," she says.

My brows frown, but I clench my teeth composing myself.

"Go Ae-ra, that's enough," Dong-min yells.

"What, am I wrong? She's just hanging around," she smirks.

"Mina, what are you still doing here."

All eyes shift to Liam as he enters, his glare locked onto me with seething fury. He stands before me, his breath heavy and tense.

"Why are you both always ganging up on her?" Dong-min asks.

"Come with me now," Liam says and storms out.

I trail after him immediately, in the hallway. He abruptly turns, gripping my shoulders, and a cold shiver courses through me. His eyes burn with rage. He sighs deeply, inhales, closing his eyes, reopening them, his expression softens, and I release a pent-up breath. Suppressing a cough, I manage to keep it at bay.

"Here," he says, handing me a credit card.

"Get me iced coffee."

My brows frown. I gaze out the window at the coffee cart sent by his fans, and he trails my gaze.

"Not from there," he mutters.

"I only drink coffee from a little cafe in Dobong-gu," my eyes widen.

It's a two-hour journey from the office.

"Is there a reason why you can't go?" he asks, and I shake my head.

"No but I need to help Soo-jin with filming," I say.

He looks around and spots Soo-jin at a distance.

"Miss Soo-jin," he calls, and she comes running.

"Can you handle things here while she runs an errand for me?" he asks.

With a cheerful smile, she turns tomato red, nodding profusely.

"Well, that's sorted," he says.

Turning back to face me and I notice Soo-jin's face fall.

"Here," he hands me a pink business card.

"It's called Zodiac Cafe. The address is on the card. You can't miss it. When you get there, ask for Jenny the Aquarius," he smirks.

Seemingly amused. His face lights up as he continues.

"Get her to make the Aries special on the secret menu. That way, she'll know I sent you," I nod.

"Liam, you're needed back on set," his manager calls out.

"Coming," he says.

"Make sure you get back before the ice melts, and it has to be made by Jenny and no one else," he emphasises.

He walks off flashing a boyish grin, and I'm momentarily caught off guard by his swift shift in demeanour. Why is he so thrilled about coffee, and who exactly is this "Jenny" their familiarity suggests he's a regular. Then I'm reminded he's an Aries. Well, that might explain a few things.

"Mina!" Rachel calls, appearing with Dong-min beside her.

"Sorry, I need to run an errand for Liam. Let's talk when I get back," I say, rushing off.

The best thing about Liam's errands is avoiding Rachel and her petty tantrums. I race to the train station, and my train arrives after a few minutes of waiting. I find a seat and plug in my headphones, then thoughts of Liam's outburst earlier in the break room flashback, and then my brows frown, recalling how giddy he was speaking of Jenny.

"Excuse me, excuse me."

I hear a distant voice calling, my eyes spring open, and it's the train conductor.

"Miss, this is the last stop," he says.

I gasp, leaping up. I had overslept and missed my stop. I rush off the train and race up the stairs, but in my haste, I step on my loose shoelace and trip over, scrapping my knee.

"Ahhh!" I yelp, a member of staff rushes over to help.

"You're bleeding," he says. "Its fine," I mutter and carry on running.

I get on the next available train limping my way in. This time, I stand, holding on to the strap for balance. Another hour goes by, and I finally get to the right stop, and hop off the train. I spot a couple holding pink coffee cups with the logo on the business card Liam gave me. I approach them asking for directions.

"Just walk down this road and turn right," the lady says.

"Thank you," I reply with a bow.

I follow her directions and spot a pink sign saying, "Zodiac Cafe." It's small but charming, radiating a cosy and vibrant atmosphere, surrounded by pink flowers.

Stepping inside, I'm greeted by a pastel pink interior, adorned with zodiac-themed writings on the walls. The menu offers coffees named after each zodiac sign. There are writings on the wall detailing traits of each zodiac sign reminding me of Ji-won eliciting a bittersweet smile.

Two servers, in pink tops with zodiac signs, stand at the counter—a "Virgo" and a "Scorpio." Virgo is tall with sandy blonde hair, while Scorpio is petite with a black bob haircut. Both are perhaps too stunning to be servers. I ponder which one is Jenny.

"Hello, what would you like to order?" Scorpio asks with a sweet smile.

"Eh, hi, erm, is Jenny in?" I ask.

"Aquarius?" Scorpio murmurs, looking over at Virgo.

"Is there a problem? Please wait a moment?" Virgo mutters, and nods at Scorpio, who disappears to the back room.

My brows furrow more intrigued about Jenny's identity. Shortly after, a middle-aged lady emerges alongside Scorpio, wearing a manager's tag with Sagittarius written on her shirt. She can't be Jenny, as Scorpio called Jenny an Aquarius earlier.

"Hello, was there a problem with the coffee Aquarius… I mean, Jenny made you," she mutters.

"Oh no, not at all. I was sent to get coffee specifically made by Aquarius. I mean Jenny," I say.

They glare at me wide-eyed, as their jaws drop.

"Hold on, so you mean someone specifically asked for Jenny to make them coffee, not to make a complaint about her coffee?" the manager asks, stunned. I nod.

"He said it has to be from Jenny and no one else," I say, and they gasp.

"Is he of sound mind?" Scorpio asks.

Virgo nudges her to be quiet. My brows frown, puzzled by their response.

"Unfortunately, Jenny left a while ago due to an emergency, and I'm not sure when or if she will be back today," the manager says.

I sigh, running my hands through my hair. I'll be done for if I go back without his coffee.

"How about we make the coffee instead? I can assure you it will taste much better," the manager says.

I consider the idea briefly but dismiss it. If he discovers someone else made it, he'll insist I return. So, I decide to wait and save myself the trouble.

"Do you have any idea when she'll be back?" I ask.

"No, we don't, sorry."

I sigh, retrieving my phone to call Soo-jin and inform her of my delay, but my phone is dead. I start pacing, considering my options. Even if I ask to borrow someone else's phone, I don't have the numbers of the staff members memorised, and no one here seems to have the same phone model as mine to borrow a charger.

I can't return without the coffee, so I take a seat and wait for Jenny. My stomach growls as I missed lunch, but I can't risk missing her. I gaze through the glass wall, watching people pass by.

"Excuse me, Miss."

I open my eyes, and it's Virgo. I look around, and gasp, seeing it's gone dark out, and I'm still at the cafe. I must have dozed off.

"What about Jenny? Is she back yet?" I ask Virgo.

"Sorry, I don't think she'll be back today, but she should be in tomorrow if you would like to come back. But we're closing now."

I close my eyes and sigh. I can envision the trouble I'll be in when I return.

"Well, thanks for your help," I say and leave.

I limp towards the traffic light, feeling sore all over, my cough now worse. As the light turns amber, a motorbike abruptly stops in front of me. I step back hastily, and the biker pulls over to the side of the road, approaching me.

"Miss Mina, are you okay?" a familiar voice asks.

My eyes widen, stepping back.

He looks around then lifts the face shield on his helmet, and I gasp, lowering my head. Although I can only see his eyes, I can tell it's him.

"What happened? Why didn't you come back, and why the hell is your phone switched off? Do you know how worried I've been," he says.

He grips my shoulders, and I raise my head, meeting his gaze blinking rapidly. His eyes are filled with concern, and my eyebrows furrow taken aback by his unexpected reaction. I anticipated being scolded, yet he seems more concerned about my well-being.

"Mina, Mina," he calls out, shaking me.

"Are you okay?" he asks.

I nod, and he exhales.

"I'll take you home. Here, put this on."

He removes his jacket and places it around me, then holds my hands and rubs them to warm them up. I stare at him, lost for words. It all seems surreal; another side of Liam I wasn't expecting.

"I'm okay," I mutter.

Trying to reassure him, and his eyes soften, I'm puzzled by his sudden shift in attitude, but relieved not to be reprimanded for once. He pauses, his face contorting as if a realisation has struck him.

"Why didn't you just come back when you heard she wasn't here? Why didn't you just leave, you dummy?" he asks, sounding agitated.

I sigh. The kind and sweet Liam act didn't last long.

"Well, you said you wanted your coffee made only by Jenny and no one else, and I knew if I came back empty-handed, you'd make me come back," I say as my brows frown.

His shoulders sink, and he sighs heavily. The tortured look returns, making my heart ache.

"I just wanted to do well this time, so I'm not looked down on by you," I say. His eyes widen, seemingly taken aback.

"When have I ev…" he stops, mid-sentence and exhales.

"All week, you've done nothing but torture and patronise me, criticising and looking down on everything I do," I say.

Fighting back the tears building up, thinking back on the hardship I'd been through because of him.

"Being a star doesn't give you the right to look down on others or treat them like they don't matter."

Clutching the jacket's edge, my hands quiver. What's come over me? What if I lose my job for speaking to him rudely? He stays silent for a while. And I avoid his gaze, and then he chuckles suddenly.

"Feeling better?" he asks, seemingly amused.

Then he leans down to meet my gaze, and I freeze, holding my breath.

"I'm sorry I made you feel that way. I was only trying to…." He stops mid-sentence again.

Then he shakes his head and sighs. A smile adorns his beautiful eyes. I exhale, turning away, as my heart pounds wildly.

He repositions himself to face me, and I find myself holding my breath again. His eyes capture my attention, evoking a potent yet familiar sensation.

This feeling isn't abrupt; it's been there since our first encounter. There's an uncanny familiarity about him, and when his gaze meets mine, it's like being ensnared by a spell.

"Breathe, Mina," he says.

Placing his hands on my shoulders, and my heart contracts.

"Let's go," he says. Grabbing hold of my hands, leading me to his bike.

"You don't have to drop me…. ahhh!" I yelp.

As I take a step on my injured leg, I'd completely forgotten about my bruised knee.

"What's wrong? Are you hurt?" he asks, leaning down to examine my leg.

"Does it hurt a lot? How did you get hurt? How long has it been bleeding?" he asks.

Sounding both annoyed and concerned, I can't keep up with Liam's constant change of mood.

"Get on my back. Let's go to the hospital," he says.

Leaning down in front of me, and I get a flashback of Joon's back. He always carried me on his back whenever I got hurt.

"What are you waiting for? Get on," Liam insists, and I shake my head, stepping back.

"I'm okay. It's just a graze," I say, and he gets back up.

"What do you mean you're okay? Can't you see it bleeding," he says.

"It's just a bit of blood. This is nothing compared to how much I used to get hurt as a kid," I say.

He sighs, then takes my arm, wrapping it around his neck, and my eyes widen.

"I'll help you," he says.

He leads me to the nearest bench. I take a seat, and he reaches into his pocket, taking out his handkerchief. He folds it and leans down in front of me, staring at my now ripped jeans stained with blood and wraps the handkerchief around it.

Chapter Twenty Four

As his fingers touch my leg, I inhale sharply, blinking rapidly. He completes tying the knot, but his gaze lingers on my knee, his expression reflecting more concern than necessary. A fleeting impulse to pat his hair surfaces, but I suppress it. Then my stomach growls, and I cough to mask the sound. Things will only worsen if he finds out I starved while waiting.

"Are you okay?" he asks.

Then gets back up, placing his hands on my forehead, and I freeze, staring at him wide eye. Then I move my head away from his reach, squirming.

"I'm fine," I say.

"This won't do. Let's go. I'll drop you home," he says.

He offers his hands to help me up, and though I hesitate, I accept, aware he won't back down easily. After reaching his bike, he places the spare helmet on me and ensures it's snugly secured. We set off. Riding on a motorcycle for the first time, I conceal my jitters by clutching the top of his shirt rather than his waist.

"Hold on to me properly," he yells out.

I grip his shirt tighter as we halt at a traffic light. He reaches back and guides my hands around his waist. As the light turns green, we speed up. Having my arms around Liam Choi is surreal, but I decide to relax and enjoy the ride as the wind brushes against us. His back radiates warmth and comfort.

Familiar sights pass by, and I realise he knows the way to my home despite not informing him. We reach the alley near my building, and he stops the bike, helping me dismount.

"Erm, thanks for the ride," I mutter.

"You have a first aid kit, don't you? Make sure you clean your wound when you get in," he says, and I nod.

Then he reaches his hands out, but I shake my head.

"Don't worry, I can manage alone," I say, and he sighs.

"Helmet," he says.

Reaching his hands out, I gasp, realising I still have it on.

"Ahhh, sorry, here you go," I undo the straps and hand the helmet over to him.

"Good night," he says, smirking.

He places the shield on his helmet back on and takes off. My brows frown as I tilt my head watching him drive away. How does he know I own a first aid kit? I sigh, shaking off the thought. As I turn to ascend the stairs, I'm startled by the neighbourhood Halmeoni.

"Was that your boyfriend?" she asks.

"Definitely not Halmeoni. Good night," I say.

I hurry up the stairs to avoid more questions and fumble for my keys. I notice I'm still wearing Liam's baseball jacket, and I let out a sigh. Once inside, I drop my bag and collapse onto my bed, reflecting on my utterly chaotic day.

Liam's varying expressions linger in my mind. And how did he know my address? I sigh, dismissing the thought, then charge my phone, which revives after a few minutes. There are over thirty missed calls from an unknown number, five from Soo-jin, and numerous texts from the repeated number. I check the text messages.

Message one: "Miss Mina, where are you?"

Message two: "Are you okay? Why aren't you picking up?"

Message three: "Just come back. She isn't in today. I should have checked before asking you to go."

And the last one reads, "I'm sorry."

The others request a callback. From the context of the text messages, it must be Liam Choi. My eyes widen, and I gasp. He must have gotten my number from Soo-jin. Then my phone buzzes again. It's another text from the same number.

"Make sure you clean your wound, Miss Mina. Sleep well, LC," my heart constricts as I read it.

I sit up, reading each text repeatedly. What's his intention? Running my hands through my hair, I decide to comply and follow his instructions, feeling like I'm being watched.

Grabbing my first aid kit, I clean my wound while thoughts of Joon Oppa flood my mind. He and Liam Choi's similarity in swift mood changes strike me. Clutching my shirt, I ache at the thought of not seeing Joon and Ji-won.

"Ahem, ahem."

My cough worsens, and I head to the bathroom to wash Liam's handkerchief, hanging it to dry. Then carefully hang his baseball jacket in my wardrobe, pondering when I'll get a chance to return it. Shivering, I crawl into bed, too weak to cook. Wrapped in my duvet, my mind drifts into sleep.

Morning arrives, and my alarm persists, but I keep snoozing it. Feeling weak and feverish, I eventually rise, battling body aches. I consider calling in sick, but shake off the thought, I can't afford to skip work. Especially as I never returned yesterday, I can't leave Soo-jin on her own again today.

I grab my phone and gasp at the time. Rushing to the bathroom, I sigh, noticing my monthly visitor has arrived, an added layer of complexity to my day.

After a deep sigh, I step into the shower, insert a tampon, and get dressed. I tie my hair in a bun and hurry out, skipping breakfast.

I limp to the bus stop, my knee's improved but still aches. I catch the bus just in time. As my cramps worsen, I grip the handrail. Then, a seat frees up; I grab it, crouching as the pain intensifies. I consider getting off at the next stop for painkillers, but I can't risk being late. Entering the office, I anticipate getting scolded, but everyone's preoccupied. Then I spot Mr Park approaching so I inhale, bracing myself.

"Miss Mina, did you get home okay yesterday? Liam said he sent you on an errand that had you out till late."

I stare at him, blinking rapidly.

"Ah yes, I got home okay," I mutter.

"Good, go help Soo-jin get the equipment in the van. We'll be leaving in twenty minutes," he says.

I nod, bow slightly, and then head off to meet Soo-jin.

"Good morning," I mutter.

Soo-jin looks up at me, rolling her eyes, and my heart sinks.

"I'm so sorry about leaving you with all the workload yesterday. Something came up at the coffee shop," I say.

She holds her hands up to stop me.

"Forget it," she says. Handing me a camera bag.

"Let's go," she mutters. My head sinks as we head out.

I sigh, lost on how to make it up to her.

"Ahhh!" I yelp.

Slouching down as my cramps attack, Soo-jin turns back, scrolling at me. I stand up straight, moving my hands from my belly.

"It's nothing. I'm okay," I say.

She rolls her eyes and looks away. During our ride to the set, I struggle to endure the cramps. The road's bumps amplify the pain. Once the harsh ride concludes, we disembark from the van and unload our gear.

"Miss Mina, are you okay?" Mr Park asks.

Noticing me crouching down constantly, I get back up instantly.

"You're breaking out in cold sweats," he says.

I dab my forehead with sweaty palms, realising I have a fever. I consider admitting to being ill and requesting a day off, but Soo-jin gives me a death stare as she passes stopping me.

"I wet my face with a bit of water earlier. It's nothing," I say.

He hesitates but accepts my explanation. In the makeup room, Liam rests in the makeup chair with closed eyes as his face is worked on. After exchanging greetings, we start filming.

My cramps persist, and I clutch the tripod for support. I'm deciding to wait until break time to get painkillers, but I'm also starting to feel nauseous. Mum claimed period pain would ease with age, yet it's worsening. A sharp cramp makes me hiss, drawing everyone's attention. I cough, playing it off.

"Miss Mina, are you okay?" the makeup artist asks.

"You don't look too well," she adds.

I shake my head, wipe my forehead, putting on a grin.

"It's nothing," I say.

Soo-jin places her hands on my shoulders with a fake smile.

"Miss Mina, do you need a break?" she asks, putting on a show.

"No, I'm okay," I reply as my smile fades.

I notice Liam glaring at me from the mirror, and his frown deepens.

"Miss Mina," Liam calls.

I lift my head, teeth clenched, dreading the task he might give me. The memory of my outburst yesterday strikes, and I gasp. Is this payback? Can't handle more hurdles, but I must comply to keep my job.

"Yes, Mr Choi," I respond, as politely as I can manage.

"I need you to get a list of things for me," he says.

I gasp, a list of things. I bite down on my teeth.

"The list is in my dressing room. I'll give it to you when we leave," he adds.

I stubble a bit, holding on to a chair nearby for balance. Luckily, no one noticed. It seems Liam's gone back to being cold and icy. He must have a dissociative identity disorder; I ponder in silence.

"Are we done here?" Liam asks the makeup artist, who nods, and he gets up.

"Let's go," he says.

Soo-jin and I follow him out of the room. As we walk to his dressing room, he stops, turning to Soo-jin.

"Miss Soo-jin, right?" he asks, and she nods, grinning.

"Can you go ahead and set up? I'll be there in a minute, just need to give Miss Mina some instructions first," he says.

Flashing a sugary smile at her, Soo-jin, helpless against Liam's charms, nods and heads off to set. Then his gaze shifts to me, and his smile fades away.

"Follow me," he says with a chilling tone.

As we move along the corridor, I take slow steps, battling a growing nausea while maintaining my composure. We enter his dressing room, and his displeasure dissolves into concern as he faces me. He walks over, placing a hand on my forehead, his eyes widening as they meet mine.

"You're burning up," he says.

Then grabs my hand, leading me to the nearby couch to sit.

"Why didn't you just stay home and rest if you're ill," he scolds.

I leap up, feeling a sudden urge to vomit.

"Bathroom, where is the toilet," I ask, with my hands over my mouth as I gag.

"Woah, this way," he says.

I rush to the bathroom, lifting the toilet seat to vomit. Despite not eating since yesterday, a lot comes out. Liam stands behind me, holding my hair. After a while, my stomach eases. I sit, breathing heavily. He hands me a tissue to wipe my mouth.

"This won't do. You need to go to the hospital, or should I call an ambulance?" he asks.

Reaching for his phone, making me chuckle, and he halts.

"Did I say something funny?" he asks, staring at me, puzzled.

"No, you just remind me of someone who once reacted the same way."

I sigh as thoughts of Joon flood my mind, and then we both freeze, hearing the door to the dressing room open.

"Liam, are you in the bathroom? It's almost call time."

"Shhh, it's my manager," he says.

Another wave of vomit hits, and I can't hold it despite his glare urging me to hold it in. I lunge for the toilet bowl. Liam rushes to the door and locks it.

Knock, knock, knock.

"Liam, are you okay? Are you unwell?"

Amidst his manager's persistent knocking on the door, my stomach gradually settles, with nothing left to expel.

"Lean against the wall," Liam murmurs, and I comply.

Then he unlocks the door, opening it slightly.

"Do you have a fever? How bad is it? Let me see how you're doing," his manager says.

"Hyung, I'll be fine. Can you get me some painkillers, fever reducer and something for nausea?" he asks.

"Is that all you need? Don't we need to go to a hospital?" his manager asks, and he nods.

"I'll be fine with just those; just tell the director I'll be there a little late," he adds.

"Okay, just wait a bit. I'll be right back, hang in there," his manager mutters before heading off.

I exhale and head to the sink to rinse my mouth.

"I should leave before he gets back," I say.

Walking towards the door, he stands before me, blocking my way.

"Where do you think you're going?" he asks.

I lift my head to meet his gaze; somehow, he looks more troubled than I do.

"Just stay here and get some rest; don't worry about anything else," he insists, and I shake my head.

"What if your manager or someone else sees us together, causing a misunderstanding? I don't want to cause you trouble," I say.

Opening the bathroom door, and he grabs my arm.

"Just stay here. I'll make sure no one comes in. Can't you trust me?" he asks.

I sigh, lowering my head, beginning to waver.

"If you get back out there in this condition, you might end up passing out, which means I won't be able to focus on anything, worrying about you," he murmurs.

Meeting his concerned gaze, I'm puzzled by Liam Choi's enigmatic nature. His dual personalities are at play. His true motive remains cryptic, his unexpected kindness unclear. As the pain intensifies, making standing unbearable, I comply with his request to stay.

"Here, lay down," he says.

Knowing what I need without asking, leading me to the nearby couch. Perhaps he has sisters. I squeeze hold of the

Corner of the couch tightly as another cramp hits. He places his hands over my forehead.

"You're still burning up," he says.

He attempts to rise, but I clutch his hands tightly, enduring the escalating pain. As it subsides slightly, I let go, and he hurries to the bathroom, returning with a damp towel. Kneeling beside me, he rests it on my forehead, and I flinch at the cold temperature.

"Sorry, this will bring down your temperature," he says.

"The door," he murmurs.

Then leaps up to lock it. A few moments later, there's a pull at the handle, and I sit up, alarmed, but he pulls my shoulders back down.

"It's fine," he mutters.

He then walks over to open it just enough to slide his hands through.

"Hyung, the meds?" he asks.

"Let me in," his manager insists, pushing the door.

"Hyung, it's fine. I'm just a little embarrassed by the mess I created," Liam says.

"What do you mean? There's no need to be embarrassed with me," he says.

"Hyung, I'm sorry, I just want to be alone," his manager sighs, passing him a plastic bag.

"Can you tell the director I'll be out in twenty minutes," he says.

"I will. I got you a sandwich too. Make sure you eat it before taking the meds," he insists.

"Hyung, thank you," he says, shutting the door and locking it.

I exhale, and he rushes back to me, helping me sit up.

"Here, take a bite," he commands.

Holding the sandwich against my mouth, I shake my head lacking appetite.

"You need to eat something to take the meds," he says.

I take a few bites of the cheese sandwich, and he hands me the tablets and a water bottle.

"Stay seated for a bit so that the medicine can take effect," he says, and I nod, he smiles warmly and exhales.

"I must head back no set in a bit. Make sure you stay here and get some rest. Okay, I'll come and check on you from time to time," he swallows, hesitating to leave.

Then he raises his hands and parts my hair gently.

"Don't be sick, okay? It hurts to see you in pain," he murmurs.

As my eyes grow heavy, I succumb to drowsiness, slipping into slumber. As I awaken, everything appears hazy. Unable to decipher if this is real or a dream. Someone's seated beside me, with his head bowed. I extend my hand, running my fingers through his hair. His head lifts, and my heart quickens. It's Joon Oppa. I blink rapidly, unable to comprehend he's here, and my eyes well up.

"Joon Oppa," I call out, reaching my hands to his cheeks, and he gasps.

"Is it really you?"

He stares blankly as his eyes widen, then places his hands over mine, caressing them gently.

"Hmm Mina, it's me, Joon," he responds, and I smile through my tears.

"Oppa, what took you so long? Do you know how long I've been waiting for you?"

I leap up, pulling him into an embrace, and the towel on my forehead falls off.

"I can't believe I have finally found you," I say repeatedly, sobbing.

"I'm sorry, I'm so sorry," I mutter.

Drowsiness engulfs me once more, and I drift away. I fight to keep my eyes open, even in this dream. I wish to linger, but I surrender to sleep. As my eyes flutter open, I'm met with an all-encompassing ache. I glance around, disoriented, and then recall I'm still in Liam's dressing room. On the side, I spot a damp towel, a half-eaten sandwich, a water bottle, and medication.

I touch my forehead to check my temperature; thankfully, it's normal, and my cramps have eased. The memory of Joon Oppa resurfaces. I reason it must have been a dream, though it felt incredibly real. How can a dream be so vivid? My heart races as the door handle jiggles.

"You don't need to come in," I hear Liam's voice outside.

I immediately clear everything up, placing the meds back in the bag and picking up the wet towel.

"I want to play the song I told you they have in mind for us to sing for the OST."

Rachel mutters. I gasp as my hands begin to tremble.

"Just send it to my phone. I'll listen to it later," Liam insists.

"Why can't I play it now? It won't take long. I want your thoughts on it," she says.

"Okay, fine, let me get changed first. I'll meet you in your room," he says.

"What's going on? You're acting a bit strange. Are you hiding something in there?" she asks.

"What's there to hide?" he replies.

"Then let me in," I hear pulling at the door.

So, I hurriedly take the carrier bag and wet towel to the bathroom, and head back out, fixing up the couch.

"Hold on, wait," Liam mutters.

"Move out of the way," Rachel says sounding grim, and the door slams open, and I give a slight bow.

Chapter Twenty Five

"It's all clear for you now, Mr Choi," I say.

Attempting to appear composed, Rachel gasps and glares at Liam, who also gazes at me in disbelief, glancing around the room and exhales to find it clear. Then I head towards the door, but Rachel steps in my way.

"And just where do you think you're going," she says.

I swallow, pressing my lips together, and squeeze my top with my trembling hands. Her eyes burn with fury.

"Shouldn't you explain what you're doing here first?" she asks.

"Rachel, just let her go, so we can talk," Liam says.

Pulling her out of my way, but she yanks his hands off.

"Go on, Mina. I'm listening. Come to think of it. I haven't seen you on set all day. Were you here the whole time?" she asks, breathless.

"Mr Choi asked me to run a few errands for him, and by the time I got back, he was throwing up and had made a complete mess, so he asked me to clear it up," I say, and I swallow.

Biting my teeth as I squirm under her intense gaze, then his manager appears.

"Liam, how are you feeling? Still feel like throwing up?" his manager asks, and I exhale, then she turns to him.

"He was throwing up?" she asks.

"Yes, it sounded quite bad. He wouldn't even let me into the bathroom," he says. She sighs, moving out of the way.

I rush to Soo-jin who's now packing up. Her furrowed brows meet mine but says nothing. Getting home again, I mull over today's close call, Liam's genuine kindness lingering in my thoughts. I don't know how I would have gotten through the day without his help.

I gasp as memories of seeing Joon emerge, but I dismiss it as a fever-induced illusion. Yet, its vividness remains. I stare at my hands, recalling their warmth against his face. Then my phone buzzes with a text from Liam that reads.

"Hope you're feeling better. Make sure you take your meds; see you tomorrow, LC."

My heart starts doing that funny thing again. I try shaking off the thought, but I spend the night turning and tossing, and suddenly it's daylight again. I get up, preparing for the day. I check the shooting schedule at the office, realising we're filming out of town. We gather the necessary equipment and hit the road. After a two-hour drive, we arrive at the location.

It's my first time in the countryside in South Korea. The air is cleaner, with a slower pace compared to Seoul. As Rachel and Dong-min's cars arrive, Soo-jin and I retrieve our equipment from the van. Liam ascends shortly after, but I avoid his gaze. Although I hate to admit it, something feels different between us, getting inside Soo-jin and I proceed to set up.

Liam enters, pausing beside me, then exhales, brushing past me as his gaze lingers momentarily. I lower my head, avoiding eye contact. He settles into the makeup chair, and I exhale deeply, as my palms get sweaty, and I start fidgeting causing me to stumble into the camera stand.

"Ahh," I yelp, and Liam leaps up, to assist me.

"Are you okay? Did you get hurt? You need to be more careful," he scolds, pulling me up. I stare at him wide-eyed.

"I'm okay," I say.

All eyes fall on us, so I release my arm from his grip, then the doors spring open and Rachel walks in. We say our greetings, and she rolls her eyes. Liam clears his throat, heading back to his seat. I lift my camera stand and carry on filming.

"There isn't enough space here, so we'll all be sharing this makeup room," Rachel says, and her glam team floods in.

"Knock, knock," we all turn towards the door and Dong-min walks in.

"I heard we'll all be in one room today," he says, smiling at me.

"Stress relief, hello," he says, waving. I give a slight bow lowering my head as everyone stares.

After lunch, Dong-min and I head back to set, and my phone buzzes.

"I need to take this," I say. He nods and walks ahead.

It's Dina, I jump with glee.

"Dina, oh my gosh, I've missed you so much," I say, grinning.

"Why haven't you called? We've been worried sick. Are you okay? You're not sick or anything, are you? What about food? Are you eating regularly? Are they being nice to you at work?" she asks all in one breath.

"Woaw, woaw, one question at a time, sis," I say, giggling.

"First, I'm well. Second, the work is good, and everyone's nice and welcoming. Thirdly, I eat regularly. I'm heading back from lunch now," I say, leaving out all the hardship.

"Anyway, enough about me. How are you guys? Did you have a good honeymoon? And Mum, how's she? Unfortunately, I haven't been able to call much due to my work schedule," I say.

"Well, we're doing well, but I have to say marriage is a lot different than I imagined. It's not all roses and rainbows," she says, smirking. I gasp.

"Omg, already, shouldn't you guys still be in the honeymoon phase?" I ask.

"I think it's at this stage we fight the most because we're invading each other's space, so to speak, which isn't something we are used to, but it's also how we learn about each other, I guess," she giggles.

"Who's on the phone," I hear Terry ask in the background.

"Hey Terry, what's good? I hope you're treating my sister well," I mutter, and they laugh.

"Yo, M, you good yeah, how are you finding South Korea?" he asks.

"It's cool man, loving every second," I say.

"Great to hear. Look after yourself, okay? I'll pass it back to D."

"Mina, make sure you call Mum, okay, she misses you," Dina nags.

"I will, I will," I mutter, then check the time and gasp.

"Dina, I'll speak to you guys later. I've got to get back on set," I say, hanging up.

When I turn to leave, I yelp finding Liam behind me.

"Oh my gosh, you startled me. How long have you been standing there?" I ask, out of breath, but he just stares at me, puzzled.

"Was that your sister you were speaking to?"

"Oh, you heard, yes it was. Why do you ask?"

He frowns, and his lips fall into a hard line.

"You guys seem close," he says bitterly, ignoring my question.

"I guess we are," I mutter, then sigh, recalling the times Dina and I were at odds with each other.

"Well, we weren't always close. In fact, there was a time when we couldn't even stand to be in the same room, but somehow, we got past it, although I wish it happened sooner."

Before it got in the way of Joon and me. I sigh, shaking off my trail of thoughts.

Why was I even telling him this? Liam's eyes shoot daggers as he walks past, his shifting demeanour back again. I sigh, wishing for a way to anticipate his mood shifts. How do I keep setting him off? After the last outdoor scene, we pack our gear, ready to leave.

"Stress relief. I have another schedule tonight at the studio, so I'll be leaving first. I'll see you tomorrow back in Seoul," Dong-min says, heading off with his manager, and I nod.

I rush to the bathroom to freshen up before returning to Seoul. Looking at my reflection, I notice my bare neck, realising my necklace is missing. I gasp searching my pockets, and then around the location with no luck. The van's leaving soon, but I can't go without my necklace. It's my last link to Joon Oppa; losing it is not an option.

"Mina, I've been looking for you. We're ready to leave. Let's go," Soo-jin says.

"Uhhhh, oh erm, you guys go ahead without me," she raises her eyebrows.

"I have a friend coming to pick me up," I lie.

"Didn't realise you had friends," she smirks and exits.

The spot where we filmed the final scene was the last place. I recall wearing it, so I rush over there. Using my phone's flashlight, I begin searching. Then I hear a snapping branch and freeze as my heart rate spikes. Could it be a wild animal or worse? I clutch a nearby stick, and slowly turn to confront the approaching figure.

"Ahhhh," I yell out.

Aiming my flashlight, I gasp when I see who it is. I lower my hands exhaling.

"Why do you keep appearing out of nowhere, scaring me half to death?" I ask. He gives me a blank stare.

"What the hell are you doing here all alone? Do you realise the production van already left?" he yells.

"Oh, erm," I swallow, scratching the back of my head, trying to devise an excuse valid enough.

"I know they left; I told them I'd find my way back to Seoul. I lost something precious to me. I need to find it before leaving," I say, and his brows frown.

"What is it? What could be so important that you let them leave without you?" he yells. My brows frown. Why's he getting so worked up?

"Besides how were you planning on getting back? Do you even know where this is? How could you still be so reckless?" he yells, and I swallow.

Looking down at my fingers, feeling like an errand child.

"Ermm, a friend is picking me up," I mumble, and he gasps.

"A friend, you say? Do you expect me to believe you have a friend who would drive out here to pick you up so late at night?" he yells, veins popping out of his neck.

"Mr Choi, why are you getting so worked up about this? I'm sure you have more important matters to attend to. Just ignore me and go your way," I say, and resume my search.

He pulls my arm, leading me towards the exit. I yank my arm out of his grip.

"Why do you even care what I do or don't do? Just pretend you didn't see me and leave," I say as we both glare at each other breathlessly.

"How can I pretend not to see you and leave? Do you think I'll be able to go and leave you behind? Do you really want to see me go crazy?" he yells.

My shoulders slump, and my heart sinks. He has that tortured expression again. But I shake off the thought. I need to focus on finding my necklace before I leave.

"Stay or go. I don't care what you do, but I'm not leaving until I find what I'm looking for," I say.

Aiming my flashlight back on the ground and continuing searching, Liam remains in the same position watching me. After a while, he sighs walking in closer.

"What exactly are you looking for?" he asks, but I don't respond.

"Wouldn't it be faster if I help?" he says. I sigh.

He's right. It will be faster if we both look. I must find it at all costs.

"It's a necklace with a star pendant. This is the last place I remember having it on," I say.

"So, this is all because of…" he stops mid-sentence and gasps.

Then puts on his flashlight joining me. We search for about an hour with no luck. I halt, sinking into the grass.

"It's been over an hour. Are you sure it's even here?" he asks.

"It has to be, I've looked everywhere else, and this was the last place I recall having it," I say, getting back up to look.

"That's enough now. Just let it go," he says.

"You can go if you want. I'm going to keep looking," I say, and he kicks a branch.

"Stop being ridiculous and come with me. It's just a necklace. You can just get a new one," he says, grabbing my hands again, and I pull it off.

"It's not just a necklace to me. It's the last; it's the last thing I have of him," I say, and tears begin to fall.

"If it meant so much to you, then why, why the hell did you lose it so easily!" he yells.

My body goes numb, and I quiver. He's right. If Joon meant that much, I shouldn't have let go of him or the necklace so easily. I crouch down, sobbing, and Liam sighs.

"What I meant was…" I cut Liam off, halting my tears. I don't even deserve to cry about this.

"No, you're right. Let's go," I say, leaping up and wiping off my face.

Heading for the exit, he follows behind. We arrive at the car park but there's no car around.

"Over there," he says, pointing at his motorcycle in the far corner.

"I asked my manager to bring it along so I could ride back home and clear my head," he mutters.

He rushes ahead, grabs the spare helmet, and tries putting it on me. But I stretch my hands, collecting it and putting it on myself, and then we get on the bike.

"Here we go," he says.

We set off and I grab hold of the side of his jacket, doing my best to keep a safe distance.

"Hold on tight. There are a few bumps ahead," he warns.

I hold on tighter, but the first bump presses my face into his back. Swallowing hard, I give in and wrap my arm around his waist. His back feels familiar, reminding me of the day I rode on Joon's bike. I can't believe I've lost the last memento of him.

My heart aches suddenly, feeling a wave of longing for Joon. I lean into Liam's back, tightly clinging to his waist as tears stream down my cheeks, allowing myself to fall apart. I tell myself it's Joon's back, finding solace in its warmth.

Liam glances back during traffic stops, perhaps regretting his words earlier. After a few hours, we arrive at my building. My lungs feel stuck, and my heart's gone numb. I get off, remove the helmet, and hand it to him with a slight bow.

"Hey, erm," he murmurs, making me halt.

I turn, staring at him blankly.

"About what I said in the woods…" he sighs, stopping mid-sentence.

"Never mind. Go in and get some rest," he says.

I bow again, and head home, heading straight for the shower, as the water comes pouring, so do my tears. All cried out. I dive straight into bed, dozing off.

In the morning, I opt for sunglasses to work to conceal my puffy eyes. I stare down at my bare neck. It feels like I'm missing a piece of me. I take a deep breath and head out for the day. Today's filming has been delayed because of Liam.

"When's he getting here? We've already lost two hours of daylight," the director yells at Liam's manager, who bows apologetically.

"I'm truly sorry. He's held up in traffic. He'll be here any moment now," he pleads.

My heart sinks. Did something happen to him after he dropped me off? I begin, pacing, biting my fingers as I watch the entrance.

"But how's the actor absent, but his manager present. Shouldn't you be with him to make sure he arrives on time?" the director yells and walks off.

"I'm so sorry," Liam's manager says.

He then takes out his phone to make a phone call.

"Mr Choi, where are you? The director is losing it. I mean, why were you still at yesterday's location until dawn? Have you even slept at all?" he asks, and my jaw drops as I listen.

"This is really driving me crazy," he says, pacing back and forth.

"Oh, you're outside now. Okay, I'll be right there," he says running off.

I trail behind his manager, trying to catch a glimpse. I exhale seeing him dismount his bike. He appears haggard, with leaves, and twigs in his hair and stained clothes. My brows frown. Did he go back to the countryside after dropping me off? Why would he go back? His manager goes ballistic seeing his state of appearance.

"What the hell happened to you?" his manager asks.

"Hyung, I'll explain later. I need to freshen up and get ready for the shoot," Liam says.

His manager nods and they walk into the hallway. I hide as they head for the washroom.

"What are you looking at?" Dong-min asks.

I gasp, placing my hands on my chest.

"Why are you so startled?" he asks, tracing my eye view.

"Nothing," I mutter.

Heading back to the hair and makeup room, Liam enters, appearing much tidier. Our eyes meet briefly, and he gives me a subtle smile before taking a seat. I lower my head as my heart races. The makeup artist and hairstylist quickly attend to him. In mere minutes, he's transformed. Soo-jin and I follow behind him onto the set. Upon our arrival, Liam bows apologising for the delay to everyone.

"Where have you been, and why weren't you picking up my calls?" Rachel mutters.

"Later, I'll explain later," he says.

Liam steals glances at me in between takes but shifts his gaze when our eyes connect. Rachel catches on and glares at me. Returning to the set after lunch, I see Liam down the hall. But before I can evade, our eyes meet. I sigh, lowering my head, hoping to pass by unnoticed. But he steps in front of me as I approach.

"Erm, about yesterday, I'm sorry," he says.

I lift my head to meet his gaze, shaking my head.

"No, I'm sorry," I say, thanking him again for the ride.

I give him a slight bow and carry on walking.

"Hey, clumsy," he calls out. My eyes widen as I turn around.

"Check your pocket," he says with a big grin.

"Don't lose it again," he adds, walking off.

I slowly place my hands in my pocket, pulling out my star necklace; I gasp as my eyes widen watching him walk away. I clench the necklace with my hands against my chest feeling a sense of Deja Vu. I think back to all the moments I've shared with him and begin to put the pieces together. He's been right here all along, leaving me clues. How the hell did I miss them? I stumble backwards, placing my hands over my mouth to stop me crying out loud.

"Why, why couldn't I recognise him? How didn't I know he was Joon Oppa all along?"

Chapter Twenty Six

I start connecting the dots, he grew up in London, and he's close to Rachel, also the things he said yesterday and how he's acted towards me all make sense now. I glare at the necklace, then squeeze it tightly as tears rain down my cheeks. Before realising it, my legs start moving towards him. It begins with a walk, then a jog, until I'm full-on running. I must see him. I need to see him.

I get close, but his phone rings, making me halt. He answers the call without speaking and abruptly starts running, entering the lift. Just as the doors shut, I spot his trembling hand. The lift stops at the basement, so I rush down the staircase to meet him there.

My heart races with each step. I open the door and find a group of men in black surrounding him. One shoves him against the wall. I gasp, covering my mouth. The door shuts, and all eyes fall on me. Joon's head sinks and one of the men lunges to throw a punch.

"Watch out," I scream.

Joon docks, escaping the blow, then kicks the man in his crotch making him release his grip. Joon crouches down panting, glaring at me.

"Get out of here," he yells out.

But my legs won't budge. I've finally found him again. How can I leave him in danger? I step closer, but another man closes in, putting him in a headlock. The others start punching him, landing blows to his stomach.

"Stop it," I scream.

But they carry on. I search for my phone to call for help.

"Hang in there, I'll get help," I say.

"Mina!" he yells.

Shaking his head, they finally stop, letting go of him. He falls to the ground, panting.

"I told you I'd pay after the movie premieres. Has there ever been a time when I didn't keep my promise," Joon says.

Talking to the biggest one, who's bald with a snake neck tattoo. He walks in close to Joon, grabbing his collar. I rush over, pulling his hands off.

"Leave him alone," I say, wrapping my arm around Joon as I tremble. He pulls my hands off.

"I told you to leave. Get out of here," he yells.

I shake my head, spreading my arms to shield him.

"Well, who do we have here," the bald guy says, closing in on me.

Joon pulls me away, hiding me behind his back.

"Leave her out of it," Joon says.

He grabs Joon's collar bringing him to his eye level. Then his grim expression turns into a grin.

"Hey, come on, we're not bad guys. You know that we just wanted to remind you that your next payment is coming up," he says, putting him down and adjusting his clothing.

"You know how considerate I can be, see I even made sure the boys caused no harm to your face," he chuckles, pinching Joon's cheeks.

"Just make sure you finish up the movie nicely and pay up or else we'll have to visit your little sister's coffee shop," he says, and Joon leans in, grabbing him by the collar.

"You will get the payment on time, so don't you dare go anywhere near her, do you understand me," he says.

All the veins in his neck pop out, and his breathing quickens. The man pulls Joon's hands away and smirks.

"Let's go, boys," he says.

And they all enter a black van and drive off, and I step in front of Joon.

"Mr Choi, are you okay?" I ask.

Checking around his body for injuries, he winces and turns away from me, lowering his head and avoiding my gaze.

"I'm fine," he says, heading back inside.

"Wait," I say, and he halts but doesn't turn.

"I don't think you should go back looking like that. I'll help you clean your wound. Come with me," I say, pulling his arm along.

"Ahhhh," he yelps, and I let go.

"Sorry, does it hurt a lot?" I ask.

He nods, and I begin to tear up again.

Then he displays a sweet smile that melts me like butter. How did I not notice it was him all along?

"But it's bearable, lead the way, and I'll follow," he says. I nod, turning to hide my trembling hands.

"This way," I say, leading him to a storeroom filled with chairs and tables.

"Wait here. I will be right back," I mutter.

I head to set grabbing a first aid kit while everyone's engrossed in the kiss scene between Rachel and Dong-min's characters. I also grab a spare shirt from the prop room. Getting back, Joon straightens up as I walk in. I place the kit and shirt beside him. I swallow trying to stay composed.

"Let's see what we have here," I murmur.

Attempting to sound calm, I reach to unbutton his shirt, but he places his hands over mine, and my breathing hitches.

"I'll do it," he says.

Unbuttoning his shirt, I gasp at the sight of his ribs covered in cuts and bruises; it's clear this isn't the first time. With trembling hands, I gently touch each wound, choked up as I pass each one. I bite my bottom lip, suppressing the urge to cry. Opening the first aid kit, I begin cleaning his wounds.

I feel his intense glare but pretend not to notice. Memories of tending to his wounds in school flood back, and my hands halt as I fight back my tears. I thought he was doing well, but he seems to be involved in something dangerous. Finally, I lay a plaster on the cut by his ribs, and he winces, and a tear escapes my eye involuntarily.

"I'm sorry, I'm so sorry," I repeat, sobbing.

I hide my face in my hands, and he gently uncovers them. As our eyes meet, his eyes probe mine, puzzled by my reaction. But I lower my gaze, wiping my face with my sleeves. He lifts my chin, searching my eyes for answers. I fidget under his gaze as I scrutinise every detail, looking for familiar traits. It truly was Joon Oppa all along. Tears stream down once more, and I shut my eyes tightly, feeling his touch as he brushes away my tears.

"I'm sorry," he says, and my eyes spring open.

"Seeing such violence must have frightened you," he adds.

He continues wiping away my tears as they fall, making me cry more intensely. Then he stands, gently enveloping me in his warmth, patting my back. I want to utter his name and reveal that I now recognise him, but the words won't come out.

I feel like I've forfeited that right after the pain I've caused him. Imagining how hurt he must have felt, seeing me right there without recognition, makes my heart ache.

Recollections flood in of the first time we reunited, he knew who I was instantly, also thoughts of Rachel asking if I'd recognise him if I ever saw him again flashback along with the anguish etched on his face that day, and I tighten my grip around him.

"Joon Oppa, I'm so sorry," I say repeatedly in my head, unable to voice it out. Eventually, he disengages from our embrace, wiping away the remnants of my tears.

"Feeling better?" he asks, smiling, and I nod.

"Let me finish up," I say.

Applying another plaster to the cut above his chest, handing him the T-shirt to change, then exiting the room to give him privacy. Pausing for a moment, the thought strikes me, and I set out in search of Rachel. Returning to the set, I find filming has concluded.

"Soo-jin, have you seen Rachel?" I ask. She looks at me, puzzled.

"Ahh, sorry, Miss Go Ae-ra," she raises her eyebrows.

"I think she's back in her changing room. Why?" she asks.

"Thanks," I reply, heading off to look for her.

When I get to her room, her manager opens the door, leaving, and I bow to greet her.

"Ae-ra, it's your high school friend," she mutters.

Letting me in as she leaves, Rachel's sat on her makeup chair, taking off her jewellery.

"What Is it?" she asks.

Looking at me through the mirror, my hands form a fist as I glare at her. She turns after my lack of response and approaches me.

"Why, why the hell did you lie to me?" I yell, and her eyes widen as her brows frown.

"Wha, what are you talking about?" she says, smirking, and heads back to sit.

"You know exactly what I'm talking about, Rachel. Why didn't you tell me Liam was Joon Oppa?"

She stops abruptly, and silence fills the room. Then, she pivots, approaching me, her gaze locked onto mine. Her hands fall on my shoulders, and she exhales, as the intensity in her eyes grows.

"Does he…"

She stops squeezing her eyes shut, taking another deep breath and reopens them.

"Does he know?" she asks, searching my eyes as she trembles, awaiting my response. My brows frown.

"Does he know you recognise him?" she yells out, shaking me.

I gasp, taken aback by her distressed reaction, and tears begin to stream down her cheeks.

"No, he doesn't," I say.

Her hands clasp down as she exhales. She then wipes off her tears, composing herself.

"So, how did you finally figure it out?" she asks, then shakes her head.

"No, that's not important, Mina," she mutters, resting her hands on my shoulders.

"You can't tell him you know who he is. Promise me, promise you won't tell him?" she yells, shaking me.

My lips fall into a hard line, and I pull her hands off, turning to leave.

"I'm not saying it for my benefit. If you tell him, you know who he is, you will only destroy him," I halt, turning back around.

"What do you mean it'll destroy him?" I gasp.

"Is this another one of your tricks?" I ask.

"Tricks, you say," she smirks, sinking down into the chair beside her.

"Do you know what he has been through these past few years? You weren't there for any of it. I was. I've been by his side through it all," she mutters, sobbing.

"I'm sure you've been curious as to why he and his family left the UK so abruptly, selling all they had," she shuts her eyes as she recalls the memory.

"Joon's dad suffered a heart attack after a major business deal went south. He lost everything. He had invested all they had, even borrowing from loan sharks, as a trusted partner assured him it was a done deal, so when everything collapsed, his health deteriorated," my eyes widen as I listened.

"So, when his Mum received the news, she immediately put their flat on the market, selling it below market value to get some cash. When I heard about it, I pleaded with my Mum to let me return to South Korea to be there for them," she sighs.

"From that point on, things got worse. Those who invested in his dad's business came to their house, attacking them and damaging their property, which the bank eventually repossessed," she gasps.

"They were constantly moving between the hospital and a motel just to get some rest. Joon changed during that time, blaming himself for being too young to assist his family. Even when I visited, he was distant, as if he wasn't really there," she adds.

My knees become weak, making me stumble. Finally, she sighs, looking down at her fingers.

"I couldn't bear to watch them suffer any longer, so I begged my father to help, but my dad said he would only help if I struck a deal with him," I raise my brows.

"A deal?" I ask. She smirks, shaking her head.

"That isn't important right now. The point is, we came to an agreement, and he paid Joon's father's hospital bills and got most of the investors to back off by paying back a percentage of what they lost," she stops and swallows.

"But unfortunately, Joon's dad died during his heart surgery."

I sink into the floor as my breathing narrows and tears flow down my cheeks. She chokes up struggling to get the words out. I squeeze hold of the couch, bracing myself.

"And soon after that, Joon's Mum also followed on."

I gasp, covering my mouth. I can't believe Joon's bright and cheerful Mum is no more.

"She'd gotten weak, unable to face it all by herself. During his father's funeral, she went to lie down to get some rest but never woke up again, and it was Joon who found her," she mutters.

I squeeze my eyes shut, placing both hands over my face, as my heart breaks into pieces. Rachel sighs deeply and continues.

"Just like that, he and Ji-won became orphans, with only their grandmother as their remaining family. Then, at his mother's funeral, loan sharks came to harass them, saying they would now be responsible for paying back their father's debt since their Mum was gone," I sigh in disbelief.

"Hold on, just hold on," I say, stopping her, needing a moment to exhale.

"You need to hear it all. At least you've had the privilege of not witnessing such a horrible sight in person," she says.

She's right. The least I can do is listen, so I nod, and she continues.

"After that, Joon asked if I could take him to my father, but wouldn't tell me why. So, I arranged the meeting, but I wasn't allowed to be present," she gets up, leaning on the table.

"I don't know the terms of their agreement, but after that day, he was signed as a trainee, and managed to rent a place for Ji-won and his grandma to live, and the loan sharks stopped bothering them. But he joined the military before starting his training, which my dad requires all male trainees to do. When he returned, he wasn't the same Joon we knew. He adopted the name Liam and started afresh, working immensely hard to build his career," she explains.

She walks up to me, and I look up to meet her firm gaze.

"That is why you can't tell him that you know who he is. Although he already knows who you are, he won't do anything, but if he finds out you recognise him, he'll begin to waver, and if that happens, what do you think will happen to his career," she sits beside me but doesn't break eye contact.

"And if word gets out to my dad about you two," she gasps.

"My dad isn't someone who'd just sit back and allow anyone to tamper with his investments. Right now, Joon is the most sought-after artist he has and if you guys threaten that, do you think he would stand by and watch?" she asks, placing her hands on my shoulder.

"Even if you were an ordinary South Korean girl, it wouldn't be easy. Fans despise seeing their idols in relationships. You're a fangirl yourself, so you understand. I've seen many careers crumble due to their secret relationships being exposed. Now, think about the storm it would create if news spread of Liam dating a foreigner," her gaze intensified.

"I hate to say it, but, especially a black foreigner," I glare at her.

"No need to give me that look. I'm only stating the obvious, it's a shame, but the world is filled with small-minded people Mina."

She gets back up, folding her arms.

"So, you can either watch him from a distance and be satisfied with that or leave this company and this country if that's too hard for you to bear," she mutters, and I gasp, lost for what to say.

"But Mina, if you jeopardise Liam's success in any way, you'll have me to deal with. This is a warning, so be careful!"

She returns to her makeup chair, reapplying her lipstick. I struggle to stand, stumbling a few times. Feeling overwhelmed with the answers to the questions I've been seeking for the past few years. I had romanticised their life for the past few years, expecting our reunion to be like a movie. Maybe I did that to avoid feeling guilty, as life would have been unbearable otherwise.

The answers I received are not as I imagined. Joon and Ji-won must have endured so much pain. Adding to it all, I broke Joon's heart just before the news about his dad broke. I open the door, taking small steps, unsure of my destination. Everything's blurry, and I struggle to breathe.

"Stress relief, stress relief, Miss Mina."

I look up at Dong-min approaching me. But lose balance, falling to the ground.

"Miss Mina, what's wrong? Are you okay?" he asks shaking me.

But I remain unresponsive, so he lifts me up and I slowly shut my eyes feeling utterly drained of energy.

My eyes spring open, and I find myself in Dong-min's changing room. He hands me a bottle of water and lifts me up to take a sip.

"Miss Mina, what's wrong? Did something happen between you and Ae-ra? I saw you leaving her changing room," he asks.

I stay silent, clutching the necklace from my pocket. Rachel was right. I don't want to hurt Joon any further. Just watching him from a distance is enough. I exhale, wipe my tears, put on the necklace, and head to the ensuite bathroom. After washing my face, I return with a smile. Dong-min's brows frown, but he sighs, forcing a smile too.

"Feeling better?" he asks. I nod.

"Umm, thanks for helping me out. I should head for the van. They must be waiting for me," I say.

Heading for the door, he runs ahead to open it.

"I'll walk you down," he says.

When the door opens, a few of Dong-min's team are standing outside, and their eyes widen.

"Omg, what were they doing in there together," one of them whispers.

"I guess the rumours were true," another adds.

Dong-min moves to speak, but I shake my head squeezing his arm. His brows frown, and he sighs but remains silent. I bow to greet them, and we head off.

"But still, couldn't he have done better than a black foreigner?" another mutter, and Dong-min halts, walking back.

"What's wrong with her being black?" he yells at the staff members.

"Why would you make such an ugly comment, are black people, not humans, too?" he asks. I squeeze my eyes shut and sigh.

"During N.O.'s rise to fame in Western countries, some of you were with us on tour. Don't you recall the racist remarks we endured in person and in articles? People saw us as less than human due to our Asian heritage, despite our skin colour not being so different from theirs. So, what sets you apart from those people if you treat her the same way?"

Their eyes widen as they lower their heads.

"Racism is racism. As minorities, shouldn't we try to stick together and be more understanding of one another instead of being a part of the problem?"

He points to the lady with long black hair and round glasses.

"Miss Ji-soo, I heard your younger brother is studying in the United States. How would you feel if someone made a racist comment to him like you just did?" She presses her lips together and looks away.

"You all should be ashamed of yourselves," Dong-min adds. I smile as he walks back to me.

"Let's go," he says.

When we turn, Joon's standing at the end of the hall, and Dong-min stops as we walk by him.

"That goes for you, too, stop treating her like your personal slave, or you'll have me to deal with."

I pull Dong-min's arms leading him out, and he exhales, turning to me.

"Your turn," he says.

I take a deep breath and exhale, feeling lighter, and we both smile.

"Stress relief, see you tomorrow," he says.

Making his way to his car, and I join Soo-jin at the production van as we prepare to leave.

"Miss Mina, do you have the camera stand?" Soo-jin asks, and I gasp.

"Sorry, I'll get it now," she rolls her eyes and sighs.

I head back in to grab the camera stand. On my way out, I walk past Rachel's changing room, which was slightly open.

"What are you talking about?" I hear Joon ask.

"Were you with her? I couldn't find you anywhere," Rachel mutters, and Joon sighs.

"Do you think I haven't noticed that you send her on errands in order to protect her by keeping her away from me," my eyes widen.

"If you want to protect her, then keep your distance because if she figures out who you are and clings unto you, and the world finds out, who do you think would get hurt the most?" she asks.

"I'm not talking to you about this," he says.

"Even if you are indifferent to losing everything or the world's opinion of you, have you considered Mina? Do you truly believe she could endure the torrent of hatred and potential physical harm that could occur?" she steps closer to him.

"Liam, just be satisfied with being able to watch her from a distance, don't let your greed become the reason she gets hurt. If you care about her, then keep your distance, and I promise to do the same."

I see his hands form a fist as she leans in, giving him a back hug, but he doesn't push her away. I squeeze my eyes shut, and the camera stand accidentally hits the door.

"Who's there?" Rachel yells.

Chapter Twenty Seven

I hide in a corner, placing my hands over my mouth.

"There's no one here. It was probably just the wind," she says, shutting the door.

I exhale, heading back to the van, and we hit the road. When I get home, I lie on my rooftop table, staring at the sky, filled with bright stars. I try blocking out thoughts of today's discoveries, so I head inside and call Mum.

"Mina, what took you so long to call? I've been worried sick. How are you? Have you eaten?" she asks. Just hearing her voice brings me to tears.

"Emm, I'm okay, and yes, I ate so much I almost exploded," I say.

"Don't overfeed yourself. You'll only get indigestion," she mutters, and I hit my chest, feeling suffocated.

"Emmm," I sit up, trying to steady my breathing.

"Mina, are you sure everything's okay? They're not giving you a hard time at work, are they?" she asks.

"Of course not. They're all nice and welcoming," she sighs.

"Thank goodness, I was worried they might be indifferent to you as a foreigner," she adds.

"No way, I think that's my charm at the office. Well, Mum, I've got to go. Talk soon," I say.

"Alright darling, it must be late over there. Get some rest. Goodnight and I love you," she says, hanging up, and those words become my undoing, and I cry myself to sleep.

Morning arrives, and I remind myself to be grateful for finding Joon while ensuring he remains unaware. Soo-jin and I set up on set as usual. Joon arrives. We exchange greetings and begin filming. He occasionally glances at me, likely concerned after the loan shark incident, but I avoid his gaze. He solely converses with Soo-jin and doesn't send me on errands. Rachel seems at ease, showering Joon with attention.

Perhaps to put me in my place, but her attempts don't affect me. She's been keeping her distance as she promised Joon she would. This carries on for the next few days, making work more bearable.

On my day off, I explore Seoul, starting with Namsan Tower. After taking a gondola to the top, I'm treated to a stunning view of the city. After looking around and taking pictures, I walk by the love lock fence, wondering how many of those relationships have lasted.

Then I gasp recalling one of the loan sharks mentioned Joon's sister's cafe. He must have been talking about Ji-won. Then I recall the Zodiac Cafe and my eyes widen. I cut my trip short heading for the exit. Thinking back to the theme, it reminds me so much of Ji-won. She loved everything to do with horoscopes and zodiac signs, and the ladies at the cafe referred to her as Aquarius.

I board the train, trembling throughout the journey. As I arrive, I approach the cafe slowly, dripping in sweat. Peering through the glass wall, I see a petite lady with black hair and pink-highlighted pigtails emerging from the back, wearing a grin. Her t-shirt reads "Aquarius." Our eyes meet, so I quickly turn putting on my face mask, and as she heads my way opening the door.

"Hi, would you like to come inside?" she asks.

I take a deep breath, put on my sunglasses, and nod, following her inside.

"What's your star sign?" she asks.

"Oh erm, I'm a Gemini," I say, her face brightens up.

"Omg really? I love Geminis," then her smile fades.

"My high school best friend's also a Gemini. If you don't mind me asking, what country are you from?" she asks, and I swallow.

"I'm from Nigeria," her jaw drops.

"OMG, she's Nigerian too. You know what, your coffee's on the house, since you brought back precious memories for me," she says.

My face mask is filled with tears, but thankfully, my eyes are covered.

"Thank you," I Mutter.

She leans in, trying to get a closer look, as my voice cracks, I clear my throat.

"Here you go," she says.

"This is a vanilla cinnamon iced coffee. I made this 'the Gemini drink' as a tribute to my memories with her. Her favourite season was autumn, you see," she mutters.

Giving a bittersweet smile, the door opens, and a few customers walk in.

"Thanks for the drink," I say, giving a slight bow.

"No, thank you. Meeting you has truly made my day. Come again soon," she says.

Stepping outside, I remove my mask and sunglasses, exhaling. I feel the urge to rush back, to embrace her and reveal my identity. But I can't. It's the only way to shield her and Joon from further pain.

I taste the coffee and it's terrible, triggering a fit of giggles. Strangely, the more I drink, the better it becomes. Perhaps it's her touch or the memories it holds, but it's the best coffee I've ever had. I spend the night wandering until my feet grow numb. It's been a day of mixed emotions.

Everyone's a bit sad as we set up for the last day of shooting for the movie. Pictures are taken, and the actors and extras share their favourite moments.

"Stress relief," I turn. Dong-min rushes in and hugs me.

I clear my throat coming out of his embrace. Joon walks in, rolling his eyes at the sight of us, and I lower my head.

"I missed you so much yesterday. No more days off, okay," he scolds, and I smirk.

"But today's the last day of filming," I say, walking ahead.

"But I'll still see you back at the company. Wait up," he yells from behind.

"Do you know what this is?" he asks, holding up a suit cover.

"A suit," I say. He gasps.

"Not just any suit, just wait and see. I'm going to transform into a cool guy. So, wait on it," he mutters, heading to hair and makeup.

Soo-jin has already set up Liam's makeup room. Today's scene is a glamorous ballroom party at an exquisite hotel with breathtaking views. On my way to join Soo-jin, I take a sneak peek at the hall and spot the producer and director by the entrance.

"She was involved in a fender bender, so she's on the way to the hospital," Miss Kang says.

"What? We can't do this without her. Do we have anyone who could replace her?" the director asks.

"Not in time," she says.

Then she turns to me, smiling, and then looks back at the director, nudging my way. He glances at me, grinning, and they both nod.

"Get her to hair and makeup immediately," the director mutters, and Miss Kang walks towards me, and I instinctively take a step back.

"Miss Mina," she calls.

"Yes," I answer hesitantly.

"Come with me," she says, leading me to the makeup artist.

"Do you have a foundation in her colour?" she asks.

"Just a moment," she says, looking through her makeup kit.

"Ahhh, found it. I recently bought one when I travelled to Kenya for a job," she says, grinning.

"What's going on?" I ask the producer.

"First, take a seat," she says, pulling me into the chair. The makeup artist begins working on me.

"So, Miss Mina, we booked a foreign actress for a cameo scene, but she got into a fender bender on the way here and can't make it, so we need you to fill in for her, please," she claps her hands together pleading, I gasp.

"Please save me just this once, uh, please say yes."

All the other staff members join in pleading on her behalf. I sigh deeply, shut my eyes and nod.

"Yes!!! Thank you so much. You're a lifesaver," she says, squeezing my hands.

"What about filming?" I ask.

"Don't worry, I'll get someone to help Soo-jin out," she says.

"But what do I need to do? I'm not an actress," I mutter.

"You don't have to worry about that. You only have a few lines, and we'll all help you out, so relax," she says, then takes out her radio.

"Can I speak to the head of styling?" she asks.

"Speaking," he responds.

"Can we get the red dress altered? There has been a change in casting," she says.

"What, this is such short notice!" he yells.

"I know, I'm so sorry, but it couldn't be helped. There shouldn't be much to adjust as they look about the same size. I'll send her up to you as soon as hair and makeup are done," she says.

"Miss Mina, I'll leave it all in your hands," she says, leaving the room.

Years have passed since I faced the camera. Butterflies flutter in my stomach. Once my makeup is done, I move to the hairstylist. As she's not experienced with Afro hair, so I assist, grabbing a nearby water bottle, sprinkling a bit into my hair to soften it as the hair stylist gawks at me in amazement. I then take out my afro comb and hair gel from my bag and begin combing out my hair before talking her through slicking it down and swerving my baby hairs to the side. Lastly I get her to wrap some straight black hair extension around the ends of my packed hair for an extended ponytail look. We both cheer as the outcome exceeds our expectations. Then, I head up to styling immediately after. When I get upstairs, the head stylist glares at me for about twenty seconds, and I stare down at my hands.

"Hmm, I can work with this," he finally mutters.

Then he claps his hands, and a group of people surround me. After about twenty minutes, I'm ready to be unveiled. When I step out of the changing room, all their jaws drop.

"Now, this is what I'm talking about. I just played Fairy Godmother," the head of styling says, giggling.

I approach the nearby mirror and gasp at my reflection. My hair is intricately pinned up, a subtle smokey eye emphasises my eyes, and my lips shimmer with red lipstick. I'm dressed in a captivating red mermaid dress, featuring a deep plunge neckline, draped shoulders, and a trailing back, exuding a princess-like charm. Just then, Miss Kang enters the room.

"Miss Mina, is that you? Wow, you look stunning. Good job, everyone."

When we get behind the ballroom door, I exhale, adjusting my feet in the heels. They are a size too small, but I do my best to walk in them. Finally, the doors open, and I walk in, taking small steps. When I look up, all eyes in the room fall on me. I begin to squirm, causing me to stumble. Then someone grabs my hands, breaking my fall.

I turn to express my gratitude and gasp when I see Joon. My lips press together. I lower my gaze momentarily, then slowly lift it again. He gazes at me softly, smiling with his eyes and his lips path. I swallow as I drink him in. He looks dashing in his tuxedo. The room grows quiet as all eyes fall on us. He clears his throat to hide his smile.

"Careful," he mutters.

"Is Miss Go Ae-ra still not ready yet?" the director asks.

"Not yet," the producer replies.

"Liam let's do a run-through with the lady beside you until Miss Ae-ra arrives," he says, and Joon smiles.

"Ready," Joon asks, and I gasp.

"Wait? I'm just an extra. I can't fill in for the main actress," I murmur. He walks in close lifting my hands.

"Trust me, I must admit you look breathtaking, Miss Mina," he whispers, and I melt like butter.

I swallow, taking his hands, and his smile gets more prominent. As he leads me down the hall, everyone stares whispering, I lower my head and he turns to me as we get to the middle of the dance floor.

"Miss Mina, always keep your head high, especially when people are watching," he says.

Then sways me into a dance position grabbing my waist, and I bite my bottom lip.

"Just trust and follow my lead," he says.

As we move, his eyes stay locked on mine unwaveringly. He turns me into a graceful dancer as I follow his lead effortlessly, thanks to the rehearsals I've observed. It's surreal that I'm dancing with Joon.

This could be the happiest moment of my life. Joon's eyes mirror mine, and I feel our heartbeats dancing to the same rhythm. I hope the music never stops. It feels like we're the only ones in the room.

As the song ends, he gently dips me, leaving us both breathless. We drink each other in panting. The director calls "cut" but we remain locked in our moment, oblivious to the world around us.

"Yeppeo," he mutters in Korean, making me blush and slowly lifting me back up.

"Woow, amazing, nicely done," the director says.

A bit of hair falls to my face. I raise my hands to tuck it, but he beats me to it. I watch his gaze as he gently tucks my hair behind my ears. Then his hands travel down to my cheeks, slowly reaching my lips.

"Liam!"

We both turn to find a very furious Rachel dressed in a stunning pink ball gown.

"What the hell are you both doing!" she screams.

"Miss Ae-ra."

The director tries getting her attention, likely to tell her it was his idea to have me stand in for her. Still, she walks towards us with full force and stumbles, inadvertently knocking into a light stand that starts tilting my way. I see it coming, but my feet stay rooted to the ground, perhaps stunned by the chaos. Joon swiftly pivots me and takes the hit. We tumble to the ground, and he's now unconscious, lying on top of me.

"Opp…"

I catch myself just in time before I accidentally refer to him as I used to as the crew rush in to help.

"Mr Choi, Mr Choi, are you okay?" I call but get no response.

When they finally get the light off him, I turn over, laying him flat on the ground, and shake him but he remains unconscious.

"Call the ambulance," the director yells.

"Liam, Liam, wake up," Rachel rushes over shoving me off him.

"Get away from him. This is all your fault," she yells burning with fury.

"Calm down Ae-ra, it was an accident," Dong-min mutters trying to calm her.

Rachel persists in shaking Liam, but he remains unresponsive. Tears stream down my cheeks as I tremble. Shortly after the ambulance arrives, administering CPR and successfully reviving him. They rush him into the ambulance, accompanied by Rachel and Liam's manager.

The shoot is abruptly cancelled, and everyone stares at me, whispering, calling me bad luck. I pace with my head down, and then Dong-min pulls my arm leading me away. When we get to the hall, he lets go.

"Go get changed. I'll wait for you."

Exhaling deeply, I enter the vacant changing room and settle in front of the mirror to remove my makeup. Mascara streaks mark my tear-stained face. After discarding the gown onto a hanger, I change and head out.

"Any news on his condition?" I ask, and Dong-min shakes his head and drives me home.

"Don't think of anything. Try and get some rest, okay," he says, as we arrive.

Getting in, I scour the web for updates, but there's a void of information. The situation appears to be tightly under wraps. My gaze lingers on his number in my phonebook, wanting to press the call button but resisting in case someone else picks up. I lie in bed, staring at the walls, sobbing. Whenever my phone buzzes, I instantly pick it up, hoping it's news about Joon, but it isn't.

The mood at the office is grim today as everyone is worried about Liam's condition. Nobody knows if he's conscious yet, and the C.E.O. has completely blocked access to him.

"Miss Mina, can you start editing the behind-the-scenes footage?" Mr Park asks.

"Yes, sir," I respond.

"What's the point? We don't even know if the movie would still premiere," the team leader says.

"Let's stay positive and carry on working, Liam will be fine, and the movie will be released as scheduled," Mr Lee says, cheering on the team.

Seeking distraction, I immerse myself in work. While reviewing the clips, I discover instances of Joon discreetly watching over me. There was a moment when he requested his hand fan, seemingly a trivial task as he instructed me to hold it facing myself, but he had noticed me struggling in the heat and wanted me to stay cool.

There was also a scene involving a cat, and he sent me to fetch allergy tablets. When I returned, he declined them, suggesting I keep them instead. I now realise he knew about my allergy. Another clip shows him asking me to sort out the green Skittles, claiming he disliked them. However, his true motive was likely to ensure I took a break after hours of standing.

All this time, I perceived him as heartless, completely misjudging his true intentions. I rush to the bathroom, seeking solace in a stall as I weep. After composing myself, I bump into Dong-min and other N.O. members in the hallway.

"Stress re…" he stops mid-sentence.

I bow and walk off, in no mood for his banter. I remain in the office until the lights dim, and then I leave. While on the bus, I silently pray for Joon, clutching my star pendant and recalling how he had stayed up that night searching for it.

Joon's always given me things, yet all I seem to do is bring him pain and misery. Back home, I retrieve the jacket he gave me at the coffee shop, inhaling his lingering scent. I lie in bed, hugging the jacket tightly and crying.

It has been three days since the incident, and still no news about Joon's condition. Unable to wait any longer, I start searching for Dong-min. Checking the practice room, studio, and snack bar, with no luck, and then I remember our first meeting spot and head there.

Opening the back door, I spot him lighting a cigarette. He gasps, dropping it, then quickly hides his hands behind his back, stepping over it.

"I didn't smoke, I promise," he mutters. I walk up to him.

"Okay, I was about to, but then you caught me. Anyway, I haven't broken my word yet, so no need to give me that look," he says.

I stare at him, unable to find the words to ask for what I want. His brows frown.

"Hey, what's wrong?" he asks. I look down at my fingers.

"Mina, talk to me. What's the matter?" he asks. Placing his hands on my shoulders, I lift my head slowly.

"Dong-min Oppa, please help me," I say before breaking down in tears. He searches my eyes.

"What is it? Tell me," he says. I take a deep breath.

"Can you help me find a way to see Liam Choi?" his eyes widen.

"I need to make sure he's okay, Dong-min Oppa. Please, do me this one favour," I rub my palms together pleading. He exhales.

"Okay," he mutters, my eyes widen.

"Really, you will?" I ask, and he nods.

"But it won't be easy. The C.E.O. has security watching him twenty-four seven so news about his condition doesn't get out, but don't worry, leave it to me," he says, and I sob harder.

"Stop crying. It's breaking my heart. It's not your fault he got hurt, so you don't have to feel so guilty, but if seeing him puts you at ease, I'll help," he says, wiping off my tears.

"Let's go," he murmurs.

Giving me his hands, and I take it. We drive down to the back of the hospital, and he brings out a box. It's filled with disguises, makeup, and props. I watch as he changes his appearance with makeup appearing older and then wears a wig to hide his bleached hair.

"Pass me the bag behind," he says.

I hand over the bag, and he takes out a doctor's robe and a nurse's uniform.

"Why do you have these in your car?" I ask.

"It's for my upcoming role. I picked up the costumes today. I'll leave the car so you can get changed," he says.

I put on the nurse's uniform, wearing gloves and a face mask along with a wig and exit the car.

"Oppa, what about my face?" I ask.

"Don't worry about that. Just make sure you stay behind me," he says, and I nod.

"Get down," he mutters, and we duck.

"What is it?" I ask.

"It's Ae-ra and her dad. They are leaving," he says, and I exhale.

When they leave, we get to the floor where Joon's room is located, and there are three guards in front of the door.

"Wait here," he says, leaving me in the corner, and walking up to the guards.

"Hey, I saw a few reporters trying to get up here. You should go check it out."

"Both of you, go evaluate the situation," the head of security says.

"Two people won't be able to stop them," he adds. They stare at each other puzzled.

"Don't worry. I'll stay and make sure no one gets in," Dong-min mutters and they all rush off.

When the coast is clear, Dong-min stands guard, and I head inside taking off my face mask. The sound of his heart monitor fills the room. Joon's lying down, seemingly unconscious. Tears begin to stream down my cheeks as I walk in closer.

"O Oppa," I mutter, grabbing his hands.

"Joon Oppa, why are you lying here like this? Please, wake up. It's all my fault. I'm so sorry."

I lay my head on the bed as I sob then I feel hands on my head.

"Mina?" Joon's voice calls.

I gasp, leaping up, my eyes widen seeing him conscious. He sits up and I spin around, wiping my face before turning back to bow.

"Hello, Mr Choi. I just wanted to check in and make sure you're okay. Now that I see you're fine, I'll take my leave," I mutter racing to the door.

"Mina!" he calls, making me halt, and I gasp.

"How long have you known it was me, Joon, or have you known all along?"

The Strings Trilogy

Romantic, addictive, and a total page turner,
The Strings Trilogy will have you hooked and captivated,
and the characters will possess you, forever lingering
in your thoughts.

Book 2 – The Strings Blurred

By Fatima Alabi

Discover what happens next for Mina and Joon: the second novel in the addictive Strings Trilogy.

Acknowledgements

First, I would like to thank God Almighty for without him I am nothing.

My loving family for always supporting my dreams, especially my parents, for the sacrifices they made to get me to where I am today. I love you endlessly.

A special shout-out to my big brother Hakeem Alabi. This book would not have been written if not for the conversation we had that day. You encouraged me to get back to creating after taking a hiatus, inspiring me to finally write this book, which was a long-time dream of mine. Thank you for always lifting me up.

To my younger brother Mustapha Alabi, words can't express the gratitude I have towards you. It's a fact that this book wouldn't be what it is without your participation. Thank you for helping me edit, critique, and improve this book. For the hours and hours of conversations about the storyline, plot, and characters, you are not just a brother, but a dear friend.

Nancy Cameron, thank you for always being one call away and offering a listening ear, for always being honest and open about your thoughts and point of view, which pushed me to improve the characters and storyline, and for your endless support in everything I do. You are not just a dear friend but my sister.

I would also like to thank my amazing friends who cheered me throughout this journey and believed in me.

Thank you to Tony Crook, who pre-ordered my book way before it was even close to being out, just because he loved my story. Thank you for believing in me.

Thank you to every single person who has purchased this book. You are part of my dream come true and I hope this book left your heart filled and healed.

Abigail McIntosh, my book was an absolute mess when it first met you. I was a complete beginner and your honesty as an editor truly helped shape me into the knowledgeable writer I am today. I am forever grateful for your contribution to my journey as a first-time writer trying to navigate my way through this process.

Sarshar Jehangir, thank you for helping me with my edits and for loving my story so much that you were determined to get through the edits even while your country suffered a flood disaster and you had lost your home. I truly appreciate you.

Thank you to Susmita Dutta and Savy Loy along with the Global Book Publishing family for helping me get my book to the finish line.

About the Author

Fatima Alabi was not much of a reader growing up, but that was until she came across the trilogy by E.L. James titled "Fifty Shades of Grey," at a time when she needed an escape from reality, at the time she was nineteen years old and homeless, secretly squatting at the office building where she interned. She became completely wrapped up in the love story between the characters, reading all three novels from the series in under a week. After that experience, a new ambition grew inside her and that was the desire to write a novel just as captivating that would turn a non-reader like she once was into the page-turner that she became, and to also help anyone going through a difficult phase in life escape their reality by immersing themselves in her stories.

You can connect with her through her socials below.

To keep up to date with her future releases, sign up for her newsletter at www.fatimaalabi.com.

@authorfatimaalabi

@authorfatimaalabi

@authorfatimaalabi

@authorfatimaalabi

Printed in Dunstable, United Kingdom

77076849R00198